THE SERGEANT
AND THE GIRL NEXT DOOR

OTHER COVENANT BOOKS
AND AUDIOBOOKS
BY LAURA (HATCH) RUPPER

Nora and the Sacred Stones

THE
SERGEANT
AND THE GIRL NEXT DOOR

A NOVEL

LAURA RUPPER

Covenant Communications, Inc.

Cover image: *Couple* © Abigail_Miles, Arcangel.com.

Cover design by Kevin Jorgensen
Cover design copyright © 2023 by Covenant Communications, Inc.

Published by Covenant Communications, Inc.
American Fork, Utah

Library of Congress Cataloging-in-Publication Data

Name: Laura Rupper
Title: The sergeant and the girl next door / Laura Rupper
Description: American Fork, UT : Covenant Communications, Inc. [2023]
Identifiers: Library of Congress Control Number 2022944930 | ISBN Number: 978-1-52442-116-8
LC record available at https://lccn.loc.gov/2022944930

Printed in the United States of America
First Printing: April 2023

29 28 27 26 25 24 23   10 9 8 7 6 5 4 3 2 1

PRAISE FOR
LAURA RUPPER

THE SERGEANT AND THE GIRL NEXT DOOR

"Laura Rupper's romance novel, *The Sergeant and the Girl Next Door*, is a gentle, comfortable read that truly speaks to the heart. The author alternates between the viewpoints of Davis and Faith. They both have a past that needs resolution, and both are reluctant to set their sights on the other. Too much has happened, too much has changed, and too many loved ones have been lost since Davis went overseas so many years before. The story is told with compassion but is refreshingly clean. The characters are well developed, and the author uses a descriptive narrative to effectively set the scene and create the mood and inner conflict of the main characters. A sweet story that will warm your heart."

—Readers' Favorite Five-Star Review

NORA AND THE SACRED STONES

"Magic, villains, treachery and romantic tension—this book has it all!"

—Alexandra H.

"Charming and beautiful story for middle graders."

—Daria S.

"A fabulous adventure story that will keep middle readers engaged through the end."

—Terressa T.

I have long been fascinated by the World War II generation. My grandparents Rae and Frank Barney and Alice and Lyle Davis Hatch were newlyweds during World War II. Frank served in Patton's Third Army during the final days of the war. He was shot in the head and spent a month recovering in a hospital in England. Lyle was a radio operator in the merchant marines. His boat was torpedoed but never hit.

This book is dedicated to all four of my grandparents. They embodied the World War II generation—they did what they considered to be their duty. They made great sacrifices for their country, and like many of their generation, they came home and got on with their lives with no thought that they were remarkable or heroic.

October 1949

They seemed terribly pathetic to me. They weren't warriors. They were American boys who by mere chance of fate had wound up with guns in their hands, sneaking up a death-laden street in a strange and shattered city in a faraway country in a driving rain. They were afraid, but it was beyond their power to quit. . . . And even though they weren't warriors born to the kill, they won their battles. That's the point.

—Ernie Pyle, war correspondent

CHAPTER 1

April 1946

"Is he awake?" the little girl asked.

Davis Wilson kept his eyes closed and his face relaxed. He'd answered approximately a hundred questions from the two young kids who shared his train compartment and had finally resorted to faking sleep.

The boy leaned forward, and Davis felt a sharp little elbow dig into his arm. The boy, his warm breath laced with chocolate, exhaled right into Davis's face.

Davis let his breath out slowly, giving an imitation of sound sleep.

"Aw, darn," the boy said. "I wanted to ask him how many Nazis he killed."

"I bet a thousand," the little girl said.

These children couldn't possibly understand the horrific realities of that question. *Don't flinch. Don't let your face show anything.* He'd used the same technique scores of times for inspections in the army.

Davis added a little snore as if to say, "Now I'm in a deep sleep." It worked. The two siblings moved back.

He sank a little more into the side of his seat and absorbed the motion of the train that was carrying him home.

Home. Butterflies fluttered in his gut.

"Next stop, Blanchester," the conductor called.

"That's us, kids," their mom said. She had read and left her kids unsupervised the entire train ride. Davis liked kids, but these two had penetrated his peace just when he needed to gather his thoughts. Thank heavens he would have quiet the last hour of his ride.

The family exited and Davis opened his eyes. An older white-haired gentleman entered the car and took the seat opposite him. They nodded at each other. The old man pulled a newspaper out from under his cardigan.

Davis stared out the window as they lurched back into motion. The fields and trees were greening up. He'd forgotten how beautiful April in Ohio was.

"Where'd you serve, Sergeant?"

Pulling his attention back inside the train car, he focused on the old man across from him. "European theater, sir." Davis gave what he hoped was a smile. "Third Army under Patton."

"Welcome home," the white-haired man said with an answering smile.

Davis nodded and turned his gaze back to the blur of green fields. Home. His heart had been pounding since pulling out from Blanchester. He rubbed his palms on his khaki pants.

"Nervous?" the old man asked.

Davis opened his mouth to lie, then remembered he didn't have to be tough. There was no company to lead—there were no men who needed their sergeant to show constant confidence. "Yes, sir."

"I fought in the first war," the old man said. He pulled a handful of lemon drops from his pocket and held them out across the rocking train. There was pocket lint stuck to the candy. Davis popped one into his mouth, letting the lint roll to the side. He'd eaten far, far worse over the past few years.

"Not an easy thing, coming home."

"No, sir." The old man couldn't know the half of it.

They sucked their lemon drops in silence for a few minutes.

"Were you army?" Davis asked.

"Fought at Marne." The old man sat up straighter.

Davis and the old man nodded at each other again with a bob of respect. The train car jolted and the old man, caught off guard, dropped the newspaper he'd been holding. Davis picked it up, noting a headline about the Nuremberg Trials. A horrible image of Buchenwald came unbidden to his mind. He folded the paper so all that showed were the advertisements and handed it back to his companion.

The old man nodded his thanks and said incongruously, "I'll tell you the secret."

Davis's eyebrows lifted. "What secret?"

The old man leaned forward and tapped Davis's knee. "To coming home."

"There's a secret to coming home?" Was he joking?

The old man wasn't smiling. He looked more than serious as he tugged at his cardigan. "Didn't you have a buddy in the army who taught you the tricks to staying alive? You know, the secrets you never learned in basic training?"

Davis nodded. A few soldiers had taught him the finer points of war. Things like keeping a pair of dry socks in your helmet—there was nothing worse than trench foot—or the art of digging a good foxhole.

"Well," the old man poked a finger in the direction of Davis's uniformed chest. "There are tricks to coming home too."

"Oh?" Davis sat back in his seat.

"First thing, you get yourself a good job that you love."

Davis rubbed his forehead. He was twenty-four and still had years left of college and law school before he could join his father's law practice. A good job was a long way away.

"Then you get yourself a sweetheart."

Davis frowned. He had had a sweetheart when he left. He'd never forget opening Daisy's letter on a miserable, rainy day near the front. The letter had taken two months to reach him, and by then she'd been married for weeks and there was nothing he could do about it. The very thought of her brought a taste of bile to his mouth. He swallowed hard. No, thank you. There was no plan for a sweetheart in his near future. He shifted in his seat. Too much of what had always been home for him was gone now. It was why he hadn't fought to be in the first group of returning soldiers.

"And last," the old man said, "—and this is the most important of all—just get on with your life."

It sounded easy—get on with life. But how? How did he get on with it when everything felt so uncertain? But the friendly old man seemed to mean well, so Davis offered him one more smile and glanced at his wristwatch. After four long life-changing years, he was almost home. A half hour more and the train would pull into Payson. Was the saying true that a person could never go home again?

His heart beat too fast, trying to match the rhythm of the train's wheels clanking over the tracks. They moved in sync with the old man's advice—*get on with life, get on with life, get on with life.*

Davis closed his eyes. His thoughts drifted and filled with Patrick. The first time he'd ridden a train had been with Patrick when they were cocky thirteen-year-olds. They'd spent all their money on peanuts and taffy. Patrick had thrown up in the train's lavatory from an overstuffed stomach that couldn't handle the train's rocking motion. But that hadn't dampened either boy's enthusiasm for the trip.

His thoughts jumped to the last time he and Patrick had been together on a train. They'd been less cocky, much quieter, and sad about what they were leaving behind. But they'd had each other and a sense of being part of something noble.

The train rounded a curve and Davis's cheek pressed against the smooth, cool window. Eyes still closed, he sighed. Maybe this was the same train he and Patrick had left together on over four years ago. For a moment, he could imagine that Patrick was sitting next to him in that quiet way of his. They would laugh about the linty lemon drops as they made their way out of the train, placing bets on whose mother would be the most excited to see her son.

The feeling of Patrick's presence was so real that Davis opened his eyes half expecting to see his best friend sitting next to him. His breath caught. The seat, of course, was empty.

CHAPTER 2

FAITH PENWILLIGER NEVER MINDED DRYING the dishes, thanks to the radio that sat on a shelf above the bread box. Energy pulsed through her to the beat of the big-band music. Mom, efficient as ever, stood at the sink washing dishes, then passing them to Faith to dry and put away in their tidy cupboards.

The Glenn Miller Orchestra's upbeat version of "The Rhumba Jumps" came on.

"I love this song." Faith bounced on the balls of her feet. Moving to the rhythm, she put away the water pitcher. Spinning, dishcloth over her head, she danced her way back to the sink for the next dish.

"You sure have energy," Mom commented as she scrubbed cherry lipstick off a glass.

Faith smiled. The music filled her, leaving no room for thoughts of the brick-store troubles or Mr. Holland's offer.

"Just practicing for the dance competition," she said with a theatrical flourish of the dish towel. Leaving her mother holding the glass out to be dried, she rhumba'd across their green-and-white-checked linoleum.

"Ah yes," Mom said, her back stiffening. "The dance competition with Freddy."

"Yes, Freddy. It's going to be a lot of fun." Mom might not get it, but Faith had needed Freddy and dancing these last few years.

"Fun," Mom echoed, eyebrows raised.

A mellow baritone announced that the next song would be "Solamente Una Vez." Faith cha-cha'd over to her mother, waving the white dishcloth back and forth to make her movements more dramatic.

"Fun." She extended her hand. "Dance with me, Mom."

"Don't be silly." Mom reached for the next dish without looking up.

Faith looped her arms and the lemon-smelling dishcloth around her mother's waist and gently pulled her away from the sink. Some people had to be forced to have fun, and Mom was definitely one of those people.

"You know you want to. Come on. Cha-cha."

Mom sighed and put the rose-patterned dinner plate back in the sudsy water. "I don't know how you always manage to talk me into your nonsense," she said, but she began to sway to the music, trying to get her feet to imitate what her daughter's were doing. "I'm not as agile as you are."

"You've got it. There you go," Faith said. She grabbed Mom's damp, soapy-smelling right hand in her left and then placed her own right hand on Mom's shoulder blade, taking the man's part. "One, two, cha-cha-cha," she encouraged as she steered her mother around the kitchen with dramatic steps and tight turns.

The band blasted the last note of the song. Faith dipped Mom down with a flare and brought her back up before she could protest. Mom's red hair bounced. Faith had always admired its vibrant color. Her own hair was a deep brown with just hints of auburn.

Movement in the backyard caught her eye. "Oh look, Mrs. Wilson is coming across."

Hurrying to the counter where the radio stood, Mom turned it off as if she didn't want to be caught listening to big-band music, let alone dancing to it. "My land, she better not have seen me trying to cha-cha," she said, confirming Faith's suspicions. She patted her carefully waved chin-length hair.

"Your hair is just fine," Faith said as her mother crossed toward the back door.

Mom shook her head with a wry look at Faith and opened the door for Cecilia Wilson, their next-door neighbor.

Faith blinked. Mrs. Wilson looked as though she had just run a race, her middle-aged, somewhat stout body trembling as she grabbed the doorjamb dramatically, pausing to gasp for breath. Beads of perspiration shone on her forehead under her bottle-blonde hair that flapped wildly. Faith eyed her scatterbrained neighbor's outfit. Even for the eccentric Mrs. Wilson, it looked a bit crazy. She sported a yellow housedress with pink roses on it, one turquoise bedroom slipper, and one white bedroom slipper. What was she so excited about?

Mom gestured for her to come in.

Mrs. Wilson stepped right to the center of the room and the center of attention as she fanned herself with a piece of paper and beamed at Faith and Mom. "The best news, the best news!" She paused to gulp a few more breaths and turned toward Mom.

"Read it!" She waved a paper that looked to be a telegram at her, the movement making it impossible to obey.

Faith gasped as understanding hit her. Oh no. How cruel for Mom to have to see this.

"You have Davy's return plans?" Mom asked in a matter-of-fact tone.

"Yes," Mrs. Wilson squealed. "He's a week early. Not that he's early. I mean, good grief, it's been almost a year since VE Day." She fanned herself with the telegram. "But his ship arrived in New York sooner than expected and he'll be here tonight." She stopped to take another big breath.

"That's absolutely wonderful, Cecilia." Mom's words were congratulatory, but her face was expressionless.

Faith felt as though she were choking and couldn't have said a word even if she had wanted to. How did Mom manage to speak? She returned to the sink and slowly, methodically continued to dry the dishes. The glasses squeaked in protest as she applied too much pressure.

"Oh, Marcia, I get to see my son today—today! Dessert. He'll be here for dessert." She paused. Was it dawning on her how this might affect the Penwilligers? Faith set the cup down and turned toward Mrs. Wilson and Mom, but Mrs. Wilson, grinning, continued. "Sergeant Wilson—it has such a ring to it. The girls are going to go crazy for him."

Faith snorted her disgust. Mom frowned at her. How annoying! Mom was worried about Mrs. Wilson's feelings even though there was no reciprocity of sensitivity as their neighbor stood there beaming, perfectly obtuse in her own happiness to the complexity of feelings in the room.

"Janet and Carrie are working on a pie," Mrs. Wilson said. "Can you help me tie the yellow ribbons up?"

Faith grabbed a mug that needed drying while Mom agreed, saying, "Just let me finish tidying up and I'll be right over."

"It almost makes it all worth it."

Faith gasped, amazed again at her neighbor's insensitivity. She peeked again over her shoulder as Mrs. Wilson smiled and hugged the precious telegram to her chest.

"We are truly pleased for you," Mom said.

Faith returned her attention to the dinnerware and rubbed vigorously with her dishcloth. There wouldn't be a molecule of water left on this mug.

"Well"—Mrs. Wilson conspiratorially lowered her voice—"I've been thinking Faith might be the girl for our Davy."

Oh good heavens, did Mrs. Wilson think Faith couldn't hear her? "I don't need to date. I have Freddy," Faith said, her voice high.

Mrs. Wilson went right on. "You've really turned into a sweet little beauty. I told James just last week you have the grace of Ginger Rogers and looks like Hedy Lamarr. I'm thinking Davy might pay some notice."

Faith frowned. How easily her neighbor dismissed Freddy. She set the mug down hard and whirled around from the sink. "Mrs. Wilson, I have no—"

"Cecilia, thank you for sharing your happy news," her mother quickly interrupted. "I'll be right over."

"I have so many people to phone," Mrs. Wilson called over her shoulder.

Faith threw her dishcloth down in disgust. Mom waved and shut the back door.

The kitchen was quiet, as if Mrs. Wilson had sucked something out of the room.

Mom gave Faith a wry smile. "I imagine that will be one costly telephone bill for the Wilsons this month."

"Oh, Mom," Faith cried. "Don't try to joke about this. How can you stand it? Waving that telegram in our faces—doesn't she know what a telegram means to us? She's simply awful!"

Mom wrapped Faith in her strong, capable arms. "She doesn't mean to be hurtful. I find that goes a long way, and as my granny used to say, 'A great person grows fat on others' happiness.'"

Faith returned the hug. Mom was too kind, too sweet, too easy for people to take advantage of. It was why Faith ran the store.

"Do you want to help me with the ribbons?"

"I need to go back into the store to look over something. I won't be there to welcome him home."

Mom nodded, but her brow furrowed.

Faith stepped back from her mother, fists balled. Thinking of Davy brought back the feelings of anger and hurt from the last time she'd seen him. Hopefully, his stay at home would be brief and their paths wouldn't cross.

CHAPTER 3

His family's love and greeting at the train station were everything Davis could have dreamed. Dad's eyes shone with tears, and he kept placing his hand on Davis's arm or around his shoulders, as if to reassure himself that Davis was real, that his son truly was home.

Carrie and Janet looked so old. His teen sisters hugged him. Janet was confident and tall now, nothing like the gawky thirteen-year-old he had left behind. His youngest sibling, Carrie, now fifteen, seemed shy of him and giggled a lot. Mom, however, was at no loss for words. She nearly plowed him over with her bear hug the moment he stepped off the train. She sobbed and talked nonstop as he gathered his duffel and made his way to the family Buick.

"Christopher and his family will be here in an hour or two. Linda is also on her way with her little ones. They can't wait to see you."

"That'll be great, Mom." Davis smiled. It would be good to see his older brother and sister and their families. It was strange to think that he had a niece and two nephews he hadn't even met yet. He settled into the back seat between his sisters. "Is Betsy still running?" he asked.

"Fired her up yesterday," Dad answered. He sounded emotional. "She's been waiting for you. She's running as well as she ever did."

Davis grinned. "As well as she ever did" wasn't very well. His old green Ford was a hunk of junk, but she was his hunk of junk. Tomorrow he'd take Betsy out for a spin. He rested his hand on the seat. "So soft," he murmured.

"What's soft?" Janet asked.

"The upholstery."

Carrie giggled, but Davis hadn't meant to be funny. It was the first time in years that he had been in a sedan. Trucks and jeeps weren't meant for comfort.

Dad pulled away from the station, and they headed toward home. Davis had also forgotten that transportation could be anything but bumpy. He leaned back, letting the luxury of it all wash over him.

Downtown Payson was just as he had remembered it. Everything looked so clean, so well-kept, so modern.

"What are you thinking, son?" Dad asked, glancing at Davis in the rear-view mirror.

"How lucky Payson is to have two gas stations, both open," he said as they passed the bright-red pumps outside of Clyde's Auto.

"Thank heavens the gas rationing is over," Dad responded.

"The stores are all open too," Davis said.

Carrie giggled again. "Of course they are."

Dad drove the Buick past Greenfeld's Grocery, the bakery, the butcher store, and Marshal's Drugstore. Did his family know how lucky they were to have these luxuries? There was no sign in Payson of war deprivation.

"You don't have much luggage," Mom said.

"No," Davis agreed.

"No souvenirs?" Janet asked.

"I might have some French perfume wrapped up in an old army sock in the bottom of my duffel."

Carrie squealed, and he gave her ponytail a tug.

Mom turned around from the front seat. "You can only wear it on special occasions."

"Aw, Mom," Carrie said.

"I mean it."

Carrie and Janet grumbled, and Davis grinned at the normalcy of it all. What was it about his sisters? They glowed. He'd seen so many miserable people the last few years. Was it their look of vitality and health that caught at him? He stared at Carrie and then over at Janet on his other side when she told him about her new kitten, Bubbleboo. No, it wasn't just the look of health; it was something more.

"Did Faith name your cat?"

"Yeah, how'd you know?"

"That kid always came up with ridiculous pet names." Davis couldn't help grinning.

Mom turned back from the front seat again. "Faith isn't a kid anymore. She's very, very pretty and a hard worker. She'll be a real catch for the right man."

And there it was. Davis shook his head. It was all coming back to him—how irritating Mom could be and how she thought she was so subtle.

"Faith is rationed," Janet said.

What did that mean?

"She teaches our Sunday School class," Carrie interrupted.

"Faith teaches Sunday School?" That was hard to believe. "She used to laugh her way through church services. She gave Pastor Clemmons h—" Davis caught himself. He wasn't in the army anymore.

The girls giggled. Distracted by the happy sound, his arms around his sisters, he gave them each a squeeze. That something about them was more than health. He knew what his family had that he hadn't seen for so long.

"You're happy," he said. Happy and carefree.

More giggles. They pulled up to the white-painted home with its green shutters. Davis hauled his duffel out of the trunk and stared. He'd slept in barracks, tents, barns, and foxholes, and he was overwhelmed. Beautiful. It was beautiful and perfect. How had he forgotten how glorious their home was? He swung his duffel onto his shoulder and followed his family onto the yellow-ribboned front porch.

"It was like the tulips knew you were coming home and bloomed for you this week," Mom said.

He smiled at the cheerful flowers that lined the front walk and went inside. Everyone followed him up to his room and watched as he threw his duffel onto his bed and turned around, taking it all in. His pictures and posters were still thumbtacked to the wall. The room was full of memories that belonged to a different life—to Davy. Had the room always been so large?

"I kept everything just as you left it," Mom said.

Davis touched the signed picture of Joe DiMaggio. Patrick had had an identical one. Was it still in Patrick's room, or had Mrs. Penwilliger thrown it away? He hoped not. Patrick had been so proud of it. But why did the thought of the picture being thrown out trouble Davis so much? A stupid DiMaggio picture was the least of what Mrs. Penwilliger and Faith must have dealt with the last few years.

Davis spent the next hour being pulled from room to room while Mom updated him on anything that had changed while he'd been gone. Outside, the sun had set, and Dad turned on a lamp in the front room. Mom showed Davis how the lampshade could be angled to hit Dad's easy chair and provide perfect reading light. Did she really think he cared about the new lamp? But he cared about her, so he nodded meekly. Then they went to the kitchen, where she demonstrated her new toaster. Dad watched too, not saying much. It was weird to be given a tour. It made Davis feel like a guest in his own home.

"The girls made your favorite for dessert," Mom said. "Apple pie and ice cream."

"Wonderful." Was that his favorite? He couldn't remember anymore. He'd eaten too many MREs to be picky.

"I'll just warm it back up."

"I'm going to pop over and say hi to the Penwilligers," Davis said. He didn't want to put it off. "I won't be long."

"Want me to come with?" Dad asked softly.

Davis shook his head. He needed to see Mrs. Penwilliger alone.

Soon he was at the Penwilligers' red front door. Faith must have painted it. She always did love bright, cheerful colors. His heart hammered, and for a moment, he thought of retreating. But no, he was a soldier, and if the last few years had taught him anything, they'd taught him to face things head-on. He knocked, three soft raps.

As he waited, he let his eyes wander over the house and lawn. What was wrong with that board on the edge of the porch? It looked like it needed to be pounded down. How many times had he stood in this very spot, banging to interrupt Patrick's piano practicing and hollering for him to come play ball?

The porch light went on, and Davis's heartbeat accelerated as the door swung open. Marcia Penwilliger blinked and looked up at him. She looked older. There were gray streaks in her red hair and wrinkle lines around her eyes. They stood staring at each other for a moment, and then Mrs. Penwilliger opened her arms and Davis stepped into them, giving her a tight hug.

"Come in," she said.

Davis followed her into the front room, and they each took a seat. The room was exactly how he remembered it. Except Patrick's piano was shut.

"You look good, Davy. More handsome than ever."

"Thank you. I go by Davis now." Davy had been a carefree boy; he no longer existed.

"I forgot Davis is your real name." She smiled. "It suits you."

"Thanks."

"I've prayed for you every night."

He cleared his throat. "That means a lot to me. How are you and Faith?"

"We're doing just fine." Mrs. Penwilliger ran her hand through her hair. Patrick's had been red and wavy like his mom's. "I've appreciated your letters," she added.

They chatted about everything except Patrick.

It was strange to see the piano closed. It had always been open, with stacks of music ready to play.

"Does Faith still play the piano?" Davis asked.

"No. Not since Patrick's death."

And there were the words, solemn and stark. Davis had come home, but Patrick never would.

Davis shifted on the sofa. "I felt his loss sharply when news first reached me, but I'm feeling it all over again now." He swallowed hard. "Home isn't going to be home without him here."

"You two always were inseparable." Mrs. Penwilliger's smile was watery.

Davis rubbed his knee. "We didn't seem to be a logical combination. Patrick was so talented and serious, and I was so—"

"So good for him," Mrs. Penwilliger finished. They sat for a while, neither of them saying anything, but the silence was comfortable and even restful.

Then Davis stood. "Is Faith here? I wanted to say hi." She had been so angry the last time he'd seen her. He wanted to make sure all was forgiven between them.

"No, uh, no. She went back into the store to finish up a little business."

"She works at the store?"

"She's been running it ever since Charles died."

That was a lot to take in. Skinny little Faith, with the huge brown eyes, the cheerful tagalong without a serious bone in her body, running a business? Davis blinked. It seemed impossible. Perhaps Mrs. Penwilliger meant Faith was helping run it.

"I was so sorry to hear of Mr. Penwilliger's death."

Mrs. Penwilliger's eyes filled with tears again. "It was unexpected. The week after we got the telegram about Patrick, he had a heart attack. I think the shock and stress were too much for him."

There were no words to make it better. Davis's hands twisted together. "Can I stop by tomorrow to fix your porch?" he asked.

"My porch?"

"There's a loose board."

Mrs. Penwilliger looked puzzled. "Why, yes, there is."

As Davis walked home a few minutes later, he didn't need to wonder what Patrick would want if he were here. The future was hazy and Davis's path forward uncertain. Going back to college, then law school, and joining Dad's practice had always been the plan, but now that plan seemed shaky and unappealing.

There was one thing, though, that he was sure of—Patrick would want him to look out for Marcia and little Faith.

CHAPTER 4

FAITH WAS TOO DISTRACTED TO get anything done at work. Coming in had been an excuse, at any rate, to avoid Davy. It was going to be painful and embarrassing to see him again. She would postpone that misery as long as she could, thank you very much.

She walked around thinking—just thinking. The warehouse part of Penwilliger Brick Store was cold and filled with the earthy smell of bricks. Faith wandered down the long room, in no hurry to go home. Lester's workbench, no surprise, was a mess. She frowned. He knew how she felt about cleaning up. He was a good brickmason but couldn't handle having a twenty-year-old boss who, of all things, was a girl. The middle-aged man was surly with a bad attitude as hard as the bricks he worked with.

Faith sighed, filled a bucket with water, and put Lester's caked trowel in it to soak. Man, she would love to fire him, but she was too shorthanded. At least Juan and Frank respected her. Juan, the eighteen-year-old who had come from Mexico to help with the labor shortage, was a godsend. He was hardworking and respectful with a quirky sense of humor. Frank, her right-hand man, had been waiting for the boys to come home from the war before he retired. The physical work was getting hard on the seventy-year-old.

She moved through the door that led to the front of the store, where the offer from Mr. Holland sat on her desk. Faith picked up the envelope and tapped it on her palm. If she accepted his offer to buy the store, she could start at Ohio State in the fall. She twirled, still holding the envelope. To think, by fall she could be attending college dances. College—she could become a teacher or a nurse or even study dance. And Freddy loved Columbus. She was certain he'd come up to visit and dance every weekend.

The envelope flew out of her hand and hit the wall. As she bent to pick it up, the pictures hanging on the wall caught her eye: Dad, young and smiling in front of his new brick store on opening day. Patrick, at a piano competition—all seriousness and concentration. A young Mom standing next to Dad, her hand in his. Little beaming ballerina Faith grinning for the picture.

Faith groaned. What was she thinking? She couldn't sell her family's store and heritage. She couldn't leave Mom. She was stuck here forever. Faith threw the envelope into a drawer. It was time to go home. It was almost ten and Mom would be starting to worry.

Faith put her bolero jacket on and placed the matching periwinkle tam at a jaunty angle over her shoulder-length hair. The bright colors usually cheered her up, but tonight she felt out of sorts.

She left through the warehouse, hopping into the truck she had nicknamed Abbot. The nickname was apt; it was a joke of a truck, making all kinds of exaggerated noises. Faith turned the key, popped the clutch, and bounced down the street. Abbot's shocks, from carrying heavy brick loads, were all but gone.

She turned the radio on to cover the truck's spluttering. A popular but sad war song, "Wonder When My Baby's Coming Home," blared. As Faith gave a little grunt of disgust and reached to turn the radio off, the truck hit a big pothole. She bounced, came down hard, and bit her tongue. She slapped the steering wheel with the palm of her hand in frustration, and a little tear rolled down her cheek. The day was catching up to her. The news of Davy coming home had her tied up in knots. Their argument from four years ago pulled forward in her mind and burned there like a hot lump of coal. But Patrick wasn't coming home.

More tears. No, that wasn't who she was. She was cheerful and strong. She didn't have to be sad. She turned the radio off and hummed "Somewhere over the Rainbow."

The Wilsons' home was all lit up as Faith pulled into her dark driveway. She opened the creaky truck door and did a hurried, inelegant shimmy to get down from the high seat, her A-line skirt riding up as she lowered herself, keys in hand, to the drive.

Turning to make her way inside, she heard a throat clear on the Wilsons' large veranda-style front porch.

She froze, knowing someone had just gotten quite the view of her legs. *Please don't let it be Davy.* Keeping her back to the Wilsons' house, she walked rapidly toward the safety of her own front porch. The smell of cigarette smoke hung in the night air.

"Faith!" a familiar voice exclaimed—a voice that had coaxed her to walk the fallen log over Miller's creek, a voice that had told Patrick to leave his practicing and "live a little," a voice that had been the first to laugh inappropriately in church, a voice Faith could still hear in her head, saying coldly, "Stop being such a spoiled princess."

She stopped again and turned reluctantly toward the tall, lean man. "Davy." He sat in a white rocking chair, smoking on his family's porch that was drowning in yellow ribbon. She couldn't help staring. Davy had always been attractive, with his wavy light-brown hair and blue eyes, but now he looked like a soldier, not the college boy she remembered.

He stood up from the rocking chair. "You drive?"

"I have for some time now. You smoke?"

He mimicked her answer. "I have for some time now."

"Ah well," she mumbled. "Welcome home."

"Thank you."

The sound of laughter coming from the Wilson home seemed out of sync with the serious-looking soldier on the porch. Not knowing what else to do, Faith waved and continued toward her front door.

Hopefully, Davy wasn't thinking of the last time he'd seen her, on that miserable January day of 1942. She could feel his eyes on her as she fumbled nervously with the keys. Her shaking hands dropped them to the porch with a clink. She scooped them up. Finally, she managed to get the key in the lock. It twisted and she slipped inside, closing the door softly behind her. She leaned against the door and said aloud, "Well, thank heavens that's over."

"What's over?" Mom asked.

Startled, Faith jumped and let out a little squeak. "You scared me!"

"You saw Davy?"

"Um, yeah." Faith's face went warm.

"Poor Davy—Davis, that is. He's had nonstop love and loudness since he arrived."

"Davis?"

Mom frowned just a bit. "He told me he goes by Davis now. He seems so much older that I suppose it is fitting," she said uncertainly.

"How was your evening? I imagine Mrs. Wilson ran you ragged."

Mom chuckled. "It wasn't too bad. I do love all the Wilson kids. Linda drove over with her family, and Christopher and his wife came down too. It's been so fun to see them all today, and words can't describe seeing Davy—Davis—again. He came over to see me earlier. He's changed." She paused, probably waiting for Faith to ask how he had changed, but Faith said nothing. Mom wrinkled her brow, as if searching for the words to describe the new Davis. "Don't you think he looks the same but different?"

Faith shrugged. "I guess so." He was as handsome as ever, but she wasn't going to admit that.

"He's a man now," Mom said. "Serious and self-assured."

"I imagine he had a hero's welcome." Faith couldn't hide the tinge of irritation in her voice.

"Well, Cecilia did her best. James found out she planned to purchase a piece of red carpet and roll it down the front steps. He talked her out of it, but I think there are over three hundred yellow ribbons in the trees and front porch. It took ten of us tying for an hour to get them all up, and I'm not looking forward to removing them."

"You don't have to help with everything," Faith said.

Mom changed the subject. "Come up to my room. I want to see what you think of a letter that came from Rose in the evening post."

Good. Faith would a million times rather talk about her cousin Rose than Davy's homecoming. She followed Mom up the stairs. The door to Patrick's room was, as always, closed. It seemed to be calling to her tonight. Was that because Davy was back? She often wondered why her mother had sorted through her father's things and given them away but couldn't do the same in Patrick's room.

She stepped into Mom's pretty lavender room. The decorations were floral pictures and lace. It was a feminine, dainty room that reflected Mom in its beauty, neatness, and details.

Faith kicked off her shoes, took off her jacket and tam and threw them onto the bed, then plopped down lengthwise over her mother's lavender lace bedspread.

"I feel like something isn't right with Rose." Mom pulled a pale-yellow envelope from a stack on her vanity and walked it over to Faith, who sat up with more energy to take it.

Her cousin Rose had grown up across the state in Cleveland, and although they saw each other only a few times a year, the two girls were extremely close. Two years ago, right before Patrick and Dad died, Rose had been working as a secretary in Washington, D.C. She'd met a handsome sailor, Joey Russo, who was on a two-week shore leave, and married him before he'd shipped back out.

Joey had returned home a month ago and moved Rose to his home in Brooklyn. This letter was the Penwilligers' first news of how Rose was liking married life and a new home.

Pulling the letter from the envelope, Faith asked, "Shall I read it out loud?"

"I've read it, but I would love to hear it again. I wasn't sure what to make of it," Mom said, coming over to sit on the bed next to Faith.

Faith moved her jacket to the other side of herself and started reading.

"Dear Faith and Aunt Marcia,

It feels as though so much has happened since I last wrote. I hope you are in good health and that the business is going well. Faith, let me know more about your dancing. It sounds like so much fun. You'll have to teach me the new steps next time we're together. Give Freddy a big hug for me.

New York this spring is quite the place to be. There are returning servicemen all over the place—they bring so much energy. In fact, energy and newness of life seem to be the theme right now. I had the chance to see Central Park last week, and it was just as pretty as I imagined, everything in bloom. The callery pear trees were my favorite. I love the color and the smells. I could close my eyes and imagine for a minute that I was back home.

It certainly is an adventure. I was on First Avenue last week, making my way toward my office, when I passed by a rather large group. Turns out it was a huge party from the United Nations made up, of course, of people from all over the world. They were on some type of tour. I felt like I was witnessing history, and a huge lump of hope rose in my throat—hope that the UN will be the answer our weary world needs. I don't believe we can endure another world war.

Good news—I was able to secure a job. I work nine to five as a secretary for a law firm in Manhattan. Mostly I take dictation and type letters. It takes a while to get there from Brooklyn, but I bring novels to read on the train or sometimes look around at my fellow commuters and try to picture what they do. I've decided that the grumpy man who sits kitty-corner from me nearly every morning is either a Nazi spy who doesn't know the war is over, a newsman, or has severe indigestion.

My job is a good one in a nice office, and I feel lucky to have it. Brooklyn has been eye-opening for me. I thought Washington, D.C., was a melting pot, but it doesn't even compare to Brooklyn. I've met neighbors of nearly every nationality.

Joey's three sisters have to sleep in the living room, and we sleep in their room. With my first paycheck we plan to find a little apartment of our own. I think Joey will be happier when we have our own place.

I long to hear from you. I miss you so much. Please write. Dance your heart out for me and know I think of you every day.

Love and kisses,
Your Rose

P.S. Faith, women here are wearing black-and-white houndstooth suits with crewnecks underneath and matching berets. A jade-green crewneck would bring out your chocolatey eyes and the copper high-lights of your gorgeous hair—how I wish mine weren't just plain red. Anyway, I digress. It's not exactly a summer outfit, but if you made one up for fall, it would put you as the next thing in style. Your mom is so good with a needle. I'll see if I can find a picture to send you so you can be the trendsetter for Payson."

Neither Faith nor Mom said anything for a moment. Then Mom tapped the bedspread with her fingers. "Does that letter strike you as odd?"

"Yes," Faith said. "There's really nothing about her marriage in there. Rose was always gushing about Joey when she was living in D.C. and he was at sea."

"I imagine this is a very hard adjustment. She sounds homesick. And she really didn't know much about Joey when they married. Maybe we should give her a call tomorrow."

Faith nodded. "Good idea." Calling Rose marked how worried Mom was. Faith could count on one hand the number of times Mom had placed a long-distance call. "Let's phone her tomorrow evening when I'm home from work."

"These wartime marriages are so . . . ," Mom said.

"Rushed," Faith finished. "That's why Freddy and I aren't official. We're taking things slow. We're just enjoying being dance partners." *And the occasional good-night kiss*, Faith added in her head.

Mom opened her mouth, then closed it, and mother and daughter were quiet for some time. Faith should get up and go to bed, but there was one more thing she needed to talk to Mom about, something she wanted to nip in the bud. She squirmed on the bed. "Don't let Mrs. Wilson get any ideas about Davy and me. I'm not interested, and he'll be looking for another Daisy Phillips anyway."

"Don't forget he was only twenty when he dated Daisy," Mom said.

"Thank heavens Patrick had more common sense than that," Faith said. "Davy probably doesn't even realize what a narrow escape he had. Daisy is as pretty as a picture and as shallow as the canvas it's painted on." Ha. Mom wasn't the only one who could fling Granny's sayings around.

"You didn't like Daisy because you had a schoolgirl crush on Davis," Mom said matter-of-factly.

Faith felt her cheeks grow warm, embarrassed that her mother remembered that. She shook her head as if to dislodge the memory and then stood up. Her hand went to her hip. "Well, it was pretty easy to see the attraction didn't involve Daisy's mind. Just for the record, my crush is long since over and you could do me a huge favor by squelching Mrs. Wilson's expectations." She leaned down and gave her mother's shoulder a gentle squeeze. She had the best mother in the world, but her goal was to avoid Davy Wilson at all costs. Some things shouldn't have to be revisited. There was too much embarrassment, hurt, and anger.

Mom gave a funny look that Faith couldn't decipher and said, "Leave your jacket behind. It's a bit wrinkly. I'll press it for you."

She gave Mom a good-night kiss. "You're a doll."

Mom's voice stopped her at the door. "Just for the record, I think you two would make a good match too."

Faith scowled and kept right on walking. Handsome soldier or not, there was absolutely no chance Davy was her match.

***

The next day, following dinner, Mom and Faith placed their call to Rose. They shared the handset, standing close to each other so they could both hear.

The phone rang three times, and then a young female voice answered. "Russos."

"May I please speak with Rose?" Mom asked.

"You her mom?" the girl on the other end asked.

"No, this is her aunt Marcia."

"And her cousin Faith," Faith said.

There was a loud sound. Was the girl popping her gum?

"You want to speak to the princess?"

Faith could feel the sneer through the phone without seeing it. My, Joey's sister had attitude. Princess? Rose was one of the most levelheaded people Faith knew. She was far from a pampered princess. Faith frowned and looked at Mom, who was also frowning.

"Could you get Rose?" Mom tapped her toes and looked at her watch. Time was money on these pricey long-distance calls.

"Rose!" the girl hollered so loudly that even from five-hundred miles away, Faith and Mom both jumped. "Telephone!"

"Aunt Marcia? Faith?" Faith leaned in closer and rested her head on Mom's shoulder so she could hear better. Rose sounded out of breath. "Is something wrong?"

Mom and Faith exchanged glances. That was exactly what they had hoped to find out from Rose.

"No, no," Mom reassured her. "We just wanted to see how you're doing."

Angry voices screamed at each other in the background, but Faith couldn't make out the words. She gripped the phone tighter.

"Oh, well," Rose said. Her voice shook. "I'm fine."

"It sounds like we called at a bad time," Faith said.

Rose whispered. "Mr. and Mrs. Russo are having words. I'm so sorry." She sounded embarrassed. "The apartment is awfully small. I think things will be better once we get our own place."

The chaos in the background continued. Faith put her arm around Mom's waist and squeezed.

"Could I speak with Joey?" Mom asked. Faith wondered what Mom would say to Rose's husband.

"He's out dancing."

Faith frowned. Why was Joey out without his wife?

"Can we send you some money to help with moving into your own place?" Mom asked.

Rose gasped. "I wouldn't dream of it! I'm making a good salary. We should be able to move out soon. Thanks for your love though." Her voice faltered again. "I could use your prayers more than anything. It's been so hard for Joey, coming home from the war and all."

"I see," Mom said. "We'll be praying for you. We love you, Rose."

"I love you too," Rose said.

There was nothing more to say, and the minutes were adding up. "Bye, sweetie. Take a bite out of the Big Apple for me," Faith said.

Rose gave a little laugh that made Faith feel a bit better. "Will do."

"Goodbye," Mom said.

Rose rang off and Mom set the handset back in its cradle. "That didn't sound good," she said, her tone flat and unhappy.

"No, it really didn't," Faith agreed, wrapping her arms tighter around Mom and hugging her for comfort. What kind of marriage was Rose in?

CHAPTER 5

"So Freddy Casper and Faith, huh? They been dating long?" Davis asked.

He was in the process of changing a leaky pipe in the Penwilligers' upstairs bathroom. He'd like to ask Faith about Freddy, but he'd been home two weeks now and hadn't seen her other than at church.

Mrs. Penwilliger hesitated. "After Patrick and Charles died, Faith took on a lot." She frowned. "She was just eighteen and needed an outlet. You know, Freddy is a marvelous dancer."

Davis just grunted.

"They started going out and entering competitions. They practice two or three times a week."

He frowned. Two or three times a week? Faith was out late with Freddy Casper two or three times a week? This was what Janet had been trying to tell him when she'd said Faith was rationed. Davis yanked the wrench and it hit his thumb. It smarted like crazy, but he couldn't curse in front of Marcia Penwilliger. He shook his hand out. Smoking and cursing were two habits he'd acquired in the army that weren't translating well at home. Mom hated the smoking, and he was constantly having to choke back curse words.

"Are they going steady?"

"No." Mrs. Penwilliger shook her head. "They've been dance partners for the last two years, but they aren't exclusive."

"Two years?" He felt out of touch with dating, but that sounded serious to him.

Mrs. Penwilliger met his eyes and sighed. "Two years they've been dancing together. Faith says Freddy isn't her boyfriend, but everyone in Payson thinks of them as a couple." She grimaced. "I don't think she'll be able to date anyone seriously until she stops spending so much time with Freddy." She paused and rubbed her chin. "He doesn't seem to have any plan to further their relationship."

Was that true or simply what Mrs. Penwilliger wanted to believe? Faith had changed, more than a little. She was a woman, and a very kind, beautiful, competent one at that. Freddy would be a fool not to marry her. Watching out for Faith, like he knew Patrick and Mr. Penwilliger would want him to do, was going to be a challenge for Davis.

He hadn't been sleeping well. Was that what made him feel so grumpy about the idea of Faith spending so much time with Freddy Casper? No, it was more than that. He remembered Freddy quite well from high school. They'd graduated in the same class. The man was shallow, and unless he had changed, he wasn't the right man for Faith.

Davis stared at the pipe. Two years? Two years could mean a lack of courage on Freddy's part, or it might mean that he and Faith were firmly dug into their trenches and wouldn't be easily pulled out. Still, taking no action for two years, staying in the same trench—it made you a sitting duck. A sitting duck that Davis was sure Mr. Penwilliger and Patrick would want him to get rid of.

He came out from under the sink and exchanged his wrench for a larger one. Mrs. Penwilliger frowned. He'd bet anything she didn't like Freddy any more than he did. She was just too polite to ever say so.

"So how did Faith end up running the brick store?"

Mrs. Penwilliger sighed. "When Charles died, Faith had just graduated from high school and was going to leave for Ohio State. I wanted to stick to the plan, but she refused to leave me alone."

The pipe threaded correctly this time, and Davis gave it a strong twist. "Oh?"

"I tried my hand at the store, but I was a failure. I was horrible at managing the men and the accounts. Faith stepped in and insisted I run the house and she run the store. She's been making it work ever since."

Faith reminded Davis of a Captain Jones he'd fought with. Jonesy, as they'd called him, had been an English teacher before the war. He was soft-spoken and slight of stature, but he'd proved himself to be much more than his mild looks and manners. He was brave in battle and took care of his men. Faith, it seemed, just like Jonesy, was more than she appeared. She had risen to her challenges and proved that she was far more than the young girl Davis had left behind.

"How do the men like having a female boss?" he asked.

Mrs. Penwilliger sighed. "Faith doesn't tell me much. Frank, of course, is wonderful—he's like a grandfather looking out for her—but I can tell Lester is a problem. He isn't at all respectful to Faith. On the other hand, Juan is amazing. At first I thought he was shy, but I think he was just homesick and figuring out English. When his English improved, we realized he has a hilarious sense of humor."

"I know and respect Frank. Juan sounds great, but why doesn't Faith fire Lester?"

"We need him. He does good work, and it isn't like there have been many men around to hire. Juan came from Mexico as part of the Bracero Treaty to help with our labor shortage. Frank stayed on to help until the war was over, and Faith keeps begging him to stay a little longer, but the physical work is hard for him." She exhaled. "Faith might seem frivolous to some, with her dancing, but she works hard and she needs the spot of fun it provides. She reminds me of one of my granny's sayings: 'The light heart lives long.'"

Davis jiggled the new piece of pipe to make sure it was in securely.

Sure, Faith needed an outlet, but why did it have to be with Freddy Casper? Freddy was from a wealthy family and had always been beyond spoiled. How would Davis describe him? He wiped his hands on his slacks.

Patrick had once said about Freddy, *"There's no there, there."* Davis smiled. That was it exactly. Freddy had never had any depth to him. Not to mention how artfully he had evaded military service. Freddy and Faith? No, no, and no. But how could he stop it?

Looking out for Marcia Penwilliger was simple. He fixed things for her, and they enjoyed each other's company. But Faith was going to be another story. She was certainly no longer "little Faith." An image of her getting out of the truck came to mind. She and her long legs were trouble.

Before Davis could think about what that meant, they were interrupted by Faith's voice calling from downstairs, "I'm home, Mom," followed by a laugh Davis remembered from high school. Freddy Casper always had sounded like a donkey when he laughed. Davis pounded the pipe a little harder than necessary.

"I left your dinner on the table," Mrs. Penwilliger called back. "Davis and I are working on a little plumbing problem up here."

"Thanks, Mom," Faith's voice floated up. Was it his imagination, or did she sound uncomfortable? He hoped so. "I'm going to eat and then practice some steps with Freddy."

"We'll be dancing in the Coconut and Avocado Club tonight," Freddy hollered up.

"Coconut and Avocado?" Davis asked. Freddy's voice irritated him, and not just because of his lack of sleep.

Mrs. Penwilliger whispered, "He calls our kitchen the Coconut and Avocado Club because of the green-and-white-checked linoleum."

Davis took a good look at her face. She wasn't happy. Apparently, he had an ally. If she was Great Britain, he was the United States, coming late to the war.

He gathered his tools and chatted a little more with her. She showed him a jammed window that would be simple to sand down and oil.

Faith and Freddy's dance music filled the house. The record player was in the front room, and they must have cranked the volume up so they could hear it in the kitchen.

"Sorry about the noise. I hope you two don't mind the music," Faith yelled up the stairs.

"We're fine," her mother called back. She turned to Davis and sighed. "'He who keeps his tongue keeps his friends.'"

Davis laughed. He had forgotten how much she loved her Irish sayings. "Is there anything else I can do for you?" He was in no hurry to go home. Faith was finally around, and he wanted to observe her with Freddy.

Mrs. Penwilliger gave him a thoughtful look. "You've already done so much. I can't tell you how much I appreciate all the little things you've fixed."

Davis cleared his throat and rubbed his hands on his slacks. "It's nothing. I love being in your home." He felt as though Patrick would have wanted this.

He glanced at Patrick's door. It was always shut. Was Patrick's stuff in there, futilely waiting for him to return from the war? Davis didn't have the heart to ask.

"Let's get a cold drink," Mrs. Penwilliger said.

Good. He would get to see what Faith and Freddy were doing. Davis followed Mrs. Penwilliger back down to the kitchen, where they walked into a sight that made his stomach turn. Freddy was rubbing Faith's shoulders. She looked gorgeous in a bright-pink blouse.

"Relax," Freddy said. "Why're you so tense?"

Faith made eye contact with Davis and stepped away quickly from Freddy. Davis scowled at them.

"Hi, old man."

Old man? He and Freddy were the same age. But in a way, it was true; Davis felt decades older than the over-groomed man next to him. It was satisfying to look down at Freddy, who was Faith's height, a head shorter than Davis.

Freddy looked him up and down, seemingly unimpressed with his jeans and plaid work shirt. Davis returned the appraisal. Freddy's hair was carefully slicked back, his tie was in place, and his clothes were pressed to perfection. *Hypergroomed*—that was the word to describe Freddy. The man looked like he had never done a day's worth of work in his life. Which, come to think of it, was probably true.

"I saw your hunk of green junk about town and was surprised you're back home already."

Davis's fists balled. *Already?* He'd been gone for four years that had felt like forty. "Yes," he said without expression. "The war sure went fast." He supposed if one evaded serving, like Freddy had, the war would have gone by quickly.

Freddy laughed loudly, patting Davis on the back. "Good one."

Davis's jaw started twitching—the same jaw twitch that had happened years ago, right before he'd slugged Kent Presley for mimicking the walk of a little girl who had recovered from polio but still needed braces.

Faith grabbed Freddy's arm and tugged him away from Davis, looking between the two men.

"How about a soda?" Mrs. Penwilliger asked.

Davis relaxed his jaw. "Sounds good."

Faith scowled at him. It was disconcerting to have her, the girl who had always tagged along after him and Patrick with admiration in her eyes, looking at him with dislike. What had he done to deserve a look like that?

An uncomfortable feeling settled inside his chest. Maybe it wasn't a coincidence that he hadn't seen her in the two weeks he'd been home. She was avoiding him. He rubbed the back of his neck. Was this about their angry words the night he'd told her that he and Patrick had enlisted? Good heavens, that had been over four years ago.

He frowned as his memory of that fight resurfaced. Faith had been how old? Let's see, she was four years younger than he and Patrick. She must have been sixteen. He'd thought she would be proud of their decision to enlist. Her unexpected anger had caught him off guard. He could easily admit now that she'd been right about Daisy, but she'd been wrong about Patrick enlisting.

Fine. If she wanted to nurse a grudge, he could handle it. He had survived sleeping in a foxhole for weeks last winter, and he could handle Freddy Casper too. Davis straightened and held his soldier posture, looking Faith right in the eyes.

Mrs. Penwilliger pulled four cold root beers out of the refrigerator, popped the caps off, and led the awkward group into the front room.

Freddy seemed completely oblivious of the tension as he sat on the floral wingback sofa guzzling his root beer and telling Mrs. Penwilliger about the preparations for some dance competition. He put his root beer down directly on the coffee table. Davis flinched. Did Freddy not notice the coaster Mrs. Penwilliger had set out? Davis stood and moved Freddy's root beer onto the coaster, then sat back down with a thud. Freddy, still oblivious, pulled Faith up to demonstrate some tricky footwork they had mastered for the swing dance. She made eye contact again with Davis and flushed.

"Show them the jazz hands you do while I swing you around my middle," Freddy said.

Freddy lifted her on his hip and began to spin in place. Faith didn't look excited, but she showed her jazz hands while Freddy spun enthusiastically. Davis couldn't make himself look away from her tucked up tightly against Freddy's side.

She narrowly missed kicking the lamp on the end table and squirmed out of Freddy's grasp. "This room isn't set up for dancing," she said. She tugged her skirt down and returned to her seat followed by a beaming Freddy.

"Pretty swell stuff, huh? We're cookin' with helium, as they say in the clubs."

Davis rolled his eyes. Good grief, was Freddy completely oblivious to the mood in the room? Davis sipped his root beer and scowled at him while Mrs. Penwilliger twisted her hands together and responded to the grinning Freddy with, "Yes, that's quite impressive." She added softly, "My niece, Rose's, husband likes to go out dancing a lot too."

Davis knew she was worried about what type of man her niece had married. A subtle insult. He liked it. Faith frowned at her mother.

"Her anchor clanker?" Freddy grinned.

"Yes, Joey was in the navy." Mrs. Penwilliger's lips pursed, and the room went silent.

Faith cleared her throat. "Isn't this root beer delicious?" The cheerfulness of her voice sounded forced.

Freddy leaned back against the sofa, took a gulp of his soda, and turned to Davis. "I hear the Germans don't like root beer; is that true?"

"It's hard to ask them beverage preferences when you're shooting at each other," Davis responded in a flat voice.

Freddy guffawed and slapped his knee. "Christopher Columbus! *Nein,* no *rutbir für die* bad boyz."

Davis turned and stared at Faith, who blushed. He gave her the same look he'd given fifteen-year-old Patrick when he'd tried to blacken his red hair with shoe polish. Patrick had explained that nobody would take a redheaded musician seriously. He'd said Davis's look had been what finally convinced him to go wash the black off. Faith dropped her eyes and squirmed on the couch.

"How is your mother getting along?" Mrs. Penwilliger asked, ever the expert on changing the subject.

"Oh, the old girl is in fine spirits. The war really kept her from traveling. She's missed France, and she's having a grand time planning a trip for later in the summer."

Davis couldn't keep his foot from beating a rapid tattoo on the carpet.

"Oh," Mrs. Penwilliger said. "I imagine she will be so happy to be in Paris again."

"She's just hoping her favorite seamstress didn't get displaced by the war and that she's still making her creations," Freddy said. "The girl is Jewish, and I guess a lot of them were relocated during the war."

This was too much. Davis set his soda down on his coaster with a thud. "Displaced? Relocated? Or do you mean murdered in a concentration camp? I was with the Third Army when we liberated Buchenwald. Trust me, the Jews weren't 'displaced.'"

"Yes, yes, old man. I read all about it in the paper." Freddy paused to take more root beer. "We were all affected by the war." He reached up to pat his slicked-back hair.

Davis gripped the hand-crocheted doily from the arm of the couch. Affected? Oh yeah, Freddy was affected, just not in the way he meant. Across from him Faith fidgeted and looked to her mother. Mrs. Penwilliger cleared her throat and said, "Faith, would you play something for us?"

Jumping up, Faith crossed quickly to the piano, sat down, and raised the lid. She stopped just before her fingers touched the keys. That's right. This must be a big moment for her. Mrs. Penwilliger had said Faith hadn't played since Patrick died. Davis leaned forward, relaxing his hold on the doily.

There was nothing in the Penwilliger home that evoked Patrick like the upright Steinway piano. Mr. Penwilliger had purchased it when it became apparent that Patrick wasn't going to just be a proficient pianist—he was going to be a master. By age twelve Patrick was spending hours memorizing concertos. It was Davis, knocking at the front door, who constantly pulled the serious Patrick outside and into mischief. Davis would assure him, "You can practice later. There's a game going at the park, and we need a good batter."

He could picture in his mind's eye Patrick's hands flying over the keys, a look of pure concentration on his face, his red hair poking out as if energized by the music. Davis shook his head and forced the image out of his mind. He leaned back in his seat and focused on Faith. She lowered her hands to the keys, then lifted them and looked to her mother. Mrs. Penwilliger gave her daughter an encouraging smile. Faith's hands hovered for a long moment. Davis leaned forward. He didn't know exactly why, but he knew Faith needed to play that piano. The war had taken so much. Had it stolen Faith's love of playing the piano too?

Slowly, she lowered her hands back to the keys. Freddy coughed and Davis shot him a glare. And then Faith began playing Pachelbel's "Canon in D." She was an accomplished pianist in her own right. The music built and it seemed that so did her confidence. The song pulled at Davis's anger over Freddy, tugging it gently away.

Faith finished and turned to her mother. They smiled at each other. Davis felt a surge of pride in the Penwilligers. It was as if Faith playing the piano was one more victory over Hitler. One little way to say that the war might have stolen Patrick and Mr. Penwilliger, but it couldn't stop the goodness of this piano's music—Faith was too strong, too resilient, for that. Davis smiled at her.

Freddy yawned and asked, "Can you play something I could sing to?"

And just like that, Davis's irritation was back. "I would love to hear some Chopin," he said. He'd be darned if he was going to listen to Freddy sing.

"Oh, that would be lovely," Mrs. Penwilliger agreed, jumping up. She pulled a book from the chest next to the piano. Davis couldn't help a little smug smile. He had a powerful ally.

Faith looked annoyed but played the piece anyway. Mrs. Penwilliger and Davis applauded, and Freddy yawned again and started to request something else. "Could you play—"

"That was beautiful," Davis interrupted.

Faith shrugged. "You must hear that I'm missing a lot of notes." She turned back to the piano.

Davis stared at her profile. She was more than pretty. "Beautiful," he said again and then quickly clamped his mouth shut. What was he thinking? This was Patrick's little sister he was admiring. He shouldn't be thinking of her like that. Besides, he was a mess. He couldn't sleep at night, and he had no idea what his future held. He didn't even know if he could make himself go back to college, for crying out loud. He jumped up and walked to the piano. He flipped the page over to some Bach and said, "How about that?"

Faith nodded. She played and played. Her mother and Davis seemed to understand each other perfectly. They never did let Freddy get a request in. After about a half hour of classical music, Freddy couldn't stop yawning and got up to leave in the middle of a number. He patted Faith on the shoulder. "See you later, alligator," he said and bounded out the front door. They could hear him gunning his Alfa Romeo and then peeling off down Forest Drive as Faith played the last few notes of "Mozart's Minuet in G."

"Thank you," Davis said, smiling. "That was wonderful." The music had been amazing, and he had won the first battle in the Great Freddy Casper War. No need to stay and gloat. He stood up, nodded to each of the women, and said, "I'll be back tomorrow, Mrs. Penwilliger, to take care of those shrubs."

Faith said, "Don't worry about it. I'll hire someone," just as Mrs. Penwilliger responded with, "That would be wonderful. And call me Marcia."

Davis left, whistling.

CHAPTER 6

FAITH STOOD UP FROM THE piano. She didn't know whether to laugh or cry. The Steinway had been opened and the music had poured out. Most importantly, it hadn't made her grieve for Patrick. The two strikingly opposite men in her front room had been all she could think of. But Davy was far too comfortable in the Penwilliger home. He had no right to scowl at Freddy, and what exactly was going on while she was at work? Why was Davy always here fixing things?

Mom hummed while she gathered the empty root beer bottles. Faith interrupted. "*Marcia?* You want Davy to call you Marcia? You told Freddy you preferred he call you Mrs. Penwilliger."

Mom paused her humming. "I consider Davis a friend."

"A friend? A friend who is always here. What are you doing, Mom? You never take help from others. Why are you letting Davy help?"

Mom set the bottles back down. Her head tilted thoughtfully. "He seems to love helping me. Davis and Cecilia are driving each other crazy. He has a long wait until he goes back to college in the fall and is awfully bored sitting at home. He wants a job but isn't sure what kind. Cecilia doesn't know what to do with this new Davis." Mom paused. "He came home lost. All he knows is that he wants to do something meaningful, and until he figures out what that is, I believe he is getting great satisfaction in doing little things for me that he knows Patrick or your father would have taken care of."

"He can't replace Dad or Patrick," Faith cried. "And I'm not sure I like you spending time with him."

"He's just trying to help, and I am certain I don't like who you are spending time with," Mom said, her tone as crisp as her ironing.

Faith gasped in hurt. "Freddy is fun. I've needed him, to stay sane."

Mom stood ramrod straight. "You can do better—much better—than Freddy Casper."

"Do you know how hard it was to . . ." She wanted to say, "To fill in for Daddy, to learn a new business, to give up my dreams of college?" but feelings of being underappreciated choked her throat closed. She simply said, "I needed the dancing and Freddy was available. I like him!"

Mom's cheeks were pink and her eyes narrowed. They both stood tall, facing each other with fists clenched at their sides, for a long moment. Faith broke eye contact first, turned, and ran up the stairs. She rushed into her room, slammed the door behind her, and flopped onto the bed. She rolled onto her back, kicking her pumps off onto the floor, and stared at her ceiling, thinking about the unfairness of it all. She had stepped up to be the head of the family, given up college, and taken the weight of Penwilliger Brick on her shoulders, and yet her mom and Davy didn't think she was old enough to decide on her boyfriend. Well, she wasn't trapped. Mr. Holland's offer sat in her desk drawer at work.

Faith scowled. Her mom had tolerated Freddy just fine these last two years—this was because of Davy—Davis. Somehow he was ruining the status quo. Her anger continued to build. She punched her pillow. She and Mom never fought—this was Davis's darn interfering. If he was going to be a fixture around home, then college and Mr. Holland's offer were sounding better and better. Freddy loved the clubs in Columbus. He'd probably come visit her every weekend.

Mom and Davis's opinion had glared through the awkward conversation and music. Freddy didn't measure up in their eyes. She knew full well that Freddy wasn't some hero returning from the war. He was fun, though, and handsome; not to mention he was a great dancer. Who were they to judge her for wanting to be with him? Why did Davis get to have an opinion of her relationship with Freddy? It was none of his business.

But it wasn't the first time she'd been judged by him. When Davis had told her that he and Patrick had enlisted, she had yelled at him in fury. Patrick was a musician and an only son. He shouldn't have enlisted. Davis had looked coldly at her and told her she was unaware and uncaring of what was happening in the real world. Harsh words indeed from the neighbor she had first idolized as a young girl and then fantasized about in her early teens. She couldn't bear to think about what she had said to him about Daisy. He hadn't responded to that comment, but her feelings had been further crushed by his response that cold January day. "Stop being such a spoiled princess. This isn't about you."

Those had been his last words to her as she had run up the stairs, leaving him in the front room, much the same way she had just left her mother. Those words had festered and troubled her all through the interminable war years, Patrick's death, her father's death, and the responsibilities of running the business. Faith stared at the ceiling and made a vow to herself. *I am not a silly girl or a princess. I am not pampered, and I will not let Davis Wilson boss me around.*

CHAPTER 7

SWEAT RAN DOWN DAVIS'S BACK. The sun had only been up for an hour and he was already overheated in the muggy May morning. He moved the shovel steadily, not allowing himself a break. It had rained overnight, and the soft ground gave off an earthy smell, mingling with the sweet scent of the wisteria that ran along the back porch.

Dad came out, mug in hand. He watched Davis silently while sipping his coffee. "The neighbors are going to think I'm using you for free labor."

Davis laughed but kept shoveling.

"What are you doing, son?"

"Didn't Mom tell you? I'm getting this area level, prepping it for cement. She's all excited about her backyard patio."

Dad's brow furrowed. "That's not what I meant. I know about the patio."

That got Davis's attention. He stopped shoveling, resting his boot on the edge of the shovel. "I just figured I could get the dirt moved and leveled before breakfast."

"So you got up early?"

Davis looked down. "Yep."

"Looks like you've done a couple of hours of work already."

"Yeah, that's right." Why did Dad look troubled?

"You got up around four?"

Davis grunted.

"Seems like you're burning the candle on both ends. I heard you come in after midnight."

What was his point? Davis started shoveling again. He'd been smoking out on the front porch, waiting for Freddy to drop Faith off. They'd been out dancing, which—he had to admit—was a major win for Freddy. Davis had wanted to make sure there was no good-night kiss. He smiled a teeny smile. Freddy had been moving closer to Faith when Davis had interrupted with a cheerful, "Hi there." Faith had slipped into the house, and Freddy had turned and glared at Davis. Davis had just waved as Freddy stomped off. Sometimes faking friendly with the enemy was a good tactic.

"I'm sorry if I kept you up," he finally said.

Dad shook his head. "That's not it. I woke when the door closed, and then I went back to sleep. I'm just worried about how little you're sleeping."

"I only need a few hours. The army changed my sleep habits."

"Nightmares?"

Davis frowned. "No."

"You know your uncle Grayson had shell shock after the First World War. He'd scream at the least sound."

Davis grunted again and went at the dirt a little harder. He wasn't ready to discuss his sleep problems.

"Linda said you worked fifteen hours straight at her house last week."

Davis nodded. "It felt good to help. They're so busy with their little ones." He'd driven Betsy up to visit his sister in Marion and had ended up building a fence for her. It looked professional, if he did say so himself.

Dad sighed and Davis looked up to see worry lines popping out like train tracks on his brow. Davis offered a smile he hoped was convincing. "I figured out in the army that I like working with my hands. The physical work feels good."

"Linda mentioned the fence turned out beautifully, but she was a little concerned about you."

"Concerned?"

Dad shifted from foot to foot. "She feels like you're punishing yourself."

"I'm just trying to fill time." He shifted his weight off the shovel.

"Your mother and I appreciate it. You've done a lot of work around the house. To tell you the truth, I've never seen anyone work as hard as you have since coming home. But we, uh, we want to encourage you to, uh . . ."

"Date?"

Dad rubbed his chin. "I see your mother has been talking to you. Yes, she'd like you to date. I just want to see you do something fun."

Fun? Davis shook his head. The work he was doing was satisfying. He honestly couldn't think of anything "fun" that he wanted to do.

Dad's voice softened. "You know, go dancing. Go to the movies. Things kids your age should be doing."

Kids his age? Things they should be doing? Unwanted images filled his head. He'd watched kids his age do unspeakable things the last four years.

"Davis?"

He snapped his attention back to Dad. "I just have all this nervous energy. It feels better to keep moving than sit around." That was half of it, anyway. Would he ever feel right again? He turned back to the digging. How could he explain war to someone like Dad who had never experienced holding a friend while he died? How could he explain the misery of a foxhole in the winter or the exhaustion of the front lines? How would he ever be able to reconcile the ugliness and evil he'd seen with his comfortable home? What was that old man from the train's advice? "I'm just trying to get on with life," Davis said.

"Good, good," Dad said with fake cheerfulness. "You'll be back at Ohio State in no time and getting on with your dreams."

Davis nodded. What else could he do? College? How could he possibly fit in with that carefree life again? He'd be with kids who were straight out of high school, kids who had been fourteen when Davis left to fight. A rock stopped his progress with the shovel. He turned his attention to prying it out of the dirt, scraping the shovel's blade behind the rock and leveraging it up.

"If you need to talk, I'm here for you."

"Thanks, Dad." There was no better father in the world, but it was better not to talk. He gave another massive thrust and the rock came free. His plan really was to get on with his life.

"And, uh, try to sleep more."

Davis sighed and said, "Will do."

But it wasn't nightmares that kept him awake. It was the thoughts that came to him when he laid down at night. Thoughts of Patrick's death at the battle of Kwajalein in the Marshall Islands. Had he suffered? What had the battle been like? What had his wounds been like? Marcia didn't know any details, and Davis often lay awake as these questions stabbed at him. He went back to his digging, letting the dirt fly in a frenzy of frustration. Along with questions about Patrick that would never be answered, his thoughts turned to things he *had* seen— starving people, hatred, misery, and men he'd watched die. The images took over his head, one after another, in a horrible nightly death parade. How could he try to sleep more with thoughts like that in his head?

CHAPTER 8

FAITH AND MOM SAT AT the kitchen table enjoying a pre-church meal of scrambled eggs and bacon. They hadn't spoken of their argument a week ago and there was an awkwardness between them that manifested itself in determined politeness. Faith had thanked her mother for nearly every item at the breakfast table and Mom had responded with false cheerfulness.

The table was too quiet. Faith cleared her throat. "It seems like we're overdue for a letter from Rose."

Mom nodded. "She's on my mind a lot."

Faith reached over, squeezed Mom's hand, and said, "She must be really busy right now. She's probably preoccupied with moving with Joey into their own apartment."

Mom squeezed back. "Yes," she said slowly, "maybe that's it." She gave Faith a smile and added, "I don't know what I'd do without your positivity."

The feeling in the kitchen warmed as Faith gave Mom a huge smile. "I don't know what I'd do without your goodness."

A tear trickled down Mom's cheek, and Faith knew the argument had been patched up. Life was too short for anger.

There was a tap, the one Mrs. Wilson always used, on the back door. Mom brushed her tear away, jumped up, and ushered Mrs. Wilson in. "Would you like some freshly squeezed orange juice?" she asked.

"That would be wonderful. Thanks," Mrs. Wilson said. She plopped down into Mom's seat, seemingly unaware that there was a plate of half-eaten food in front of her.

"How are you today, Cecilia?" Mom asked as she pulled out another juice cup and poured some fresh OJ.

Mrs. Wilson sighed deeply. "I'm worried."

"What's troubling you?"

"Davy—I mean Davis—he's just so different. He's so serious now and he smokes. You know I hate smoking. It's not just that though. He's been home for over a month now, and I can't get him to do anything the young men his age are doing." Mrs. Wilson's lip trembled. "I don't think he's excited about going back to college or about following James into law. He doesn't want to go out dancing. He doesn't want to go out on dates." She glanced over at Faith as she mentioned her last grievance.

Faith jammed a big mouthful of egg into her mouth to keep from saying something rude. Maybe Davis wasn't going out on dates, but he sure enjoyed breaking her dates up. Sometimes when Freddy brought her home, she let him give her a kiss good night, but that hadn't happened since Davis got home. Every time Freddy dropped her off, there was Davis out on the porch, smoking and watching them. Every. Single. Time.

Mrs. Wilson went on, lowering her voice. "I found out he could have come home earlier, but he kept volunteering to take duties that kept him overseas longer. Can you imagine? We were praying and writing our senator to get Davis home and he didn't even try. And now that he's here, it's like he isn't even happy to be home." Mrs. Wilson's voice shook on the last thought.

"I'm sure he's happy," Mom said. She pulled a chair closer to her friend, sat down, and covered Mrs. Wilson's hand with her own. "It must just be such a big adjustment."

"I irritate him," Mrs. Wilson said sadly with what Faith thought was uncharacteristic perception. She paused as if waiting for someone to contradict her. The Penwilligers remained uncomfortably quiet.

"Every time I try to talk to him about the war, he treats me like I don't know what I'm talking about. Marcia, he talks to you. What am I doing wrong?"

Mom took a moment, seeming to gather her thoughts. She and Mrs. Wilson were opposites in so many ways, but they had been neighbors for twenty years, and Faith knew Mom really did care about Mrs. Wilson. Tears welled in their irritating neighbor's eyes, and Faith couldn't help but feel a twinge of compassion for her.

"Well," Mom said slowly, "I think it might not be a matter of asking him to tell you about his experiences in the war but catching him in moments when he is willing to talk."

Mrs. Wilson looked at Mom blankly. "He can talk to me anytime he wants about the war. He doesn't want to."

Faith set her fork down. Listening really wasn't Mrs. Wilson's forte, but maybe she could play to her strengths. "Perhaps you could find a way to tell Davis how happy you are to have him home, like write him a letter or something."

Mrs. Wilson looked at Faith with a spark of interest. "You mean like a grand gesture, to show him how much we love him?"

"I don't know that it has to be grand exactly." Faith and Mom exchanged wary looks.

Mrs. Wilson didn't seem to hear. She sat up straight in her chair. "I know what I'll do. I'll plan a reception for him and invite guests to welcome him home. He could put on his dress uniform and look so handsome. I'm sure if he sees how many people care about him that he will cheer up." She looked tremendously pleased with her idea. She picked up Mom's fork and ate the last few bites on the plate while Faith and Mom silently watched.

"You'll help me?" she asked, looking perkier by the moment.

"That wasn't what I meant at all," Faith said. Good grief, the woman was going to change a simple idea into a lot of work.

"We will need some spectacular decorations and lots and lots of great refreshments."

"Slow down, Cecilia," Mom cautioned. "I don't think that's what Faith meant."

"Faith, will you play the piano for us as background music?" Mrs. Wilson stared off into space, smiling.

"Mrs. Wilson, I think that Davy—Davis that is—would—"

"Marcia, you could be in charge of the kitchen."

Mom spoke up again. "Maybe you should make sure Davis wants this. He doesn't seem to like being thought of as a hero."

"He'll love it!" Mrs. Wilson said, her grand gesture taking the shape of food, music, and a spotlight moment for her son. "Thanks for the idea, ladies."

Faith shrugged. "Don't give me credit—it isn't what I meant."

"I think right before the Fourth of July would be ideal. We must get the invitations out soon though. It'll be marvelous."

"I just don't think Davis will like it," Mom said in one last attempt to dissuade Mrs. Wilson from an idea that had no chance of pleasing her son.

"He'll love it," Mrs. Wilson repeated with a vigorous nod of her head.

Mom sighed with resignation. "I'll help."

Mrs. Wilson looked positively delighted. She drank the last of her orange juice and then cheerfully went home to what Faith imagined would be a long day of list making and party planning.

"Davis is going to hate this," Mom said, frowning.

"He certainly will," Faith said with a smug grin. "I don't want Mrs. Wilson going around saying it was my idea, but since she's determined, I think I might enjoy watching this. Put me down for pianist. I'll have a front-row seat to this debacle."

"Well, at least Cecilia will be happy."

"The next few weeks will be a dream come true for her. A party to plan and lots of people to boss around!"

Mom just shook her head and responded sadly. "Davis is not going to like having his war service put on display."

She and Faith tidied up the kitchen, took off the aprons that had been protecting their new spring dresses, put their hats and gloves on, and checked themselves one last time in the parlor mirror. Faith's brown eyes sparkled underneath her pale-blue halo hat. Mom had sewn a beautiful summer dress for her. It was made of pale-blue silk and gathered in the front and had darling mother-of-pearl buttons and a bow around the neck that added a feminine touch. Mom's own pale-green dress was made from the same pattern but without the bow or extra flounce on the bottom.

"You look like summer," Mom said as she picked up her handbag.

"All thanks to you." Faith winked at Mom. "You look awfully beautiful yourself. Those widowers are going to be turning their necks for a second look."

Mom shook her head, but she smiled back.

It was too beautiful a morning to drive, and the church was only a twenty-minute walk. They headed up Forest Drive. It was good to have things patched up with Mom. Davis Wilson didn't need to come between them. Life felt charmed as Faith listened to the chirps of birds and smelled the fresh grass, knowing she looked good. She held her head high and smiled. The joy of summer filled her.

They passed Mrs. O'Malley, who was on her front porch, watering flowers.

"Do you need a saying for her?" Mom asked Faith. The Penwilligers and Mrs. O'Malley liked to remind each other of their roots with Irish sayings.

"I got this one covered." Faith called out, "'May neighbors respect you, trouble neglect you, the angels protect you, and heaven accept you.'"

Mrs. O'Malley rubbed her hands in delight. "You two certainly look beautiful."

"Thank you," Faith said.

"'Here's to Hades. May the stay there be as fun as the way there!'"

Mom gasped while Faith laughed.

"That's something we'll take right into church with us," Faith said.

"I don't go myself—too boring."

The Penwilligers continued on down the road. When they were out of earshot, Mom said, "That certainly doesn't seem appropriate. What did she say? 'Here's to Hades'?"

Faith just smiled and pointed out the Robinsons' tulips.

Pastor Clemmons greeted them at the door. Mrs. O'Malley was right; the pastor could be boring, but he lived what he preached, and Faith felt a rush of affection for him. On the horrible day Patrick's telegram had come, and then Dad's heart attack a week later with their futile rush to the hospital, Pastor Clemmons had known exactly what they needed. He stood guard over their home after they came back from the hospital, Faith as numb with grief as Mom. She had few memories of the following week, and they were all foggy. One, though, was of Pastor and Alicia Clemmons taking over at the house. They had answered the door, accepting flowers and food from well-meaning neighbors but refusing them entry to the home, where Mom and Faith had huddled in pain and shock. Pastor Clemmons had made the funeral arrangements and walked them through financial paperwork.

He had never once told them that it was God's will or that everything would be fine. He and Alicia had just puttered about the house, making themselves quietly indispensable.

He didn't give the most interesting sermons, but Faith still loved being there. She sat down with Mom in a pew in the middle of the chapel, where they always sat. Faith had promised herself she'd be there every Sunday as a kind of thank-you to God for putting Pastor and Alicia Clemmons into their lives.

Mom reached over and squeezed Faith's hand. No words were needed for her to read her mother's emotions; Mom, too, was grateful to be in their beautiful little church.

The Wilsons were already seated in their pew a few rows ahead of the Penwilligers, but Mrs. Wilson was missing. She must be home already planning Davis's party. Faith couldn't help a smug smile. Davis was going to hate the fuss.

Pastor Clemmons's dry sermon began, and Faith tried not to wiggle. Ahead of her Davis Wilson sat, back ramrod straight, unflinching. He still looked like a soldier. What a change from the past. It wasn't that many years ago that he was shooting spit wads during church, trying to look innocent, until his mom inevitably put a stop to it. Faith smiled at the memory. Patrick had been too well-behaved for that kind of mischief, but he had sat by Faith, shaking with laughter, watching his troublemaking friend.

The sound of birds chirping floated in through the open windows and seemed to be harmonizing with the congregation as they sang "Rock of Ages."

The main service ended, and Faith left to teach her Sunday School class. Eight teenagers filed in. Janet Wilson complimented her on her dress while the boys joked around until Faith started her lesson on kindness with an attention-grabbing story. She ended the lesson by having the teens read Paul's words on charity. She was a good teacher, and her students liked her, so why did she feel so flat?

She packed up her little classroom and found Mom chatting with a friend about gardening woes. "I'm going to stay a bit longer," Faith said.

"That's fine. I'll have lunch ready when you get back."

Faith waited patiently for the last of the congregants to file out, then walked over to where Pastor Clemmons stood by the door. "Can we talk?" she asked.

"Certainly." He led her down the hall that led to his little office. He sat down in his well-worn desk chair and motioned for her to take the padded seat across from him.

She took a moment to admire his eclectic pictures. There were several of Christ, several of his children and grandchildren, and a few from the Grand Canyon and Yellowstone National Park. The office had an organized but homey feel to it.

"What can I do for you, Faith?"

She sagged in her chair. She hated to admit she was failing at something, but the truth was she was a fraud. "I shouldn't be teaching Sunday School."

Pastor Clemmons didn't say anything, but his eyebrows went up.

It was painful to disappoint this good man. "I just don't think I'm the right role model for teenagers." Tears welled, and Faith blinked them back.

Pastor Clemmons handed her a handkerchief. "Do you remember what I asked you when I called you to be a teacher?"

Faith nodded. "You asked if I had faith in Christ." She dabbed at her eyes.

"Has anything changed in that regard?"

Faith gave him a watery smile. "I still have faith."

"You were aptly named."

Faith clutched at the handkerchief. "But sometimes that's all I feel I have."

"Is there anything in your conduct that would lead our youth astray?"

"I like dancing a lot, and music, but I don't think it hurts my faith." She could have added that along with dancing and music, she liked to kiss Freddy good night, but kissing wasn't something she wanted to discuss with her pastor. Anyway, she hadn't been able to kiss Freddy since Davis had come home.

"I don't either," the pastor said with his usual gruffness. "Your faith, energy, and cheerfulness make you a wonderful role model. So what is the trouble?"

Faith sighed. The pastor didn't seem to want to accept her resignation. How did she explain the anger in her heart? Maybe he didn't need to know everything, but she'd tell him about her uncertainties. "I'm just not someone who has things figured out. I'm trying so hard to keep the business going and to enjoy it, but I feel so young and uncertain sometimes. I should be hiring new help, and I feel paralyzed by the enormity of the decision. I always try to act like I know what I'm doing to give our employees and customers confidence in me and keep my mother from worrying, but I don't know what I'm doing. I'm scared, and for two years I've felt constantly in over my head. I should be in college right now, not bumbling about trying to run a business or set myself up as a role model for teenagers. And on top of that, my mom thinks something big is wrong with my cousin. I'm trying to stay optimistic, but I'm worried about her too."

"Your mother discussed Rose's situation with me," Pastor Clemmons said. "I'm concerned as well."

Faith swallowed a lump in her throat. "Thank you. We've been so worried about her."

Pastor Clemmons nodded with a sympathetic look, reached out, and squeezed her hand. "Let's talk about you. It seems you feel inadequate to the tasks you face."

Faith nodded. "That's exactly it. I don't feel like a good person. I feel like a fake."

"You aren't a fake. You're just learning on the job, the same way Christ's Apostles did. They were ordinary men who accepted a calling and became better people along the way. You fit Christ into your life and the stresses will come into better perspective. Not only that but you will also have more confidence in yourself."

"You think so?"

"I know so." There was a moment of quiet as Pastor Clemmons looked kindly at Faith.

She fidgeted. "There's something else." She rubbed her hands down the sides of her dress. She was going to have to explain the feelings in her heart, and she hated talking about her own shortcomings. "I just taught a lesson about being kind, but I'm a fraud. I'm having a hard time feeling charitable right now. I'm angry that Patrick isn't coming home. I see some of our returned soldiers around town, and feelings of loss wash over me." Her voice shook a little.

"Are you angry with God?"

"No." Faith's lips twisted. "My anger is much more realistic. I'm furious with a specific person who talked my brother into enlisting. Patrick should never have gone. He was a musician, not a soldier, and as an only son, he didn't have to go." She ran her fingers over the cool, solid wood of her seat, then lowered her voice to a whisper. "If Patrick hadn't enlisted, he'd be home writing music, and my dad wouldn't have died from a broken heart."

"I see." He rubbed his chin. "I'm not going to lecture you on forgiveness, but I will say that every Christlike quality takes time to develop. It's a process. Forgiveness may take time, and that's all right. In the meantime, I still feel strongly that you are the right teacher for this class."

How could that be? Was she really the best choice?

Pastor Clemmons leaned toward Faith. "Just today I was thinking of Robert Sullivan. He should be in your class, but he's been refusing to attend church with his family."

Faith nodded. She knew the Sullivans. Robert's older brother, George, had died in Normandy.

"Robert stopped coming after his brother was killed. Maybe you could try to talk to him. You could be someone he would relate to."

The little office filled with silence. How could she say no? Maybe she was a fake, but the pastor knew the worst of her heart now, and he still wanted her to try. She looked up to see him still smiling kindly. She twisted her hands, took a big breath, and said, "If you're sure about this, I'll keep teaching."

"Thank you, my dear. I don't think you'll be sorry."

"I'll feel like a hypocrite teaching them to be Christian when I don't feel so Christian myself, but as long as you're okay with that, I'll do my best."

"That's all I can ask."

She reached over and squeezed the pastor's hand, then stood up, and silently walked toward the door, turning to say, "I hope you don't expect me to be as good an example as you are."

She could hear him chuckling behind her as she walked down the hallway. She might never be able to forgive Davis Wilson, but at least Pastor Clemmons didn't think she was an awful person.

CHAPTER 9

Davis, perched on the ladder that rested against his house, put his gloved hand into the rain gutter and scooped out the gunk. It had rained overnight, a June deluge, and the trees had dropped some debris. He threw the muddy leaves into a bucket. He'd have this side of the house finished before breakfast.

He felt cheerful this morning, probably because he'd slept well. He smiled. He'd won another battle in the Great Freddy Casper War. He'd gone into his house, smug and triumphant. Then, lying in bed, clarity had come to him— clarity and peace. He'd made a decision and it felt so right. He was going to ask Faith if he could work for Penwilliger Brick. Davis threw another scoop of gunk into the bucket. Hopefully, Dad would see the sense in it. Law school had no appeal for Davis. He wanted to work with his hands. He wanted to help the Penwilligers, and he wanted to be part of a business that built things. Last night, when he'd had the realization that he wanted to work for Faith, it had felt like a puzzle piece falling into place.

After Davis had made his decision, instead of his usual dark thoughts, he'd fallen into a deep sleep. Maybe knowing what one's purpose was did that to a man. There would be obstacles, but at least he knew what he wanted, and it wasn't law school.

Across the street, the Penwilligers' front door opened, and a flash of color caught his eye. Faith, on her way to work. He wasn't the only one working long hours. He hurried down the ladder, pulled his gloves off, and threw them to the side. Faith had her hand on the door handle of her truck. Her hair caught some of the morning sun in a glint of rich brown-gold.

"Good morning," Davis called out to her. If he wanted her to hire him, he would have to clear the air between them.

Faith paused. Her pretty pink lips pinched together. "I see you're still out on your front porch. It's funny how often I see you there."

Davis tried not to smile; he really did. He walked down the porch steps.

Faith jingled the keys in her hand and frowned at him. "What were you doing out on your porch at midnight?"

Waiting for Freddy to bring her home and making sure there wouldn't be a good-night kiss. But he wasn't dumb enough to say that out loud. "Smoking."

Her eyes narrowed. "At midnight?"

Davis had learned a few things as a sergeant. Sometimes the best defense was a counterattack. "Are you trying to avoid me?"

She full-out glared. "Avoid you? Every time Freddy brings me home, you're outside, spying on us."

Davis walked over and leaned on the truck, standing next to her. She smelled like lavender and looked like spring—all fresh and crisp. He shook his head. It shouldn't matter to him what she looked like—or smelled like, for that matter. That line of thinking wasn't helpful. "But are you trying to avoid me?"

"What reason could I possibly have to avoid you?" she asked, tilting her chin at him, her tone curt.

Davis narrowed his eyes. Why did women ask questions they didn't want answered? If Faith had a problem with him, it was because of either the Great Freddy Casper War—a war neither of them had openly acknowledged—or what had happened the night he and Patrick had enlisted.

Faith pulled the truck door open. "I'm a working woman. We've been extraordinarily busy, and any free time I have outside of work I've been practicing dance steps for the competition at the Swingin' Stars Club."

Davis frowned. "And you have to practice with Freddy every night?"

"That's right." Up went her chin again. "We make a great team."

Team? Team? No. The men from Davis's company came to mind. Men who'd literally taken bullets for each other. He'd been part of teams and Freddy Casper was no team player. Patrick would have hated knowing Faith was spending so much time with the man. Mr. Penwilliger would have hated it too.

Davis pushed away from the truck. "You shouldn't be spending time with him," he said in the firm sergeant voice that had worked so well with his men.

Faith flushed. She looked prettier than ever, but angry. "Don't tell me what to do. I'm not sixteen."

"I can see that." And so could Freddy Casper—that was the problem. Davis straightened and took another step toward Faith, resting his hand lightly on her shoulder. Maybe he should have tried a softer approach. She froze, facing away from him, looking into her truck.

"Patrick and your father wouldn't want you dating Freddy," he said in a gentler voice.

Faith spun around, knocking his hand off her shoulder, and glared. "Don't you dare tell me what they would have wanted! Remember what happened the last time you told me what Patrick wanted?"

Davis's head whipped back as if he'd been slapped. He took a step away. Faith pulled herself up into the truck and slammed the rusty door. She and her truck left in a cloud of angry exhaust and loud backfires.

Davis swore quietly. He rubbed his neck and stared down Forest Drive at the old red truck that bumped along. This wasn't good. Faith's grudge was worse than he'd thought. What was wrong with women? She'd probably written the whole argument out in her diary and reread it anytime she came close to forgetting the details.

Davis returned to the ladder and shoved his gloves back on, frowning. He hadn't thought about their argument during the four years he'd been gone, but it seemed Faith had.

His mind went back to that January in 1942 when his world had changed so dramatically. The attack on Pearl Harbor had just happened a few weeks earlier. Davis had been shocked by the news. President Roosevelt had signed the joint resolution the next day, and suddenly the US was at war and Davis had a huge decision to make.

Patrick and Davis, students at Ohio State, had spent hours together discussing the war and how pulled they felt to enlist. Finally, they'd withdrawn from school and made their way to the army enrollment center. They'd enlisted together. Patrick had known his family would take it hard and begged Davis to go home and break the news to the Penwilligers while he stayed and cleaned out his dorm room.

The day after enlisting, Davis, proudly wearing his new uniform, had taken the train home to Payson. He'd knocked on the Penwilligers' door, and Faith, the only one home, had answered.

He took a step up the ladder now and paused as the memory came back to him. Skinny Faith, with her huge brown eyes, had opened the door and let him in. She'd taken in his uniform and stared at him without saying a word. He'd grinned at her, confident that she would be excited for him and Patrick. He'd ruffled her hair, and what had he said? Oh yes, he'd broken the news with, "Patrick and I are Uncle Sam's newest nephews."

The fury from sweet Faith had caught him off guard. He had expected hero worship, not hot anger. He hadn't taken her response well, but back then he was a cocky twenty-year-old, sure of himself and assuming he'd always be adored by his little neighbor.

Davis shook his head and reached back into the gutter. He scooped another handful of debris and flung it so hard into his bucket that some of the mud came back up and splattered on his cheek. He knew he'd said angry words back to Faith that day, but he couldn't remember what exactly he'd said.

She probably wanted some big apology, but how could he apologize for something he wasn't sorry for? It had been the right thing to enlist.

Davis groaned. There had been something in the argument about Daisy too. He remembered that had made him even angrier with Faith, and he probably hadn't been kind in his response. Great. He frowned. Just great. How could he address the argument when Faith didn't want anything to do with him? And what would this mean for getting a job at Penwilliger Brick? It was what he wanted, and he'd give his best effort, but Faith's grudge would make his next steps all the more difficult. He sighed and threw a couple more scoops of muddy leaves into his bucket. Considering Faith's anger, his chances of her hiring him were probably around one in twenty. One in twenty—in the army his company had faced those kinds of odds more than once and come out on top. Davis climbed down the ladder, carrying the bucket of gunk. Would Faith be able to see how much he had to offer Penwilliger Brick? Or would her grudge stand in the way?

CHAPTER 10

FRANK LEANED AGAINST FAITH'S DESK. He had come in before Juan and Lester and was interrupting her coffee-making and cleaning routine. She had been thinking of dance steps for the competition later tonight. She sighed and dragged her thoughts away from dancing and back to the present.

"You can't keep putting this off, Faith. You have to hire more help. I'm too old for this job. I'm officially giving you until November. That's five months. It should be enough time to find and train a new man."

"I can't possibly replace you that soon!" Faith said, panic rising in her voice.

She looked over at the old walnut desk. There was a manila envelope inside a drawer, waiting patiently for her to make up her mind about Mr. Holland's offer—a very reasonable offer. Her eyes moved to the picture of her father that was hanging on the wall. She knew her dad wouldn't want her to sell, but it felt unbearable to think of going on without Frank, her greatest support.

Frank cleared his throat. "I told you almost a year ago, when the war ended, that I needed to retire. I'll help you train a new bricklayer, but it's past time for me to retire."

"I know, I know," Faith moaned sadly. "I just can't imagine running this business without you."

"You aren't the eighteen-year-old girl who took over. You've got experience under your belt now, and you can make it work. You're a fabulous business-woman. Just hire a couple of men who are home from the war and ready to make a name for themselves."

"I don't know if I can hire the right men," she responded.

Frank rubbed his jaw. "I've never told you this, but when your dad hired me, he went with his gut." His voice shook a little. "I had served some time in jail, and your father overlooked that and gave me a job—a really good job. You'll find the right men for this business. They're out there; just go with your gut."

Faith tried to mask her shock, but her eyebrows shot up. He had done time? Dad had never said a word about Frank's record. She wondered if he had even told Mom. The world would never cease to surprise her.

"How can I trust my judgment?" She tipped her head toward Frank. "My dad got it right, but I don't know if I can find that. I mean, really, what man wants a twenty-year-old female boss?"

"If they don't work out, then you fire them."

"I can't even fire Lester and you see how belligerent he is toward me."

Frank frowned. "Hire some new men who will respect you, and then you won't be so dependent on Lester's help. You can do it." He thumped Faith encouragingly on the back.

Her spirits sank. She had always been able to talk Frank into giving her a little more time before he retired, but now he seemed determined. She searched her mind for a new argument that might persuade him. Nothing came to her. Oh, how tempting Mr. Holland's offer was now. The man's investors could figure out who to hire, and she could be enrolled in classes at Ohio State for the fall.

The bell rang, and she pushed her thoughts away as Davis Wilson stepped through the door. He looked sharp in his light-gray, double-breasted suit. His light-brown hair was smoothed down with just a hint of a wave in the front. Around his neck a blue-striped tie brought out the color of his eyes. Faith tried not to notice how handsome his face was. Why was he so dressed up? Faith didn't move. She had spent the last seven weeks avoiding him. He might look good, but she wasn't happy to see him on her territory.

"Davy," Frank said, grinning and coming over from behind the desk to shake his hand. "How are you?"

"Good, thanks." Davis's eyes flashed to Faith's for a brief moment. "Just adjusting to being home and trying to keep out of my mom's way."

"How are the plans for your reception coming along?" Faith asked with fake sweetness as she drummed her fingers along the top of the desk.

"You're getting married?" Frank straightened his lanky form to his full height. "Who's the lucky lady?"

Davis shook his head and grimaced. "My mom is planning a welcome-home reception for me. I'm sure your invitation will be delivered soon."

Faith couldn't keep herself from smiling at his discomfort. It helped her feel a little kindlier toward him. "What brings you into Penwilliger's?" she asked politely, standing up from behind the desk.

"Well . . ." He paused and tugged at his tie. Why did he look nervous? "I hear you need a bricklayer and wondered if you would be willing to take me on."

Faith sat with a loud thunk. What was Davis playing at?

"An answer to prayers!" Frank exclaimed with what Faith thought was too much enthusiasm.

She shook her head emphatically. Her voice lost its politeness. "Absolutely not! I do the hiring, not Frank. I know what you're doing, and the answer is no."

Both men stared at Faith. Frank looked surprised by her rudeness and Davis looked amused.

"What am I doing, Faith?" he asked, maintaining eye contact, his blue eyes clear and sparkling with a challenge in them.

She jumped up again from her seat. "Trying to worm your way into the Penwilliger family." She took a determined step around the desk toward him. "You have my mom wrapped around your little finger. It's like you're trying to be a son to her, but you're *not* my brother."

Davis's blue eyes sparked. He took a step forward, chin jutting out. "I like spending time with your mother, but I don't think of you as a sister."

Faith flushed and balled her fist. She took a step back and broke eye contact. Frank looked from one to the other with big round eyes; even his white mustache seemed shocked, poking straight out.

Clearing his throat, Davis continued. "You know I'm a hard worker. I've thought a lot about what I want to do. I want to stay here in Payson, and I want to work in construction."

"Suddenly you've decided on the brick business?" Faith spluttered. "Does your dad know? What about law school?"

"Don't look a gift horse in the mouth," Frank interjected.

"My dad understands and supports this choice. Your business has all kinds of possibilities." Davis gestured with his arm to Faith's brick display. "I've always liked working with my hands and think I could be trained to be an excellent brickmason." He nodded at Frank, who looked like he had been given a longed-for Christmas gift; he positively beamed.

Faith looked Davis in the eyes, stood ramrod straight, and said, "No." She stepped back over to the desk and picked up her ledger. She pulled out a stack of receipts that needed to be recorded and began entering them in the accounts-receivable column, keeping her head down, purposely ignoring the two men who stood watching her.

"Faith," Frank said, "could I speak with you in the back?"

Faith slammed the ledger shut, trapping the receipts inside, and followed Frank back to the warehouse without looking at Davis.

"Are you crazy?" Frank asked as soon as the door shut behind them. "He would be fantastic. You won't find anyone as competent as Davy Wilson."

"It's complicated."

"It's business. It isn't complicated. You hire the best person for the job, and you don't turn down a worker like Davy Wilson."

"He goes by Davis now. He acts like he's still a sergeant bossing his men around, and I don't want to work with him."

Frank frowned and fingered his white mustache, curling the waxy ends with his fingertips. "I didn't want to work the last four years, but I sacrificed for the good of the business. You can't just think of yourself." He left Faith before she could respond and walked back to the front. She pulled her foot back to kick a cement bag and stopped herself. The last thing she needed was a broken toe on the day of the dance competition. She stomped instead. How unfair life was! If she were thinking of just herself, she would have already accepted Mr. Holland's offer. She would be headed to college instead of being stuck in a warehouse surrounded by bricks, the stress of keeping the business afloat, and infuriating men.

Frank came back a moment later with a fidgety Davis in tow.

"I propose we let Davy—Davis that is—work here on a trial basis. We can pay him for helping me instead of paying Juan and Lester a boatload of overtime. He'll get a sense of what being a bricklayer is all about, and you two can decide whether this is a good fit."

Davis jammed his hands into his pockets and looked over at Faith. She dug her fingernails into the palms of her hands. The last thing in the world she wanted was to work with Davis, to have him around daily. But Frank was right. Everyone had made sacrifices. It looked like life wasn't about to get fairer just because the war was over. She thought again of the manila envelope containing Mr. Holland's proposal—she did have an out if having Davis around was too miserable. She gave the men a very small, almost imperceptible, nod.

That was enough for them. Frank put his arm around a pleased-looking Davis. "Come on," he said. "Let's load Costello up, and then we'll swing by your house and get you some work clothes. I'm headed out to a job on the east side of town."

"Costello?"

"Faith named our trucks Abbott and Costello—their names suit."

Davis laughed as they made their way toward the back of the warehouse. "That sounds like something Faith would come up with. She was always giving cats ridiculous names when we were kids."

Faith sniffed. Gumyum, Poppykins, and Angelfluff were fine names.

"Did you know the size of a brick is made to fit in a man's hand?"

"That makes sense. What's the job and what needs to be loaded?" Davis asked eagerly.

Their voices faded from Faith's hearing; Frank's reply was too soft for her to hear. Completely agitated, she made her way back to her desk in the front, plopped down, and drummed her fingers with nervous energy on the ledger. She didn't know if she could handle having Davis around at work as well as at home. His interfering and acting like a big brother got under her skin like nothing else could.

Around noon she looked up to see Mom coming in the front door with a basket over her arm. She wore her yellow "going to town" pillbox hat with a snood that covered her red-gray hair. She had a yellow-and-white-striped shirt on, a gray fitted skirt, and sensible-looking shoes. Faith watched her sharply dressed mother come in and marveled that Mom, the consummate housewife, could look so put together.

"I wanted to bring you and the men some hot biscuits," Mom said.

"Thank you," Faith replied, rising from her chair to take them. "The men are all out on jobs, but I'll save them some." She pulled a napkin and a soft biscuit from the basket, waving Mom to the seat opposite. Spreading the napkin out to protect her desk, Faith leaned over and bit into the warm, flaky biscuit. "Delicious!" she said. "Did you hear from Rose today?"

Mom shook her head and sighed. Something was definitely wrong. Throughout the war Rose had written them every week, long newsy letters, about what it was like to live in D.C. and work at the Pentagon. Her letters had often been the highlight of their week. It was more than strange that there had been no letters in weeks. Mom had tried twice more to call, but nobody had answered.

"I'll try to call again this evening."

Faith nodded. They prayed for Rose every time they said grace. Her lovely cousin was daily on their minds.

"As Granny Penwilliger used to say, 'No news gives your imagination scope to run wild like children just let out of school,'" Mom said.

Faith smiled. "Granny sure had a way with words. Hopefully, Rose is just busy setting up a new apartment with Joey."

"Hopefully." But Mom's brow was furrowed.

Faith ate three biscuits while Mom talked about her garden, but she knew Mom wasn't here to talk about Rose or the garden. It was time to address the elephant in the room. Faith folded the napkin, replaced it in the basket, and turned to confront her mother. "You told him we were looking for a bricklayer, didn't you?"

Mom didn't pretend to misunderstand. "Yes, he needs a job, and I think you need him."

"I'm doing fine."

Mom pursed her lips. "That's not what Frank or the hours you're keeping tell me. You need help, and Davis can give it."

"I don't want more help from Davis. You think all the pruning, planting, landscaping, painting, gutter cleaning, drawer unsticking, banister fixing, and picture hanging are wonderful. I hate it. It puts us in his debt, and he is *not* family." She clenched her fists. "I don't like Davis Wilson. I don't want to be in his debt, and I certainly don't want to work with him."

Mom started to answer when a customer came in. Faith put a smile on her face, and her tone immediately changed to a welcoming one. "What can I do for you?" she asked as she rose to greet a young couple.

"We're looking to have brickwork done on a home we're building out in the Riverside development."

"I know that development well," Faith said. "We bricked a home there for the Smythes. Have you seen it?"

She spent the next half hour getting to know the young couple, showing them brick samples, and talking over pricing while Mom waited patiently in her seat by the desk.

The couple left, promising to get back to Faith after they looked at all their options.

"You're a very good saleswoman," Mom said.

"Thank you. I've learned a lot the last two years." She really had learned a lot—a lot of accounting, business practices, brickmasonry, general construction, and customer skills.

She sat back down, and mother and daughter stared at each other. Faith broke the silence first. "Mom, do you think I'm spoiled?"

"Not in the least." Mom leaned toward her. "No spoiled girl could do what you have these last few years with so much grace and spunk." Looking at her thoughtfully, she added, "Davis said he has some bridges to mend with you. I think it would be good for both of you to make up and be friends again."

"We were never friends. He was Patrick's friend and tolerated me. He thinks I am spoiled. I never told you this, but we had a huge fight the night after he and Patrick enlisted. It makes it awkward to be around him." She picked up her fountain pen and fiddled with it.

"Do you want to tell me about it?" Mom asked.

"No, I'm trying to forget it. I'm not proud of my behavior that night."

"I knew something happened between you two. Maybe you need to clear the air with him and start a new friendship."

"I don't see that happening." Faith tapped the desk with her pen. "He still treats me like a little girl. Every time I go out with Freddy, he's smoking on his porch when Freddy drops me off. He doesn't say anything, but we both know he's checking up on me. I hate it. I don't want him trying to take Dad's place or Patrick's. Do you understand why it would be unbearable for me to have him here?" Faith finished saying just as the phone rang.

"Penwilliger's Brick Store, this is Miss Penwilliger."

"Hiya, kiddo," a cheerful voice said.

"Freddy, what are you doing up so early?" Mom looked at the clock on the wall that said 12:30 and rolled her eyes. Freddy worked for his family business, but he didn't have to keep regular hours like Faith, or even go in that often.

"Just too excited about the competition tonight. I think we got this one in the bag." They had never won a competition. They'd placed but never taken home the grand prize. They'd been practicing like never before. Surely it'd pay off and they'd come home tonight with a hundred dollars. "I'm going to come at seven," he added.

"All right, sounds good."

"Don't forget to wear your green dress. I've got my matching bow tie."

"Check. I'm all good to go. See you tonight."

Faith rang off and looked over at Mom, who pursed her lips. The thought crossed her mind that it might be Mom putting Davis up to waiting on the porch for her.

Mom picked up her handbag. "Granny always said that the key to a happy life was in forgetting what was best forgotten," she said and walked out without even saying goodbye.

Faith returned to her accounting. She would never be able to forget her feelings from the night Davis told her he and Patrick had enlisted. The hurt was still very real. She entered more numbers in the ledger and rolled her shoulders back in an attempt to ease the tension she felt. Davis was ever present—darn him—and Rose was on her mind, along with selling the brick store, but she had become an expert during the war at pushing unpleasantness out of her head and focusing on things she could control, on being happy even when worries pressed. She entered another page of numbers, and her mood improved. When her mind started to think of Davis, she redirected her thoughts toward the excitement of the dance-off. She and Freddy had never been so prepared for a win.

The door opened and Janet and Carrie Wilson entered the store.

"Is Davis here?" Janet asked.

"No, he's out on a job."

"He's going to be a great bricklayer." Carrie's blue eyes were full of pride.

"Ah," Faith faltered. Not hiring Davis could cause a rift between the two families. She hadn't thought about that. She smiled at the girls and changed the subject. "Tonight's the night of the big dance competition. Come over around seven and I'll show you the dress my mom made."

"You'll be wonderful!" Carrie gushed.

"Break a leg," Janet said. "Is that okay to say to a dancer?"

Faith laughed. "The words might be off, but the intent is just right."

"Are you nervous?" Carrie asked. "I hear there are couples coming from as far away as Illinois to compete."

"I'm really nervous, but luckily all those nerves just help me have more energy for dancing."

"You're so gorgeous," Carrie looked with adoring eyes as she reached out to touch Faith's hair. "I wish I could come watch you dance, but my parents say I'm too young for the Swingin' Stars Club."

"I'll tell you all about it tomorrow," Faith promised.

The girls each gave her a hug and wished her good luck again before leaving. At five thirty she ushered the last customer out of the store and locked the front door. Humming "Till the End of Time," she moved to the warehouse to check up on the men. Lester and Juan were unloading some supplies from their truck.

"How did the brick wall go today?" she asked.

Lester ignored her and continued to unload the unused brick.

"It will dry fast in this weather," Faith said, determined to be cheerful and civil. "I'm sure the Thompsons will be delighted with your excellent work."

Lester didn't respond but threw his dirty trowel down onto one of the workbenches. Faith flinched. She hated dealing with him. He knew her expectations for cleaning tools at the end of the day.

She said politely, "Don't forget to clean your trowel and bucket."

"You do it," Lester said. "I'm tired."

Juan looked uncomfortably at Lester.

Davis's voice rang out from across the warehouse, "The lady asked you to clean the trowel." He strode toward their conflict, looking tall, stern, and intimidating in his mortar-spattered work clothes and military bearing. Frank was behind Davis, coming along at a slower pace.

Lester stared at Davis for a moment and then nodded and went to the work sink, Juan following him.

Faith frowned. She should feel appreciative, but how irritating that Lester would do what Davis asked simply because he was a man.

Davis nodded at Faith and said, "I'll go unload the truck and get Frank's tools cleaned up."

Frank and Faith watched him walk away.

"He's fantastic," Frank said. "He peppered me with questions about the business and technique all day. He understood on my first explanation how to do a corbel, and he figured out on his own how to kerf. That soldier works harder than anyone I've ever seen, your father included—made me wish I was in my twenties again and just starting out. He already has the hang of the trowel."

"You're gushing, Frank," Faith said with irritation.

He continued earnestly. "You won't find anyone better for this job."

She just shrugged. "You and my mom are in love with the idea, but I'm the one who will have to work with him."

Frank shook his head at her and walked off muttering something about stubbornness and youth being a bad combination.

CHAPTER 11

CARRIE BURST INTO THE DINING room, followed by Janet. The girls looked excited. "What color would you call her dress?"

Janet's eyes were soft and dreamy. "Seafoam green."

"Sit down," Mom said to the girls. Davis's sisters were quiet for a brief moment while Dad said grace.

"So I'm on trial to see if things go well," Davis explained to Dad after the food was blessed.

"I'm sure you will make more than a success of it." Dad had been first-rate in the way he'd handled the news that Davis wouldn't be going to law school. Davis smiled. It had been a satisfying day. There was just one little fly in the ointment of today's happiness.

"Did you notice the silver bows on her shoes? They match Freddy's buckles." There was the fly. Faith, Freddy, and the dance competition. Davis rubbed his knee.

Dad tapped the newspaper and looked at Davis. "The US Energy Commission is recommending that the UN be in control of all nuclear weapons. Do you think that's a good idea?"

"Uh," Davis said.

"Did you see Freddy's plaid tie? It matches her dress perfectly," Janet said.

Davis passed the bowl of potatoes to Dad, forgetting to dish himself up any.

"They look like Fred Astaire and Ginger Rogers," Carrie said. "Mom, can we go watch the dance competition?"

"They serve alcohol at the Swingin' Stars."

"I don't think the US will want to cede control of our nuclear weapons, do you?" Dad asked.

"Aw, Mom," Carrie said, "we wouldn't drink any. We just want to watch Faith and Freddy."

Faith and Freddy. Davis crumbled the roll he was holding. Dad looked at him, waiting for an answer. "Yes," Davis said.

"Really? You think we should let the United Nations control our nuclear weapons?"

"Please, Mom?"

"No," Mom and Davis said in unison.

Carrie and Janet looked pouty. Dad went back to reading the newspaper.

Janet turned to Carrie. "Have you seen anything prettier than Faith in that lovely phantom dress?"

Davis set his fork down. It was over an hour's drive to the Swingin' Stars Club. Freddy would be alone in his Alfa Romeo with Faith and her lovely phantom dress—whatever that meant—for a very long time.

"I love the wide waistband," Janet said.

"And all the tucks and pleats. Did you see how the skirt floats when she spins?" Carrie asked.

"And the pearl buttons." Janet sighed.

"The patio is going to be perfect for the reception. But can you string up lights around the perimeter?" Mom asked.

Davis grunted. He didn't mind doing work, but he couldn't be less excited about the reception Mom was planning. Man, was he dreading it. Mom wanted to set him up as some kind of hero, but the only heroes, in his mind, were dead. But he shrugged. It'd be one night. He would survive it.

"Did you hear what Freddy said when Faith came down the stairs?" Carrie whispered to Janet.

Janet giggled and whispered back, "'That's one dish I want to sample.'"

Davis scooted back in his chair. One night. One night of Faith dancing in Freddy's arms. This called for more than waiting up on the porch to make sure there was no good-night kiss.

"Something wrong?" Mom asked.

"Ah . . . no," Davis said. Everyone stared at him. What should he wear? Carrie and Janet seemed to think the choice of clothing you danced in was important. He grimaced. He'd never win a fashion contest with Freddy Casper. He clenched his fist. Too bad Freddy didn't box. In the army they had often settled differences with boxing matches. Nothing would be more satisfying than going a round or two with Freddy. But sometimes a man had to accept a battle on the enemy's terms. Sunday clothes it would be. "I'm going to head out for a while."

Everyone at the table gaped at him.

He threw his napkin down. "You know, to have some fun." Or to interrupt some fun.

The table was silent as Davis hurried out of the room.

"But you didn't even eat anything," Mom called after him.

Davis changed his clothes in record time. Just as he tied his shoes, Janet knocked. "Wear the blue bow tie," she said. "It brings out your striking eyes."

His eyes were striking? Good to know.

"Do you know any of the new steps?" she asked.

How did she know where he was going? Davis gave her a little grin. "Not many chances to dance the last four years."

She nodded.

He tugged his tie off and put on the blue one Janet handed him. If he was going into battle, he should use every asset he had. Janet pursed her lips and studied him. "You look sharp. But if you get the chance to dance, just keep it simple and bob in place."

He nodded, eyes wide. Bob in place. He could do that.

CHAPTER 12

"I'm wondering," Faith said, "if we should do our bump-lift at the beginning of the swing or at the end. I think it's our best move and I'd like it at the end, but I want enough energy to do it justice." She twisted her fingers together.

Freddy ignored her and cranked up the radio. "My Dreams are Getting Better All the Time" by Les Brown came on. He belted the words out while Faith looked out the window at the rolling green hills and tapped her foot nervously.

Dayton was an hour away, but tonight it felt like two, even with Freddy speeding. When they pulled into the Swingin' Stars Club, the young valet looked like he was in heaven as he took the Alfa Romeo from Freddy. The freckled teen slid behind the wheel of the sleek car, revved the powerful engine, and left them standing in the circular brick driveway. Soft evening shadows fell over the drive, and the air was rich with the smell of June roses. Freddy offered Faith his arm.

"Why, thank you, sir," she said.

"Let's make our entrance." Freddy's chin tilted up. He pushed his chest out and angled his hat. "Here comes the best-looking couple of the night!"

She smiled at him. Freddy did look sharp.

They made their way up the wide steps and past the doorman who held the heavy grand oak door open for them. He recognized them as regulars and wished them luck in the competition.

Freddy checked his suit coat and hat while Faith checked her purse in at the cloakroom. They made their way through another set of double oak doors into the grand ballroom, where the band was setting up on the stage. Faith caught her breath in excitement. The polished hickory dance floor gleamed. It seemed to be begging her to come dance.

Freddy grabbed her by the hand and pointed at the judges' tables set up along the side. "Let's get our numbers."

Faith nodded and let him lead her over to the tables.

"Frederick Casper and Faith Penwilliger," he told the official.

The efficient-looking woman checked them off her list and gave them their numbers.

"I hope thirty-seven is lucky," Faith commented.

"It will be," the ever-confident Freddy said.

"Pin them securely to your backs," the woman at the table said. "Your number must remain on at all times. You know the format tonight?"

"Yes," Freddy said, eyes roaming the room. He looked bored.

The woman continued. "No lifts in the first round. It'll be too crowded."

Faith nodded.

"Got it." Freddy grinned as he leaned toward the middle-aged woman and touched her hand. "Wish us luck." He leaned even closer. Good grief. Was he trying to flirt?

The woman backed up, flustered, and handed them safety pins to pin their numbers on with. Freddy paid the entry fee and winked at the woman.

Faith grabbed him and pulled him away from the table. "You didn't need to flirt with her," she whispered.

"Are you jealous?" Freddy tipped his head at her and smirked.

Faith rolled her eyes, ignored the question, and said, "It looks like we have twenty minutes. I'm going to go freshen up. I'll be back five minutes before start time, okay?"

"Sure thing."

The competition would be in the center of the ballroom with circular tables set up all around for attendees to smoke, drink, eat, and view the competition from. The double oak doors were now pushed all the way open, and patrons and contestants filed in. The room filled rapidly.

Faith wiggled her way against the flow of traffic and crossed the foyer. The ladies' room was crowded too. Waiting in the long line did nothing to calm her nerves. She and Freddy had worked so hard on their dancing. Tonight was their moment to finally win some serious money. A hundred dollars for the first-place team. The money dangled within their reach.

Coming out of the ladies' room fifteen minutes later, she made her way through the crowded, noisy foyer into the ballroom, where scores of people were already seated. More chairs were being set up along the back wall to accommodate the huge crowd. She put her hand to her stomach to try to calm the butterflies and made her way over to where Freddy should be waiting for her. No Freddy. Where on earth could he be?

She felt a hand on her shoulder and turned. "Freddy," she started to say with relief, only to find herself looking up into the handsome face of Davis Wilson. She stared at him. He looked wonderful and smelled good too—like soap and mint. He certainly looked different than he had a few hours ago at the brick store in his dusty work coveralls.

"Good luck, Faith." A small half smile curled up one side of his mouth.

"Thank you," Faith said in surprise. "What are you doing here?"

"I came to watch the competition." He seemed to loom over her, standing close but not touching.

"Oh," Faith said softly, too anxious to figure out whether she was more worried about the missing Freddy or the thought of Davis watching her dance.

He leaned down toward her as if he were going to say something over the noise of the crowd but pulled back when they both saw Freddy striding toward them. She thought she heard Davis mutter, "Incoming."

"Let's get this show on the road," Freddy said as he loosened his green tie just a bit. Noticing Davis, he nodded. "Hi, old man."

Davis grimaced. "We're the same age."

Freddy put his arm around Faith's waist and led her onto the dance floor. She turned and glanced over her shoulder. Davis stood in the same place, watching them maneuver to the center of the floor. What was the look on his face? Wistfulness? Did he wish he were dancing tonight?

"Ladies and gentlemen," a peppy emcee said into the mic, "welcome to the Swingin' Stars Dance Competition. Our contestants tonight come from at least five different states. They are the best of the best. Let's hear it for our dancers." The audience cheered.

"Our band tonight is the Duane Ludmiller Band. Let's welcome them to Dayton."

The audience clapped enthusiastically.

"Mr. Ludmiller, is the band ready?"

"The band is ready," Conductor Ludmiller called from behind the piano.

Faith's heart seemed to be trying to beat itself out of her chest.

"Dancers, are you ready to swing a wing?"

"Ready!" and "Yes!" the dancers called out enthusiastically.

"Let the competition begin!" the emcee shouted.

Ludmiller counted the band off, and they began to play "Take the A Train," a favorite jazz song of Faith's.

Freddy grabbed her hand and led her into an energetic swing dance. It was a slower jazz beat, and Faith used the opportunity to really exaggerate her movements—long kicks, lots of swiveling on the balls of her feet, twisting down to the dance floor, popping back up and sliding under Freddy's legs. Her mint dress was being put to the test! Freddy held his finger on Faith's head as if he were a record player and she was the record. She did an exaggerated series of what she liked to call "monkey steps" as she spun around under his finger, and then she did the same for him as he really hammed it up, making silly faces and circling her. The judges walked around the dancers on the floor, taking notes and carefully watching footwork. Faith turned her focus from the judges. *Ignore them. Just feel the music and smile.*

Midway through the song she finally felt the nerves leave as her body seemed to say, "I've done this a thousand times before." A saxophonist stepped to the mic for a solo. Faith's feet flew, and happiness filled her. This was why she danced, this feeling of delight and energy. Rose concerns and brick-store worries couldn't exist at the same time as this bubbling joy.

Near the end of the dance, Freddy signaled a lift. Faith yelled at him, "We can't—not allowed in the first round!"

"Oh yeah." He pulled her instead into one of their well-coordinated kick steps. They matched each other's moves perfectly. All the practicing really had paid off. One of the judges watched them and nodded her head. Ludmiller played the last note on the piano, and the dancers came to a halt, most of them smiling.

The emcee immediately stepped to the mic. "The judges want to see a foxtrot next," he said, his voice booming through the ballroom.

Faith put her head high with perfectly straight posture. Ah, the foxtrot. This was going to be good. Thanks to her years of ballet classes, the posture and grace of the foxtrot came naturally to her. She leaned back in Freddy's arms with her head turned toward her left shoulder. The music started and Freddy took a large step, Faith following his lead. They were off, gracefully making their way around the room. Their steps were long and smooth, dipping gracefully down and back up.

Midway through the dance they passed a cute couple. The man had a pained look of concentration on his face, and she could see him mouthing, "Slow, slow, quick, quick." The woman smiled and looked like she was having a lot of fun.

"They make a good team," Faith said.

"Huh?" Freddy maneuvered her toward the judges' table. "That guy is a dead hooper."

Bad dancer or not, it was sweet how hard he was trying.

"Wonderful job, dancers," the emcee called at the conclusion of the foxtrot. "Next up we would like to see your version of the Charleston."

"That's not fair!" a dancer standing near the middle of the floor called out. "You never said that could be one of our dances."

Ludmiller ignored the murmuring of the dancers and played a piano intro. His band joined in, and the Charleston began.

Freddy was an excellent improviser. They'd be fine on the Charleston. His cockiness was irritating, but it could also come in handy.

He faced Faith, bent at the waist and squatting slightly, and began to slap his thighs. Faith imitated him. He raised his right hand toward Faith's. Catching on, she lifted her hand and followed him through a series of hand-clapping rhythms to the beat. Freddy waited until a judge noticed their hand game and then Freddy sprang into the air, Faith copying his movements. Turning to her side, he worked through the classic movements of the Charleston. Faith caught on to the steps quickly. Hopefully, it looked like they were in sync. She kicked her leg out to the side. Energy and silliness—that was what the Charleston was all about.

"Well done!" Freddy said at the end of the dance. "You're fabulous at following. It's like we read each other's minds." He put his arm around Faith and gave her a sweaty hug. She shrugged out of it quickly, sensing that somewhere out in the audience, Davis was watching them. Why did that bother her?

The music began again. Faith and Freddy danced their way enthusiastically through a fast-paced swing dance, a waltz, and the last dance of the first round, a tango.

"We got this in the bag," Freddy said as the judges convened for their ten-minute break.

"I don't know," Faith said. "There are a lot of great dancers out there."

"It's ours," Freddy said with his usual bravado, wiping sweat from his forehead. "We'll see."

They walked over to the refreshment table, where Faith got herself a cup of icy lemonade.

Freddy helped himself to a cup of spiked punch.

"Do you think you should be drinking that?" she asked.

Freddy didn't respond but picked up the punch and drank it down in one long gulp, then reached for another one and quickly downed that too.

Faith frowned. Why did Freddy always have to drink? And why in the middle of a competition? Sure, two cups of punch weren't enough to harm his dancing, but if he drank two more at the next break, it wouldn't be good.

Faith sipped her lemonade while he flirted with a cute redheaded girl. Faith leaned against the wall, looking around at the spectators, and spotted Davis slowly approaching. He weaved his way in and out of the crowd gathered around the refreshment table.

"Great job on the first round," Davis said.

"Thanks."

He said something else that was lost in the noise of the crowd.

"Sorry," Faith shook her head. "I can't hear you."

Davis put his hand on her shoulder, leaned down, and said, "Your foxtrot was beautiful."

"Did my mother ask you to come and keep your eye on me?"

Davis shook his head and said, "I wanted to see your phantom dress in action." He winked at her. Faith's face went hot. He was awfully audacious for a man hoping to be hired at her store.

"Attention, please. The results are in," the emcee boomed.

The crowd quieted down, dancers and audience alike turned to face him.

"The level of competition this year has been outstanding. Let's hear it for all fifty couples."

There was a smattering of impatient applause.

"Our judges have chosen the following couples to continue. When your number is called, please come back to the dance floor in preparation for our next round."

Freddy grabbed Faith's hand and faced the judges with a big grin on his face. Davis looked down and scowled at their entwined hands. Faith shrugged and said, "Freddy thinks we'll win."

"You do make him look good," Davis said with a frown.

"Couple number twenty-seven!" Polite applause sounded as the Sorenson siblings came forward.

Five more couples were called. Faith squirmed. What if their number wasn't called? But Freddy just continued to grin.

"Couple number thirty-seven!" Freddy whooped and pulled Faith energetically back out onto the dance floor.

The remaining three couples were called. Faith looked around at their competition. She recognized several of them as extremely good dancers. Freddy was all smiles. A tinge of irritation moved through her. Did the man even know the meaning of the word *nerves*, or was the alcohol making him relaxed? Could they really pull this off?

CHAPTER 13

DAVIS SAT BACK IN HIS chair. He had a good view of the dance floor from his table.

"Let's hear it for our top ten," the emcee called.

The audience clapped politely. The couple at Davis's table ordered dinner from a waiter. The woman was annoying. She wanted to chat, and Davis didn't. He wanted to watch Faith dancing in Freddy's arms and scowl.

"Can I get you anything, sir?" the waiter asked.

Davis shook his head. He wasn't hungry.

"Mr. Ludmiller," the emcee called out, "let the band play on."

Davis's eyes stayed glued to Faith as the band played a jazz song he didn't recognize—like he'd told Janet, it wasn't as if he'd been dancing the last four years. Faith and Freddy glided over the floor, and Davis tapped a finger on his knee. Freddy really could dance. He was smooth. But Faith, Faith was more than Freddy in every way. She was grace and energy personified. Davis sighed as he watched her green dress weave effortlessly in and out of the other dancers. Carrie was right—the dress did look like sea-foam when she spun. Davis shook his head. What on earth was wrong with him? Why couldn't he take his eyes off Patrick's little sister?

The swing ended, and the dancers and audience applauded. Freddy leaned over to whisper something into Faith's ear. Even from across the ballroom, Davis could see her smile.

"Next dance is a waltz," the emcee announced.

Across the floor, Freddy held Faith in his arms. Davis flinched. The lovely sound of Strauss's "Blue Danube" contrasted starkly with Davis's mood. His jaw clenched. He had spent nearly a month last winter living in a foxhole in the cold, muddy ground while the enemy shot at him and his men. Watching

Faith in Freddy's arms felt like being back in that foxhole. Freddy grinned and tugged her a little closer. Yep, this felt like bailing water out of a hole he was going to have to sleep in.

"Who do you like?" the woman at his table asked her husband.

The man shrugged. "They all look good to me."

She shook her head. "Watch couple number fifteen. I think they'll win."

Davis's eyebrows went up. "What about couple thirty-seven?" That was Faith and Freddy. "They look pretty talented to me."

The woman shook her head. "No," she said, "watch them closer. They're proficient but they don't have any romantic spark."

"Romantic spark?" Davis asked.

"Yeah. Watch couple fifteen. You feel the romance of their dances. Couple thirty-seven doesn't have enough chemistry."

"They don't?" Davis leaned toward the woman. She wasn't so annoying after all.

"Nah," she said and repeated, "no romantic spark."

Davis laughed.

"You know them?" the woman asked.

"Yes, ma'am. They've been dancing together for two years."

The woman leaned forward and tapped Davis's arm. "Take my word for it. They won't end up together."

Sitting in that foxhole had felt helpless until the air force had come in and bombed the German army. Davis's men had cheered as they watched their fighters fly overhead and heard the sound of them strafing the enemy. The woman at his table seemed so certain that Faith and Freddy wouldn't end up together that Davis felt the same sense of hope he'd felt back in the army watching the air force come in. He sat up straighter as the dance ended.

CHAPTER 14

THE EMCEE ANNOUNCED THEY WOULD take a break before their last three dances. Freddy wiped the sweat from his brow and said, "I need a drink."

Faith put her hand on his arm. "Not spiked," she said.

Freddy ignored her and moved across the floor to the drink table.

"Could you tie my bow?" the girl with a number fifteen on her back asked.

"Sure." Faith retied the bow around the girl's waist while trying to keep her eye on Freddy. Darn him. He was gulping down the spiked punch. She hated when he drank too much. He put his hand out for a third cup just by the time Faith reached him. She shook her head at the girl behind the table and tugged Freddy away.

"Hey," he said. "I'm still thirsty."

"Water," Faith hissed. "Drink some water."

Freddy giggled. Oh no. Was he feeling the effects already?

"Dancers, get ready to swing again," the emcee called out.

Faith gripped Freddy's hand and pulled him to the center of the dance floor. The music started, and he flung her into a swing with a little too much oomph. She bobbled but quickly caught herself.

Smile. She wanted to glare at Freddy but pasted a smile on her face instead. They made it through the swing without any mishap. Next was a jive. They danced well, but Faith thought Freddy was missing his usual crispness. Darn it. She'd told him not to drink more. They did one last synchronized jump together and bowed to the last note.

"Last dance!" Mr. Ludmiller counted off the band, and they broke into "Rhumba Amalia."

"You need to dance sexier." Freddy picked up Faith's hand.

She gazed into his eyes. Sexier? Did he mean crassly? Did he want her to dance like the girl across the floor—all suggestive, with no grace? Faith wanted to tell him what she thought of his suggestion, but she bit her cheek and gave him a fake smile instead. After all, this was a courting dance, and irritation wasn't exactly inviting. She took small steps while maintaining eye contact with Freddy. They danced around the floor with what she hoped looked like the passion the rhumba called for. Freddy managed to maneuver her right in front of the judges' table at the end of the dance. He dipped her dramatically, keeping her down while he blew the judges a kiss, then raised her up for a final dramatic twirl and a synchronized bow.

"Did you see that judge smiling at me?" he asked. "We got this, baby."

Faith wasn't so sure. Those last three dances had seemed a little sloppy to her.

The emcee announced that the judges would take fifteen minutes to tally their results, and Freddy left Faith on the floor. Oh great. He was drinking more of the spiked punch.

A cute blonde girl in yellow came over to her and, with a friendly smile, said, "I've been watching you. You look classically trained."

Faith smiled back. "Thirteen years of ballet."

"It shows. You have beautiful lines. I wish my waltz was as graceful as yours."

"My partner wishes my swing and Latin were as sexy as yours."

"Don't change anything about your dancing. Anyone can do gimmicky, but your skill is a thing of beauty."

Faith's smile widened, and she said with sincerity, "Thanks! Your encouragement means a lot."

The judges finally handed a folded piece of paper to the emcee, who walked back to his mic. "We have our results in."

The room quieted. Freddy hurried back to stand by Faith and put his arm around her shoulder. She looked at the emcee, and her heart beat faster.

"The judges say they are impressed with all the dancers but that three couples really stood out tonight for their innovation and modern moves. Our third-place couple is couple number forty-two."

The audience cheered.

Faith clapped and called out, "Well done!"

"In second place is couple number twenty-two." The couple who was dressed all in black hugged and then moved forward to receive their trophy and stand by the third-place winners.

Freddy bent down and whispered into Faith's ear, "I think we won it all."

Faith didn't feel so confident. It seemed to her that the winners were winning based on edgy moves.

"And our first-place couple is Ivy Phillips and Kent Lemmon."

Luckily Freddy's disgusted cry of "No way!" was drowned out by the cheers for the winners. Faith hadn't thought that couple was anything special but clapped politely anyway. A sweaty dancer in a sparkly orange dress next to her muttered, "Ivy's cousin is one of the judges."

"All that work for nothing," Freddy said. He turned to Faith. "I told you you needed to dance sexier."

Faith opened her mouth to tell Freddy he shouldn't have been drinking spiked punch, but she bit back her retort. What was done was done. He hadn't been as crisp on those last three dances, but the bigger problem was her dancing. Faith's classic dance style simply wasn't what the judges had been looking for.

"I'm getting a drink." Freddy turned his back on Faith and walked away, clearly angry about not placing.

The remaining couples made their way off the dance floor, and Faith followed slowly, feeling a sense of loss. She sighed. Dancing had meant so much to her the last few years. It had been her bright spot, her creative outlet, a time to immerse herself in the music and forget her pain. This was the first time it had brought a sense of disappointment and letting someone else down. Tears stung her eyes. She hated the feeling that her dancing wasn't enough for the judges or for Freddy.

"You were robbed," Davis said, coming up behind her. He put his arm protectively around her shoulders.

Taken off guard, she let him lead her toward the table he had been sitting at. She was too sad to protest the fact that Davis had his arm around her.

She turned her head away from him, embarrassed that she couldn't control her tears. He handed her his handkerchief and moved to grab an extra chair from a nearby table and swing it over to Faith. She wiped her eyes, took a couple of big breaths, and handed the handkerchief back to Davis.

"You really were fabulous, Faith," he said with sincerity. His blue eyes looked at her with concern.

"Yes, you certainly were," the middle-aged woman who sat at the table by Davis said.

"Thanks." Faith looked down at the table and fiddled with the tablecloth. "You must think I'm pretty shallow to be crying about dancing."

"No," Davis said softly, "I don't."

Faith glanced up at Davis from underneath her wet lashes. "I didn't care that much about the money or winning."

"Then, why are you sad?"

"You wouldn't understand."

"Try me."

"I just feel like I let Freddy down."

Faith had seen many expressions on Davy's face over the years, but she couldn't read the one now as he looked at her across the table. A couple more tears rolled down her cheeks. Embarrassed, she tried to wipe them away quickly.

"Let's get you something to eat; that'll make you feel better." He cleared his throat gruffly. "You don't need to worry about Freddy."

Davis waved a waiter over. Her pride shouldn't let him take care of her, but hunger won out. The couple at the table with them headed out to the dance floor, leaving Faith and Davis alone. They waited in silence for the food to come, watching the audience-turned-dancers fill the dance floor.

"You can go dance while I eat," Faith said. "There are more women here than men. You'll have no problem finding a partner—lots of khaki wackies."

"I'd rather watch you eat." Davis paused, rubbed the back of his neck, and added, "The truth is I haven't danced in four years, and I was never that good anyway. Half the steps people are doing I've never even seen before. I feel out of step, figuratively and literally."

"You want to be like the old people? Sitting at their tables and just watching?"

His cheek twitched. It looked like her arrow had hit its mark. Good. Davis was way too young to give up on dancing. She wanted Davy, who was always up for fun, back.

Davis said, "I think I would look stupider bobbing than sitting here."

"Bobbing?" What did he mean?

"Never mind," he said.

Faith dug into her food, savoring her steak and potato while Davis fidgeted, opened his mouth, closed it, fidgeted some more, leaned forward as if to say something, and then leaned back in his chair, tapping his fingers on his knee. He finally said, "Have you heard from your cousin Rose lately?"

Faith shook her head and paused eating. Was that what he had wanted to ask her? It felt like he had given up on his real question. She shook her head. "No, and it's driving us crazy. We're going to worry until we hear from her. It isn't like her to go so long without writing."

"I know it's worrying your mom," he said. "Do you have a number for her?"

"Yes. We try every night to get her on the phone, but we haven't had any luck."

"Have her parents heard from her?"

"My aunt and uncle are in very poor health. We haven't asked them, because we don't want to worry them when they can't do anything for Rose anyway."

The table went quiet again, and Davis fidgeted some more while Faith finished her food. Reenergized and feeling more like herself again, she set her fork down and raised an eyebrow at Davis. "All right, say what you need to say."

He set down the napkin he'd been playing with. "What do you see in Freddy Casper anyway?"

Faith flushed. She opened her mouth to tell Davis that her dancing partner was none of his business, but he had just bought her dinner and been kind to her. She gathered her thoughts, cleared her throat, and said, "After my dad and Patrick died, life was pretty grim. I was working long hours at the store and coming home to sadness. Freddy was heaven-sent. He showed up at just the right time in my life." She smiled and looked at the dancers on the floor. "He invited me out dancing."

Davis was silent, so she went on. "He made me happy. He was sweet and a breath of fresh air in the middle of the war. I know you don't think Freddy is serious enough, but his lightheartedness did me good. I needed him. I needed the dancing."

Davis leaned forward and said, "*Made* you happy? *Needed?* Does he still do you good, or is he just a habit?"

Faith frowned. He had no right to ask her those types of questions. Good heavens, he was her employee. Setting her napkin down, she said, "Thank you for an excellent and timely meal. It was exactly what I needed. I'm going to see if Freddy is ready to leave."

She stood abruptly and hurried away, weaving in and out of the crowded tables. Was Davis following her? She sped up, pushing through the crowded room to the bar.

"Are you ready, Freddy?" Faith asked, finding him seated at the bar, leaning against it with a drink in his hand.

"Ready, Freddy—that rhymes," Freddy slurred. He lurched to his feet, set his glass down, and swaying, followed Faith out toward the coatroom. She glanced back at Davis, who was close behind, and darn, he looked angry.

Ignoring Davis, she retrieved her purse and Freddy's suit coat with his keys in the pocket. Freddy sagged against the wall, his upper body slumped over.

Davis edged his way in between Faith and Freddy and said, "I'm not letting him take you home. He's completely drunk."

"I'm aware of that."

She moved around Davis, put Freddy's arm around her shoulder, and pulled him toward the door while he grinned vacantly. Heavens, he was heavy. She wrinkled her nose. What an unpleasant mixture of beer and sweat.

Davis stepped in front of her, forcing her to stop. "I'm not letting him drive you home."

How dumb did Davis think she was? "He's not driving; I am. Move out of my way. He's heavy."

Davis clenched his jaw but moved around to help Faith pull Freddy along. His technique was a lot rougher than Faith's. He gripped Freddy around the waist and marched him out the oak doors and down the rose-rimmed drive.

"Shhhlow down," Freddy slurred.

Davis sped up.

Faith found the valet ticket in Freddy's suit-coat pocket. Davis grabbed it out of her hand and gave both his and Freddy's tickets to the valet. She frowned. He wasn't acting like a man who wanted to be hired.

His jaw jutted out. "I'm not letting you drive a drunk man home. You'll take my car and I'll drive Freddy in his." He grabbed Freddy's arm off Faith's shoulder and roughly yanked it over his own.

Faith immediately felt the relief of the deadweight taken off her shoulders, but merciful heavens, Davis had grown bossy in the army.

She stood up straight, prepared to protest, but there was steel in Davis's eyes. She vividly remembered the last time she had seen that look, the night of their huge fight. She had known that cold January evening, by the determination in his clear blue eyes, that he wasn't sorry he and Patrick had enlisted. The same determination glared back at her now.

"Yes, Sergeant," she said with sass in her voice.

She fumed while Davis loaded Freddy into the passenger seat of the Alfa Romeo, and she fumed when he tossed her his keys and said, "My car's no Alfa Romeo, but she'll get you home. Take it easy on the clutch." Did he still think she was some princess? She fumed behind the wheel of Davis's old Ford. Meddling, infuriating man! The Ford sputtered to a start, and Faith tried to come up with appropriately cutting remarks as she shifted gears and followed Freddy's sports car onto the highway.

She needed to let Davis know exactly what she thought of his interfering and that she was too old to be treated like this. For heaven's sake, she owned a business—a business he wanted to work for. She accelerated and the old car responded.

What was going on in Freddy's car? She hoped he was singing love songs to Davis like he had to her the time he'd gotten drunk in Columbus and she'd had to drive home. Faith allowed herself a teeny smile at the thought of Freddy singing Sinatra to Davis. That in itself would be some nice payback for the sergeant. Honestly! Did he think he was still in the army where he could bark out commands?

The memory of Freddy's foul breath and his drunk belches did make her a little glad she wasn't in the car with him. What did Mom always say? "'When the drop is inside, the sense is outside.'" But Davis's bossing her around and interfering with her life had to stop!

Faith fumed the entire hour drive home to Payson.

At last Davis pulled into the long drive of the Casper mansion. Faith parked behind Freddy's car but didn't get out. She watched unhappily as Davis marched Freddy up to his door, pushed him inside his house, threw his suit coat after him and slammed the door.

She slid over to the passenger seat as Davis opened the creaky driver's-side door of his car. She turned and looked out the window, ignoring him, but even without looking at him, she could feel his tenseness. He restarted the car and carefully backed out of the Casper driveway.

"I told Freddy you won't be seeing him again," Davis said, his right arm behind Faith as he looked over his shoulder to back up.

"Hah!" Faith said. There was no chance of that. She scooted closer to the window so there was no possibility of his hand touching her. Her anger with him at sixteen had been red-hot and fiery; this anger was ice-cold and deliberate—it was a mature, more deadly anger. She certainly didn't feel helpless like she had at sixteen. Davis would find out for himself that her life wasn't to be meddled with. She would most certainly be seeing Freddy again. He was her dance partner. She remained glued to her door, still looking out the window as they drove back to Forest Drive.

"Even if this means you don't hire me," Davis said, "it'll be worth it."

Faith didn't answer him. The car was silent—deathly silent.

Davis pulled into her driveway, and she jumped out of his car before he had even put it into park. She nearly ran to her front door, her green dress swishing with her anger, her dancing shoes stomping to no beat. She unlocked her front door and turned to glare at Davis before she marched in. He was standing by his car, staring after her. Even in the dark she could tell he was angry too, his chin jutting out and his arms folded across his chest.

She slammed the door shut behind her. She was fine with Davis being angry with her. She didn't want him to like her or be her friend. He had crossed a line by talking to Freddy. He wanted to interfere with her life? Then, fine—he'd better be prepared to have his own life interfered with. This was war.

CHAPTER 15

"You get in a rhythm with it," Frank said. "Yeah, that's it." He nodded in approval of Davis's technique.

Following the line of string they had carefully placed, Davis balanced on the scaffolding, picked bricks up in his left hand, flipped them onto the line of mortar, and smoothed the excess mortar off with the trowel in his right hand.

"I got an invite to the reception your mom is throwing for you this weekend."

Davis grunted his disgust and slapped another brick down.

"Careful. Not so hard. You're going to break the brick."

Davis exhaled and forced his muscles to relax. He didn't need to take his displeasure out on the bricks. "The reception is for my mom, not for me."

"Kind of like the time my wife made me dress up like Raggedy Andy for our neighbor's Halloween party. She was Raggedy Ann. I couldn't have looked stupider."

Davis couldn't help a smile. "Exactly like that."

The two men worked side by side, Frank offering direction here and there. "A little more mortar. Now check your level."

Davis placed his plumb level on the row of bricks he had just completed. They were in the English bond pattern; a brick was placed with the narrow side out—a stretcher—and then the next brick—a header—was put in lengthwise. This pattern necessitated a two-layer wall. More strength but also more work.

Davis pushed himself to work faster under the hot June sun. Sweat trickled down his back. *Keep the pace. Keep marching.* Another row of brick done. The house they were working on was going to be beautiful.

Frank's face was red from heat and exertion. "Why don't you wait in the truck," Davis suggested. "I'll finish this row before we leave for the day."

Frank didn't argue.

Davis, lost in thought, kept the bricks flying from his left hand. His right hand scooped and placed the mortar. He used the back of his trowel to smooth and even the thickness. Bricks had a distinct smell—earthy and warm. He loved it as well as the muddy odor of the mortar. He loved watching the walls of a house come up. He was meant for this business.

He finished the row, loaded his equipment, and joined Frank in the truck.

"You don't seem to feel the heat," Frank said.

"I don't mind it much," Davis answered. The truth was the heat and the hard physical labor were good for him. They were cleansing. He couldn't do anything for the dead men who haunted his nighttime thoughts, but his daytime work brought him satisfaction and purpose. Plus, he slept a little better when he was exhausted.

Frank started the truck. The breeze from the open windows felt good. They were in the truck Faith had nicknamed Costello. Davis smiled. She had a way with names.

"You think Faith will keep you on?" Frank asked. He tugged on his white mustache, glanced sideways at Davis.

Davis just shrugged. "I hope so." Surely Faith would be able to set aside their disagreement over Freddy and hire him permanently.

"You want to tell me what's going on between you two that has her so worked up?"

Davis pulled his damp T-shirt away from his chest and let the breeze dry some of his sweat. He turned away from Frank and watched the neat homes with their green gardens move by. "It's a little complicated."

Frank snorted. "It's not that complicated, is it?"

"What do you mean?" Davis turned his attention back to Frank.

"I reckon little Faith Penwilliger grew up while you were gone. You've got a thing for her, but she's your boss and you don't know how to break up what she's got going with Freddy Casper."

Davis just grunted. Frank could be really annoying. What did he know anyway? The biggest problem was that Faith had an old grudge against him for something that happened four long years ago.

"Freddy Casper." Frank sighed. "Lots of money, that one, to impress the girls. Thinks he owns the world."

Davis grunted again.

"You can't be like America, waiting and waiting to enter the war until Pearl Harbor happened." Frank reached over and thumped Davis's shoulder. "You need to get in there and fight for Faith. Show her you're interested."

"Not happening," Davis said. Sure, Faith had caught his eye. He wasn't going to deny that he was attracted to her, but he was in no position to court anyone. He folded his arms over his chest and grimaced. He was a mess. He couldn't sleep. He didn't know how to flirt with girls or dance with them anymore, let alone ask one out. Not to mention that Faith *was* his boss and didn't even like him.

"Don't be intimidated by Freddy Casper."

Frank was assuming a lot. "Oh, I'm not scared of Freddy Casper." Davis may not be in a position to ask Faith out, but that didn't mean he wasn't going to do everything he could to keep Freddy away from her. "As a matter of fact, I believe he's scared of me. I told him to stay away from Faith."

"Is that right?" Frank shifted down and took the corner on Main Street. The truck bounced as he accelerated toward the store.

"I had some time to talk to him." An hour-long drive, to be exact.

Frank's eyebrows went up. "I know Faith pretty well. I don't think she'd take too kindly to that. For a man wanting a job from her, that was dumb. For a man wanting to court her, that was *incredibly* dumb."

Davis squirmed in his seat. Maybe Frank was right. Faith was barely communicating with him. She gave Frank work directions to pass along and avoided Davis.

"Take it from an old man," Frank said. "You cross a woman, she'll get even with you."

"You saying Faith won't hire me because I told Freddy off?"

Frank nodded. "That's exactly what I'm saying, but it isn't too late. You just need to sweet-talk her."

Davis sighed. He'd spent the last four years barking orders and giving things straight to his men. Sweet talk? He stared at Frank and shook his head.

Frank gave a grim smile. "Well, don't say I didn't warn you."

"I'll have to take my chances."

Frank changed the subject abruptly. "She's thinking of selling the business, you know."

"What!" Davis started. Was Frank serious? Faith had made it through the lean war years and now she was going to sell just when the business was poised to take off? "Why would she do that?"

Frank tugged his mustache. "She doesn't know I know. She got an offer from Howard Holland, and she's tempted. It would mean her being able to go to college."

College. Just because Davis had decided not to go didn't mean it was something Faith would turn down. He braced himself against the dash. "How do you know she's tempted?"

She wouldn't sell, would she? It'd break Marcia's heart.

"She has the offer in her desk drawer. She pulls it out almost every day, looks at it, and puts it back in the drawer with a tormented look on her pretty face."

Davis's stomach lurched, and not just because of Costello's lack of shocks.

CHAPTER 16

FAITH TURNED THE RADIO UP and sang along on the way home from work. It had been a long week, and she was coming home tired and hungry. It was two hours past dinnertime, and Mom was probably getting anxious.

The June evening was still hot, so Faith had the truck windows rolled down. Hopefully, Payson appreciated her music.

She parked Abbott, and before Faith had even exited the truck, Mom hurried out of the house waving a letter.

"Rose wrote?" Faith asked as she jumped down from the truck.

Mom nodded.

"Is she all right?"

"I'm not sure." Mom tipped her head to one side. "Come inside. I'll read it to you while you eat."

Faith took her hat off and washed up. She joined Mom in the kitchen, where a warm plate of fragrant meat loaf and potatoes waited for her.

Mom unfolded the letter. Faith cut into her meat loaf, chewed slowly, and listened intently as Mom read.

> "*Dear Faith and Aunt Marcia,*
>
> "*I hope this finds you both well and in good health. I was so sorry to hear about the dance competition. I'm sure you deserved to win, Faith. Keep dancing.*
>
> "*You asked about my job. It pays the bills. It's rather monotonous, but the building is cool and a break from the heat. Sometimes, though, the work just seems so meaningless. I suppose everyone involved with the war effort is having to adjust to life not being so purposeful. Do you know what I mean? For four years I lived, breathed, dreamed,*

and prayed about the war. I suppose any job would feel mundane af-
ter working at the Pentagon. Taking shorthand on meaningless law-
suits doesn't seem world-changing somehow. Yesterday I took a long
dictation from a man who is suing his neighbor because the dog barks
during the night. I couldn't help but wonder if the man ever thought
of earplugs—they have certainly helped me. After dinner I go to my
room, put earplugs in, and read. That way I don't have to hear the
Russo family screaming at each other. I never appreciated quiet when
I had it before. Joey doesn't much like being at home either, but it
looks like, with his expenses and no job, we won't be able to move out
for some time, so I'm trying my best to learn to love earplugs.

"I've become involved with a marvelous project. Every Saturday
afternoon I go down to the Baptist church, where we work on putting
together items to send to France to help with the relief effort. The
organization is called the Cooperative for American Remittances to
Europe. We call the packages we put together CARE packages, and I
certainly hope they know Americans do care about their hardships.
I know it has meant the world to me, as I struggle to adjust to New
York and my marriage, that my family is praying for me. The letters
I get keep me going. I swear they even smell of home. I buried my
nose in a letter from my mom last week, and I could smell our lilac
bushes. I sat and cried for simpler times.

"I just reread my letter and realized how negative it sounds.
Please don't worry about me. I'm just so tired. I suppose that comes
from working long hours, commuting, and then being in a hot,
stuffy room at night.

"Love,
Rose"

Faith set her fork down as Mom dropped the letter and stared at the wall. "What do you think she means about Joey's expenses?"

Faith grimaced. "My guess is that he's a drinker or maybe a gambler."

"Poor Rose."

"I'm more worried about how tired she sounds," Faith said.

"I wonder if she's expecting. I've never been so tired as when I was expecting."

Faith moved some meat loaf around on her plate. "I feel like she isn't telling us everything."

"I don't know what to do," Mom said. "I suppose her parents must be awfully worried too."

Faith frowned. Aunt Clarice and Uncle Dell were in their late sixties and not in good health. They were very proud of Rose, but they wouldn't be of any assistance to her. "What did she call those packages again?"

"CARE packages."

"Let's send her one every month," Faith said.

"A little love from Payson to New York City?"

"Exactly. I don't think it will matter what we send. We just need to box up some love for her."

Having a plan in mind, the Penwilliger women spent their dinner discussing items for Rose's care packages. Faith was happy not to have to discuss Davis or the hecticness at the brick store. Mom was full of good ideas for the packages. Faith smiled. It wouldn't solve Rose's problems, but nobody knew how to package love like Mom.

Mom dished them each up a little bowl of homemade strawberry ice cream. Faith took a spoonful and let the sweetness melt on her tongue. "Heavenly," she said.

"Mmm." Mom seemed just as happy with the treat as Faith was. "How was work?"

"Just fine," Faith responded. "But busy."

Work was changing; business was flowing in. She rubbed her forehead. She had to either commit to hiring more men and growing with the times or selling, but thoughts of her father and his pride in his business had her paralyzed with feelings of uncertainty.

Mom swallowed her ice cream and waved her spoon. "I was busy today too. Cecilia asked me to help make some decorations for Davis's reception."

Faith rolled her eyes but said, "That's nice."

"Speaking of Davis, how is he getting along at the store?"

"All right," Faith said, her tone flat.

"A kind word never broke anyone's mouth," Mom said.

Faith rolled her eyes again and sat up straighter in her chair. If Mom was waiting for her to compliment Davis, she would have a long wait. Faith was still furious with him for interfering with Freddy. She consistently refused to discuss hiring Davis, but every few days Mom would bring the subject up to test the waters.

"A little pebble in your shoe can cause constant irritation," Faith responded, then changed the subject. "How was the junior cultus club today?"

Mom accepted the change of subject with grace.

The next evening found Faith doing yard work. It was a far cry from her usual Saturday-evening dance outings with Freddy—he had called her once in the last week, but he still hadn't asked her out dancing, and it was Davis's fault—but the mindless work gave her plenty of time to ruminate over Mr. Holland's offer.

She needed an epiphany or at least a feeling of resolution. As it was, one day she was determined to sell and the next she was determined to stay. If she stayed, should she hire Davis? How hard would it be to have him around nonstop? She kicked at a dirt clod, her garden clogs sending it flying. The backyard smelled wonderful—like roses and freshly turned earth. She didn't mind yardwork, and there *was* satisfaction in knowing Davis wouldn't have much to do when he came over on Monday, his day off. It irritated her that the only two things he seemed to have going on were shadowing Frank on his bricklaying jobs and helping Mom around the Penwilliger home. The man needed to have some fun so he'd have something better to do than interfere in her life.

Faith went to the shed and pulled out the stepladder and the saw. She would get even with Davis. She just wasn't sure when or how. For now, she would simply continue to avoid him. This took a certain level of skill. He was, after all, at work and often around home helping Mom. The key to avoidance was knowing where he was at all times. She thought of it as her Davis radar. She could sense when he was around the Penwilliger home and always knew where he was at work. If she had to talk to him, she was polite, and he responded with the same cool politeness.

"What are you up to, Faith?" Carrie Wilson asked as she wandered over from her yard.

"Just working on my mom's to-do list," she replied from the stepladder, where she sawed a dead limb off an apple tree.

"Oh, Davis would do that for you," Carrie replied with confidence in her big brother.

Faith gritted her teeth. "I know he would, but I think I can handle this."

Carrie looked up at her and sighed. "How come you look gorgeous no matter what you wear? Even in your old overalls?"

Faith laughed, dropped the saw, and gave one last tug that snapped a long branch from the tree. "Maybe because I smile. My mom says that to smile is to dress your face in its finest gown."

"Do you believe that?" Carrie asked.

"I think it's true. I really am attracted to people who smile a lot."

"Is that why you like Freddy Casper?"

Was it? "I think it is," she said carefully. She descended the ladder, picked up the heavy branch, and began tugging it to her debris pile. "Freddy is never down."

Carrie followed her closely and persisted in the uncomfortable conversation. "Are you serious with him?"

Faith's cheeks went warm. She turned her back to Carrie and pulled the branch along. How to answer that? Freddy had never even asked her to go steady, but they were more than friends. He was fun and he gave nice goodnight kisses. Of course, lately, Davis sitting on the front porch smoking had killed any attempt at all by Freddy.

"It's good to have a happy dancing partner." There. That was a good evasion of the question.

"Is that why you don't like Davis? Because he doesn't smile?"

Faith heaved the branch onto the burn pile and made an attempt to sidetrack Carrie.

"I'm going to widen the drainage ditch for my mom. Let me grab a shovel."

Carrie followed her to the shed while Faith put the saw and stepladder back and pulled the shovel out. Why was Carrie still looking expectantly at her? They went carefully through the huge victory garden Mom had patriotically planted and energetically tended the last few years. It was people like Mom who'd given her the confidence that the war would be won. She'd been asked to plant a victory garden, so she'd done it, and the number of tomatoes, zucchini, squash, peas, beans, potatoes, and corn that had come out of it so far was impressive.

Faith approached the ditch in the far corner of their yard and garden, took her first scoop of dirt to widen it, and said, "Why do you think Davis doesn't smile?"

"I don't know. He just seems so different now. I heard my mom and dad talking about him and that he can't sleep." Carrie shook her head and looked genuinely perplexed but accepted the change of focus for the conversation, to Faith's relief.

"He used to smile and laugh all the time," Faith said. "He wasn't serious about anything. Do you remember his high school graduation?"

"My dad is still embarrassed about that."

"That's when I knew for certain that he can't dance." Faith smiled as she flung dirt behind her.

"I don't think it was the dancing across the stage that got my dad, I think it was the pink boa he pulled out from under his graduation gown."

Faith laughed in appreciation of the memory and took another big scoop of dirt.

Carrie tugged at her ponytail and asked in a serious voice, "Do you think Davy will ever be back or that he'll always be Davis?"

Faith tried to gather her thoughts so she could give her fifteen-year-old neighbor a good answer. Carrie looked at her with big serious blue eyes that were so like Davis's.

"I think we all change and grow up. I was sixteen, barely older than you, when the war started. It was hard—really hard. I'm not the same girl I was then. I had to grow up faster than I wanted to. I think the same thing happened to Davis."

Carrie nodded. "Yeah, he seems so much older than how I remembered him."

"There are still lots of reasons to smile and laugh; for me, it's dancing and my mom. I suppose your brother needs to figure out what those reasons are for him."

"Maybe you could help him figure it out. My mom thinks you should date," Carrie said with such simple sweetness that Faith couldn't be irritated. But she also didn't want to discuss with Davis's cute little sister all the reasons she could never date him, starting with Freddy and ending with Davis's bossy interfering.

She changed the subject. "Do you remember how Davis was always pushing people to do fun things? I remember him convincing Patrick, when they were about fourteen, to sneak out in the middle of the night to go sledding on the golf course." She paused to smile at the scolding her usually mild-mannered father had given Patrick. "It was the first snow of winter, and I guess they couldn't pass it up. They sledded from about midnight till five a.m., then tried to sneak back into their houses. They both got caught. Patrick was grounded for two weeks and still had to go to school that morning even though he was exhausted."

Carrie giggled. "I would like a friend like that."

"Maybe you and Janet can be that friend to Davis. Push him to do things he doesn't want to do. Push him to live a little and not take himself so seriously." Faith couldn't help the irritation that crept into her voice. She hit a rock with the shovel and had to use it as a lever to pull the rock out of the ditch.

"Push him to do what kinds of things?"

"Fun things. Happy, adventurous things that will pull him away from his seriousness. You know Patrick was always the intense one. He told me after the sledding incident that he hadn't wanted to go. Davis had talked him into it, but Patrick said sledding in the moonlight in the fresh powder was worth every minute of grounding. He wasn't sorry. Find things like that to push Davis to get back into life again and remember that there are lots of reasons still left to smile."

She attacked the ditch, lost in her own thoughts. If Patrick had known how short his life was going to be, she bet he would have savored his moments even more. The dirt flew madly behind her. Carrie watched for a few minutes and then wandered back home, calling out, "See you in church tomorrow."

Faith's shovel hit another large rock, and she paused to get her breath. Sometimes when something like rocks thwarted a person, they had to regroup and make a plan. Under the warm June sun, sweat rolling down her back, a plan came to her. She grinned. She knew how she would get payback for Davis's interference. Tomorrow, after church, she would recruit Carrie and Janet. The man would never know what hit him. Operation Sledding in the Moonlight was about to commence. He would be sorry for meddling in her life. Humming, Faith went back to work digging around the rock.

The next morning she put on a cute pink summer dress with ivory lace at the sleeves and a full skirt. She paired it with ivory pumps and a lacy hat. Feeling confident in how she looked, she told Mom she would meet her at church.

Davis was out on his front porch smoking again, and she decided to give him a neighborly nod—a temporary truce, as it were. After all, in a couple of hours she would be teaching her class about the parable of the good Samaritan and what being a neighbor meant.

"You're off early," Davis said.

"I'm going to visit a Sunday School student to see if I can get him to come back to class."

"Robert Sullivan?"

"Yes," Faith said, surprised. "How did you know?"

"I knew George and heard Robert took his brother's death hard. I went to visit the Sullivans a couple of weeks ago."

"Oh," Faith responded. "Do you think I have a chance?"

Davis stubbed out his cigarette, grinned, and said, "If you, in that pink concoction you're wearing, don't make him want to come to church, nothing will."

Faith's cheeks warmed. "I think you overestimate my abilities."

"No." Davis smiled and stood. "I just understand teenage boys better than you do."

"See you at church." Faith hurried down the drive, feeling Davis's eyes on her and inwardly scolding herself for engaging in a conversation with him. Why did she always feel unnerved when she talked to him? Who did he think he was, complimenting her? It had almost felt as if he were flirting. A man shouldn't flirt with his boss or with someone he was at war with. Still, her lips tipped up. It did feel good to know that he thought she looked nice, and he had looked like Davy when he smiled.

She walked the mile to the Sullivans' in the warm, muggy morning, praying silently. She knocked on the green door of the Sullivans' well-kept home and grimaced as she saw the gold-star flag in the front window, a flash of the pain of it all running through her.

Mrs. Sullivan came to the front door in her Sunday dress with a white apron covering it. "Faith Penwilliger, how nice to see you. What brings you here this early on a Sunday?"

"I'm sorry to interrupt your breakfast. I was hoping for a word with Robert."

Mrs. Sullivan eyed Faith, opened the door wide, and smiled. "Come on in."

She left Faith sitting on a plaid couch and returned with Robert in tow. Faith recognized him as one of the quiet, studious young men around town. She knew he played as the pitcher for the high school baseball team and that he was strong for his sixteen years. He was well over six feet and would probably grow even taller.

"I'll leave you two while I clean up breakfast. We don't want to be late for church." Mrs. Sullivan beamed at Faith and then exited with a spring in her step.

Robert sat in a rocking chair. He seemed unsure of what to do with his hands and settled on folding them in his lap while nervously twiddling his thumbs.

"I'm Faith Penwilliger."

"Yes, ma'am, I know."

"I'm the Sunday School teacher for the teen class, but I haven't seen you there." Faith looked at Robert, patiently waiting for him to respond.

He sat up straight and with strength in his voice said, "I've decided not to go to church anymore. If God can let a war that kills millions of good people happen, then I'm not interested."

"I see." Faith was impressed with his directness. "So you don't believe in God?"

"No, I believe there's a God. I just think He isn't a very good God, or He wouldn't let people like my brother, George, or your brother, Patrick, die in horrible wars. Pastor Clemmons has already talked to me and he couldn't change my mind. My mom and dad can't change my mind and neither can you."

"All right," Faith said. "I will respect that. I certainly know how painful it is to lose a brother to war."

"Thank you." Robert's seriousness made him look much older than he was.

"Maybe I can leave you with three thoughts."

Robert looked at her impassively.

Faith leaned forward. "First, sometimes we do things for our parents because they have also been through a lot. I don't work long hours at our brick store because I love bricks; I work there because it's our family business. Going to church looks like it means a lot to your parents." Faith felt that God was confirming her own words to her. She felt shaken to the core. She was honoring her mother by being there for her on a daily basis.

Robert tilted his head to the side.

"Second," Faith went on, her voice shaking, "we need to find ways to honor our brothers instead of only mourning them."

"Like how?"

"By finding ways to remember what they accomplished during their lives. Monuments to them, if you will."

Robert actually looked a little interested in the idea of monuments. "What's the last point?"

Faith refocused. "Justice and mercy. I've been thinking about this all week. We know God has both qualities. We just have to look at the world around us and try to find examples of His justice and His mercy, even in the unfairness and ugliness of war. I see attempts at justice in the Tokyo Trials and the Nuremberg Trials. I see examples of mercy in the generosity of those who have donated money to help European refugees displaced by the war. Look for your own examples of God's justice and mercy in the world." Faith blinked back tears as she felt the certainty that there would be justice and compensation in her own life for the things she had lost.

Robert extended his lanky legs right out in front of him and said, "I'll think about your points; that's all I can promise."

Faith nodded, rose to shake his hand, and showed herself out. She felt happy as she walked back home. Why was that? What was that saying? Something about helping your brother's boat across the river and finding that your own boat had crossed.

CHAPTER 17

DAVIS TUGGED AT HIS COLLAR. He'd never liked wearing his dress uniform. Big breath in, big breath out. Three hours. He could do it. Three hours and the reception would be over. He looked around his bedroom with longing. What he wouldn't give not to have to leave it.

"Davis!" Mom yelled up the stairs. "We need you."

He'd learned in the army to face things head-on. Charge the enemy. Chin up. He'd feel stupid being the center of attention, but he'd hide it. Mom had written him every week throughout the entire war—long, rambling, loving letters. Sometimes he'd go weeks without the letters finding him and then he'd get a stockpile of homey goodness and love. He could do this for Mom.

He descended the stairs into a sea of red, white, and blue. Mom and the girls had spent hours decorating.

Dad, carrying a box of vases, looked a little harried. He was a good sport. It had been nonstop work around the Wilson house for the last week. Mom was like a determined General Patton when she had a goal in mind.

Dad leaned down and whispered, "It looks like Uncle Sam vomited in here."

Davis laughed. "You'll stay by me tonight?"

"Of course." Dad thumped his shoulder.

"Davis, James." Mom rushed back in carrying a huge box. She was going to hurt herself.

"Cecilia," Dad said, "let Davis take that for you."

"Put it in the kitchen," Mom said. Her face was pink, and she looked like she'd run a race. Davis grabbed the box and followed his father to the kitchen, then looked out the window. Faith and Marcia were crossing through the backyard, Faith carrying a huge cake. Dad opened the door for them, and she carefully set the cake down on the kitchen table.

"That looks delicious," Dad said.

"Thanks." Faith gave him a big smile and then turned it on Davis. "Are you ready for the reception?"

Why was she smiling at him? Faith had done nothing but ignore him and scowl since the Freddy incident. Davis took a step toward her and cleared his throat. "I'm as ready as I'll ever be."

Marcia handed Faith a stack of music.

"Oh, are you playing piano tonight?" Davis asked.

Faith, still smiling, said, "Yes. I'll be here the whole night. I won't miss a thing."

Was he crazy, or were her pretty brown eyes challenging him? Davis narrowed his eyes. "I don't think there'll be much to see."

Faith laughed. "You might be surprised."

Marcia, head cocked to the side, looked at her daughter. There was definitely something up. Davis stared at Faith, but she just shrugged and smiled.

"Davis," Mom called from upstairs, "I need those tables moved." Yesterday he and Dad, under Mom's supervision, had borrowed five tables from neighbors and arranged them on the new patio. This morning Mom had decided that the tables were too close together and needed to be better spaced.

Davis sighed and hurried out to the backyard, and the Penwilligers followed. He hefted the tables without thinking about what he was doing. His eyes stayed on Faith as she helped Janet and Carrie put carnations into vases for Mom's centerpieces. Every now and then she met his eyes and smiled again. He should have been delighted. Growing up, Faith had followed him and Patrick around with constant smiles and laughter, but today's smiles felt like there was a secret he wasn't in on.

He heard Carrie whisper to Faith, "I delivered both of them this morning, and my mom's is in the piano bench ready to give at the end of the reception."

Give? Give what?

Janet giggled. Davis pushed a little too hard on a table and it nearly tipped over. The girls were putting him on edge. What on earth were they up to? It was like waiting for the enemy to attack without knowing when or where.

Mom's frantic voice floated out from the open kitchen window. "James, James, where's the ice? We have to have the big bins of ice in the backyard *right now*. I need to put the watermelon sorbet and the punch out, and I can't because there's no ice!"

"I can't do two things at once. Do you want me to fix the bunting or get the ice?" Dad yelled back.

Marcia set the flowers down and said, "I'll find the ice."

"Praise heaven you're here," Mom said, coming into the backyard. She looked near tears. "Why didn't you come an hour ago?"

"Well, I'm here now, and we still have twenty minutes before anyone else comes. I'll find the ice. You go powder your face, and I'll make sure the refreshments are good to go."

Mom nodded and said shakily, "You have no idea what I've been through today." She turned to Carrie. "Why are you just standing there?"

"I've been working for the last five hours," Carrie said, injured.

Marcia put her arm around Mom's waist and drew her back toward the house. "I'll get Carrie and Janet to help me. You go take a minute for yourself."

Mom called out a few more directions but let Marcia lead her back inside.

"I'll go set up in the music room," Faith said.

She still smiled. Why did she look so smug?

Davis finished moving the tables and made his way back into the house. Mom wanted him in place for when the guests arrived. The callers would enter through the front door, where they would greet Mom, Dad, and him in their large front room and then file through to the backyard. Davis's siblings were fortunate. They got to mingle with the guests while he stood on display.

Faith was setting music out on the piano in the music room that opened just off the front room. The plan was for her to play the piano quietly as the guests filed through. The music would be heard but wouldn't overpower the conversations in the receiving line.

He crossed the room to speak to her. "You look happy. I'm glad someone is."

"Yes," Faith said. "I'm looking forward to this." Davis narrowed his eyes again, but Faith jumped in before he could say anything more. "How did the Critchfield home turn out?"

"It looks wonderful. We finished last night just as it was getting dark." Davis was happy to speak of something other than the reception. "I could drive you by tomorrow if you want to see for yourself how it turned out." He paused and rested a hand on the piano. "I've learned a lot from Frank. I love the work and am hoping to continue with you."

"Let's see how you feel about that after the reception."

Davis raised his brows and tipped his head to study Faith. She looked so sweet in her lacy summer dress—a perfect picture of beauty behind the piano.

A chill went down his spine. That's how the enemy got you. They would leave boxes that looked like confectionery, so sweet and good-looking. A gullible GI would open the box only to have it explode. There was something dangerous about Faith's sweetness too. He'd keep a very close eye on her tonight.

"Places, everyone, places!" Mom hustled into the room in a bright-blue dress with a huge American flag scarf draped around her front. Davis smiled. No one would ever have to question Mom's patriotism.

Linda and her family and Christopher and his family arrived at nearly the same time. Their kids, excited to see their cousins, hugged each other and ran off to the backyard to play. Lucky kids. Davis barely had a moment to say hi to his older siblings before Faith began playing Sousa's "The Stars and Stripes Forever" and Mom called him over to join the receiving line.

The first guests trickled in, and Davis politely shook hands and leaned forward to listen to each of them. Mom beamed. Her irritation had evaporated with the arrival of the guests. Dad also looked happy—happy and proud as he chatted with an old friend, his arm around Davis's shoulder.

"Best day of my life," Dad said.

Really? A lump formed in Davis's throat. The day he had come home had been the best day of Dad's life?

The crowd continued flowing by, most of them chatting for a few moments and then moving on. The Macdonald family entered and the line stalled. The four Macdonald girls were the biggest flirts in Payson. They formed a cluster around Davis, and he tugged at his collar, uncomfortable with how close they stood. It was too warm in here and too crowded.

Laura Macdonald said something about Davis's great sacrifice. She reached out and touched the ribbon on his uniform. Davis took a step back and bumped into another one of the Macdonald girls, who giggled.

"Sorry," he muttered. Laura grabbed his arm, and another sister grabbed the other.

Faith played "Over There," but she looked up from her music, made eye contact, and smirked.

"We should go out dancing," Laura said.

"Uh, I don't dance."

"We can teach you." Another sister tittered.

Christopher, checking in on the group, came over to the girls, thank heavens. "Ladies, I think you'll want to try some of my mom's sorbet."

Davis wiped his brow. The giggling girls looked over their shoulders at him, but they followed Christopher to the backyard.

Pull yourself together.

Another guest, Larissa Rogers, Payson's resident dance instructor, entered through the front door. The sixty-year-old woman looked far younger than her age with her black shoulder-length hair, erect posture, and slender form.

Faith began playing "The Lone Twister." Davis smiled. Was she choosing the music she played based on who walked through the front door? Janet and Carrie hovered around the piano. Why did his sisters look nervous?

Ms. Rogers stepped up, and instead of the usual "Welcome home," she waved her arms enthusiastically. "I was so pleased to get your note. Of course I'll teach you."

Davis stared at her. Teach him what? He looked over to the piano room just as Janet and Carrie broke into song. "First you put your feet side by side. You swing to the left and then you swing to the right. Prance around the floor nice and light. And then twist it down, twist it down with all of your might. That's how you learn to jive."

Faith met his eyes and gave him a very cocky grin. Ms. Rogers reached in and hugged him. "I'll have you dancing like a pro in no time. I have room in my Saturday class."

He didn't want dance lessons, but Ms. Rogers looked so pleased and excited. "That'll work fine," he said. What else could he say?

"Wonderful, wonderful."

He glared in the direction of the piano room, where Faith played a song that had become popular in World War I and Janet and Carrie sang along. Mr. Arnold, Payson High School's chemistry teacher, shook Davis's hand and said something, but Davis was too distracted to concentrate. He met Faith's eyes and shook his head at her. What was she playing at, signing him up for dance lessons? Mr. Arnold dropped his hand, frowned, and turned to leave. Great. He probably thought the head shake was meant for him. Davis grabbed Mr. Arnold's arm, pulled him back, shook his hand, and exchanged a few pleasantries.

Dad stepped forward to welcome the next couple in line. Davis took advantage of the small break and moved with quick steps to the music room. Janet and Carrie eyed him and moved behind the piano, away from him. Faith, however, still looked cocky as she finished the song. "Did you have a request?" she asked, honey dripping from her voice.

Janet let out a nervous giggle.

"Dancing lessons! You wrote her a note pretending to be me and said I want to take dancing lessons?" He didn't bother keeping the irritation out of his voice.

"Having someone interfere in your life is unpleasant, isn't it?"

They stared at each other, neither smiling. Faith didn't break eye contact, but her fingers began another song by memory. He rubbed the back of his neck. She had a point, but he wasn't going to admit it. Besides, he had just been doing what Mr. Penwilliger and Patrick would have wanted when he'd interfered with Freddy.

"Davis," Mom called.

He turned and left.

"Oh, he looks mad," he heard Carrie say.

"He'll be just fine." Faith's voice carried as he walked, ramrod straight, back to the receiving line.

The next half hour flew by in a flurry of old friends and neighbors. Faith played "Red River Valley" as Pastor and Mrs. Alicia Clemmons approached. Janet, Carrie, and Faith's pretty voices blended well as they sang the beautiful song. But why were they smiling at him again?

Pastor Clemmons also smiled. He patted Davis enthusiastically on the back and put his hand on his shoulder. The good pastor held a letter in his hand—a blue-papered letter in handwriting he recognized as Faith's. This wasn't good. Davis braced himself for impact.

"It's a wonderful idea," the pastor said.

What? What was a wonderful idea? What else had Faith signed him up for?

"I can't believe no one thought of it sooner," Mrs. Clemmons said.

Davis just smiled weakly.

"Let's get together this weekend to get the ball rolling."

"You're a wonderful man," Mrs. Clemmons said.

Davis shook the pastor's hand and nodded numbly. What else could he do? But Faith had crossed the line. Who was she to sign him up for all kinds of things? He took a step toward the piano room again, but another flood of neighbors stopped him. It was twenty minutes before he could break away to confront Faith.

Carrie and Janet saw him coming and scurried out of the piano room. Good. At least his sisters had some fear of him.

He watched Faith play for a moment. She looked peaceful and beautiful there at the piano. When she finally acknowledged his presence, it was with a calm nod. Unbelievable. She was committing him to hours of who knew what, and she didn't look remotely sorry. Where was the skinny kid who just appreciated being in his and Patrick's presence? Little Faith had always seemed in awe of Davis. There was certainly no awe in her face now. The only thing he saw was smugness.

He leaned on the piano. "What did you sign me up for with the Clemmonses?"

"Fundraising."

Davis gritted his teeth. He hated fundraisers, and he couldn't think of anything he wanted to fundraise for.

Faith's fingers ran up and down the keys in a waltz. She didn't miss a note. Obviously, her heart wasn't pumping in the same way his was. The adrenaline made him want to pick her music up and throw it out the window. Or, better yet, pull her into his arms and kiss her.

Wait, kiss Faith? Where had that thought come from?

He shook his head. "You volunteered me for what exactly?"

She looked up at him from under her eyelashes. How could such a sweet face be so much trouble? "You'll be organizing a fundraiser for a monument to honor Payson's fallen soldiers."

He blinked. A monument in Payson? It was actually a great idea, but she had no right to sign him up to organize it. It would take months, if not years, of work to pull something like that off. "Do you have any more surprises for me?" he asked.

"Just one, and it's the biggest."

Davis grimaced. "I was just doing what your dad and Patrick would have wanted me to do when I talked to Freddy."

Faith smiled at him. "So am I."

"Is that right? They would want you to taunt me?"

"Taunt?" Faith kept the waltz going. "I'm not taunting you. You're treating me like a little sister, and I'm treating you like I would a really obnoxious big brother."

"I told you I don't think of you like a sister," Davis said. He pushed on, wanting to force her to acknowledge what was between them. "Remember the fight you and I had the night after I enlisted?"

Faith's cheeks went pink, and she wouldn't meet his eyes. Davis leaned toward her. Before he could think through what he was going to say—to admit—he said, "You were right. Daisy and I were wrong for each other. It just took a Dear John letter and some time to admit it to myself."

Faith stuttered in the song and missed a few notes. Finally, she seemed affected.

"But," Davis said as he placed his hand on the piano and leaned even closer to her, his voice quiet but firm, "you were wrong about Patrick. He had to fight."

CHAPTER 18

FAITH STOPPED PLAYING. DAVIS'S CHIN was out, and his arms were folded over his chest. He looked like a strong, stubborn soldier. Did he remember what else she had yelled at him that night? Her already flushed face grew warmer thinking about the words her angry, impulsive, sixteen-year-old self had blurted out. She had yelled that she, not Daisy, was who Davy should be with. The feelings she had carried for him for years had burst out during their argument. Did he remember? If he did, she hoped he recognized that she no longer idolized him.

Bubbles of anger simmered inside her, and she gripped the piano bench as if it would keep her from launching herself in fury at Davis. How could he not acknowledge that it was his fault Patrick was dead? Patrick was a musician, not a soldier, but he had followed where Davy led.

Davis looked at her as if he expected her to speak, but her throat was too constricted to say anything. The words "He had to fight" hung in the air. She played "Yankee Doodle," but the song sounded angry. She pursed her lips. She wouldn't say anything more to Davis. After another minute he spun on his heels and left. He looked mad, his posture perfectly erect as he returned to the receiving line.

As the next hour went by, she noticed he had stopped looking over at her. Had she gone too far? She lifted her head and straightened her own back. Operation Sledding in the Moonlight was for his own good. He needed to stop being so somber and join the land of the living. He needed to stop trying to take Patrick's place, and he really needed to stop treating her like she was still sixteen. She was a competent businesswoman and his boss.

She kept the music flowing even though her feelings were overwhelming. Davis was supposed to be the one who was rattled after the reception, not her.

His older sister, Linda, entered the music room near the end of the reception and brought Faith some of the icy fruit punch. Faith stopped playing to sip her punch. Was the last letter overkill? *No*, she answered herself, *it wasn't*. Freddy still seemed nervous of Davis. Davis needed to learn that interfering could go two ways. Besides, this last letter and the change it would force on him would make Mrs. Wilson so happy.

"Could you please tell Janet and Carrie I'm ready for the last number?" Faith asked Linda. Linda winked before she left. Did she suspect something was up?

Faith took a big breath, opened the piano bench, and pulled out a blue envelope with *Mother* on the outside of it. She looked up to see Davis's older brother, Christopher, smiling at her, and she motioned him to come into the piano room.

"You sure have Davis wound up," Christopher said, but he looked amused.

"Trust me, he deserves it. I'm trying to help him lighten up and make the transition away from being a sergeant who orders people around."

Christopher laughed. "Thanks for making the reception entertaining."

"I have one more little surprise for him," Faith said. "Could you give this to your mother after our last special number?" She handed him the blue envelope.

His eyebrows went up, but he agreed and slipped it into his pocket.

Janet and Carrie came back into the room, and Faith nodded to them. "We're on, girls. Here's for the knockout."

The line had broken up, and a dozen people mingled in the front room. Faith stepped in and cleared her throat. "Janet, Carrie, and I have prepared a special number. Davis wants to express his appreciation to his mother."

Mrs. Wilson put her hands to her heart and beamed. It might not have been a good night for Davis, but his mother had had a wonderful evening.

"Oh, how sweet!" one of the women said.

"What a wonderful young man," the woman's husband added.

Davis looked like he might reach out and choke Faith as he ran his finger underneath his uniform collar. She moved quickly back to the piano.

"This is a little song you may be familiar with," she called out to her audience. "The music is by Theodore Morse, and the lyrics are by Howard Johnson. We present 'M-O-T-H-E-R.'"

Faith looked at the keys, her good mood coming back. She played cheerfully, and the girls sang sweetly. Mrs. Wilson sniffled as her daughters sang. Yes, Operation Sledding in the Moonlight was good for everyone. The girls ended to applause. Christopher did his part and handed the envelope to his weeping mother as the song ended. Mrs. Wilson opened the envelope with shaking hands. Davis looked nervous as his mother silently read the note.

"Oh, Davis, I can't believe it. I couldn't ask for a better gift." She cried in earnest now and waved the note. Mrs. Wilson pulled herself together and wiped her eyes on her American flag scarf.

Davis, with a look of dread, took the note from his mother and scanned it. He turned and glared at Faith as his mother launched herself at her handsome, irate son. Mrs. Wilson hugged him tightly. "I'm so glad you're going to give up smoking. What a good son you are. You know it bothered me. Oh, you sweetheart," she gushed. She stepped back and squeezed his cheeks, totally oblivious that her son looked completely unhappy.

Davis glared at Christopher, who was laughing.

Faith shut the piano. Davis had no remorse about getting Patrick to enlist; why should she feel guilty about Operation Sledding in the Moonlight?

CHAPTER 19

"Nice work," Frank said, surveying the completed wall.

Davis nodded. It was the first time he'd done the flemish bond pattern and it'd turned out perfect. He picked up his tools that were becoming more and more familiar in his hands. The trowel, especially, was almost a part of him. He'd carved its wood handle down, making an indentation for his thumb, to fit most comfortably in his hand.

Another full day's work. It felt good, much better than his evening was going to be. He and Frank took the wooden scaffolding down and placed it in the truck bed.

"You're awfully quiet today," Frank said.

Davis grunted. "I've started some things that aren't easy for me."

"Quitting smoking?"

"Yeah, that's got me on edge." Davis threw his load of wooden planks into the truck.

"I've heard quitting is a real bear," Frank said.

"There're a few curse words I could use to describe it. And dancing. I started lessons last week. I go again tonight."

"Dance lessons, huh?"

"Dance lessons," Davis said with a tone of voice that implied he'd rather have his foot cut off than dance on it.

"Is that all that's on your mind?" Frank asked. "Are you still worried about Faith hiring you on permanently?"

"I'm ready for her to make a decision." Had his feud with Faith over Freddy ruined his chances to be hired? Surely she'd be able to look beyond her irritation to see that Davis was meant for this job. He could help Penwilliger Brick soar. He knew he could.

The two men climbed into the old truck, and Frank pulled it out onto the road. With one hand on the wheel, he tugged his mustache with his other hand and stole a quick glance over at Davis. "I just can't figure out why Faith is so reluctant."

Davis shrugged but stayed quiet. He knew where Faith's reluctance stemmed from—anger. Anger over his interfering with Freddy and anger over Patrick enlisting. The question was whether she could overlook her bad feelings and see how much Davis could help her. "Do you think she's still thinking of selling?" he asked.

"The envelope is still in that desk drawer."

"Maybe she doesn't want to hire me until she decides whether to sell."

"Hmm, maybe." Frank turned the truck onto the highway leading back to town. "I think deep down she doesn't want to sell, but she also wants to know continuing to run the business won't be as hard as it was during the war years."

"That makes sense."

"She needs you to show her you're in her corner, that you've got her back."

Davis tapped his clenched fist against his knee. That was what he'd been trying to do ever since he got home three months ago.

Later that night Davis, wearing dress clothes and a tie, stood in Ms. Rogers's dance studio looking around the roomful of teenagers. He definitely wasn't the only one who had been forced into the class. A couple of the boys looked absolutely sullen. The girls, on the other hand, had a look of . . . what was it? Eagerness. They all looked eager.

Eagerness was all fine and good, but why were these young teen girls looking eagerly at *him*? He rubbed the back of his neck and bent down to whisper into Janet's ear. "Don't leave me." Good heavens, was that girl next to Janet batting her eyelashes at him? She looked all of fourteen. Davis flinched and once again wished he weren't the only adult enrolled in dance lessons.

Last week he had painfully danced with several teen girls who'd giggled and blushed and fawned over him. It had been excruciating. Faith's revenge had been accomplished in spades, but tonight he was prepared—he had an armored tank named Janet. He reached out and gripped her hand firmly. His sister grinned at him and raised her eyebrows. "Okay," she whispered, "I'll protect you from the other girls, but don't step on my toes."

She was a good sister. "I'll try," he whispered back.

"Partner up," Ms. Rogers said. "Tonight we will be learning the waltz."

Davis held on to Janet like he was a sailor who had fallen overboard and she was his life preserver. A couple of girls approached, but Janet just shook her head at them.

There was a lot of shuffling and anxious looks among the teens, but finally everyone had a partner. Ms. Rogers talked about the waltz stance. Davis held Janet, listening carefully to the instructions. The pimply boy to his right held his partner as far away as he possibly could. Ms. Rogers moved up and down the line of students, her black ponytail swinging, her posture perfect. "Look over your partner's right shoulder. The correct position begins with your head." She pushed the pimply boy closer to his partner. The poor kid was sweating profusely. Ms. Rogers adjusted Davis's right hand on Janet's upper back and said, "Your right hand is going to be your steering wheel. You'll tell your partner where you want her to turn by applying light pressure. It's called signaling the lead."

Davis nodded and thought back to watching Freddy and Faith dance. He had wondered how they moved together so flawlessly.

Ms. Rogers showed them a simple box step. Davis stared intently. He could do this. The next time he had the opportunity, he wasn't going to sit and watch; he was going to dance. The music started. "Rise and fall," Ms. Rogers called.

Davis stretched up on tiptoe, then sank down much lower.

Janet giggled. "You look like a jack-in-the-box. Try to glide."

Glide? He nodded. "Is that better?"

"Yeah," Janet said. "Now, relax and smile."

He gave a sheepish grin. A gangly boy whose sharp elbows looked like they would hurt came toward them. Using his right hand, Davis gently pushed on Janet's back. It worked. She followed his lead and they moved to open space.

Step, slide, step. Step, slide, step. This wasn't too hard. He looked down at Janet and smiled. He wouldn't say dancing was fun, but once he got the rhythm, it had a certain exactness to it. Kind of like marching in step. He could appreciate that.

***

The following week Frank brought up quitting smoking again while they finished up the house they'd been bricking. "How's giving up smoking going?"

Davis just grunted.

"That good, huh?" Frank asked. He handed over the bucket of mortar he'd mixed.

Davis hoisted it to the top of the scaffolding, climbed up, and began scooping mortar down in a wet line over the last row of bricks. "It wasn't my idea." He plopped more mortar down. "It was Faith's."

Frank climbed up next to Davis and began working from the other side. He waggled his eyebrows. "The things we do for women."

"It's not like that. I'm not doing it for Faith. She tricked me and it stinks." Davis swore and threw the mortar on so hard that some flipped up and hit him in the face. "I'm not sleeping."

"Really?" Frank's brows furrowed, and he paused, his trowel in midair.

"My sleep got messed up by the war. It was getting better for a while, but since I've given up smoking, it takes me hours to fall asleep." He rearranged the string line so he could ensure the last row was straight. Frank waited patiently for him to continue. "I began smoking in the army. It was a way to relax." His voice shook as memories flooded his head, but he kept the bricks coming. There was something therapeutic about the pattern. "Without being able to smoke, I can't relax. I just lay there in bed, thinking and thinking." He didn't add that his thoughts were of the men he'd seen die.

Frank didn't offer any platitudes or trivial advice. He simply worked side by side with Davis. The wall kept climbing, brick row after brick row, built with their muscle and sweat as payment. Finally, Frank called for a lunch break and the two men paused to eat in the shade. "Can I ask you something?" he asked.

Davis nodded, his mouth full of his ham sandwich.

"What're you going to do about it?"

Davis swallowed. "About what?"

Frank shook his head. "About your feelings for Faith."

Davis took another big bite of sandwich to buy some time. Feelings for Faith? Yeah, he had feelings for her—he wanted to shake her for her interference. He needed to rid Frank of whatever romantic notion he was telling himself. Davis chewed for a moment and then said, "What makes you think I have feelings for her? I work for her."

"Aw, come on, kid. I see the sparks between you two." Frank threw his apple core into the long grass behind them.

"Angry sparks."

Frank laughed, his mustache moving up and down. "If you say so."

"Don't get any big ideas. She's out two or three nights a week dancing with Freddy."

"You try sweet-talking yet?"

Davis groaned. "Do I seem like a man who would be good at sweet-talking?"

Frank closed his lunch box. "You've had a girlfriend before. You must have done some sweet-talking."

Daisy? For the life of him, Davis couldn't remember any conversation he'd ever had with her. He rubbed his knee. He didn't think he had sweet-talked her. In fact, he didn't think their relationship had had much talking in it. All he could remember about it was that they'd kissed a lot and Daisy had gushed over him.

He tapped his lunch box. Faith was in a different category. Faith was . . . He searched for the right word. She was sweet but fiery. She was hardworking but lighthearted. She was graceful but down-to-earth. She was soft but determined. She was dedicated to her business but toying with selling it. She was giving Davis a chance to become a bricklayer but seemed unhappy to have him around. *Contradiction*—that was the word. Faith was a contradiction. She exasperated him, but he couldn't get her out of his thoughts. He wanted to shake her, but in the moments he was being honest with himself, he also knew he wanted to kiss her. He sighed. It seemed highly unlikely that would ever happen. "I don't think Faith wants me to do any sweet-talking."

Frank put his lunch box back in the truck and took Davis's to line them up side by side. "You two'd make a mighty fine pair." He pointed a finger at Davis; his mustache ends seemed to be pointing as well. "Whatever you did to make her mad, just go tell her you're sorry."

Davis smiled. Simple advice, but what if he wasn't sorry? It was more complicated than Frank could appreciate. "I'm paying for what I did that made her mad." He shrugged. He'd already had two dance lessons, and Sunday he was meeting with the pastor again about the monument. Quitting smoking was horrible. Yes, he was paying. He sighed again and grabbed his trowel, then closed his eyes for a moment.

He had a plan. It had been filling his head at nights while he lay awake. The details were beginning to come together, but it would involve Faith agreeing not to sell the store and her being able to tolerate him as more than a bricklayer. Could he sweet-talk her into his plan?

CHAPTER 20

FAITH AND MOM SAT AT the kitchen table on a muggy August morning. Mom had prepared a delicious breakfast of French toast and bacon, and Faith sat sipping her freshly squeezed orange juice, her mind wandering back to the reception and the triumph of that day. Even though it had been weeks since the reception, the memory of getting even with Davis still made her smile.

Mom looked up from her newspaper and said, "You look like the cat that ate the canary. What are you thinking about?"

Faith laughed. "Davis's face when he found out he wouldn't be smoking any longer."

"You think that's funny?" Mom set down the newspaper and frowned at her daughter.

"Well, yes."

"Not that funny," Mom said. "It's been really hard for him to quit. Cecilia told me he spends hours pacing every night."

Faith squirmed but said, "It's a bad habit. Quitting is for his own good."

Mom looked at Faith with disappointment on her face. "Quitting may be better for his health in the long run, but the choice should have been his to make when he was ready. He's having more sleep problems now that he's quit."

Faith stopped smiling and looked down at her feet.

"Your father smoked a pipe. Why do you care if Davis smokes?"

She squirmed in her seat some more and picked up her fork to fiddle with. "It's not healthy, the way Davis smokes. Dad just had his pipe after dinner; Davis smokes a lot through the whole day, and I don't know—it just seems like he is too severe sitting over on his front porch, smoking, watching Freddy drop me off. It's like he's some kind of serious old man."

"You're awfully hard on him," Mom said. "Don't be prejudiced, Faith. Whatever your problem with Davis is, we need him."

She was hard on *him*? Davis was the one looking down his nose at her choice of dancing partner. "All we need is each other. Haven't we made it the last two years? Why does Davis have to be part of the equation now?"

Mom picked up her paper and said, "Never bolt your door with a boiled carrot."

What on earth did that mean? Faith was pretty sure she didn't want to know. She set down her fork and pointed at Mom's paper, changing the subject. "Anything in the news?"

Mom pursed her lips but said, "We exploded a nuclear bomb out in the ocean yesterday. I still can't wrap my mind around the power of it all."

"I know. It's terrifying."

"We used this one to destroy a bunch of old battleships. I think we're flexing our muscles to intimidate the rest of the world."

"I hope it works," Faith said seriously. "Because if it doesn't, it'll be the end of us all."

Mom shook her head. "I hope Truman knows what he's doing."

Faith nodded her agreement.

Mom picked up her hand and rubbed it gently. "I have some questions for you too. Why do you dislike him so much? What happened that night you fought?"

Faith shook her head. "I'm going to head out to work now." She didn't want to talk about that awful argument—the anger, embarrassment, and hurt were still too real.

Mom got up, handed Faith her lunch, and hugged her goodbye. "You look beautiful in that green blouse. It brings out your pretty brown eyes."

"Thanks." Faith planted a kiss on Mom's cheek. "After work I'm going out to dinner and dancing with Freddy. I should be home by ten." It was hard to work Saturdays, but at least she had something to look forward to that evening.

"All right, have fun."

"I always have fun when I'm dancing." Faith waved and left through the back. She made her way around to the side of the house to the driveway, where she had parked Costello.

It spluttered to life with protest. Faith put it into gear and backed out of the drive, popping the clutch at just the right moment and expertly missing the Wilsons' petunias. She put the windows down, turned the radio up, and sang along with Bing Crosby's "Deep in the Heart of Texas." She bounced in her seat, waving to the handful of people who were out early. Mrs. O'Malley must have heard Costello's noisy engine, because she ran out her front door to wave Faith to a stop. Faith pulled over and said loudly over Costello's rumble, "'Here's health to your enemies' enemies.'"

Mrs. O'Malley smoothed out her floury apron and called back, "'May the enemies of Ireland never find a friend.'"

Faith tooted Costello's horn in appreciation and pulled back out onto the road. She drove on, singing to the radio. She was energized and ready to take on a pile of bricks by the time she pulled through the back alley and parked behind the warehouse.

Juan and Lester weren't there yet, but Frank and Davis were waiting for her and turned to watch her pull the noisy truck up by the warehouse doors.

"Hiya, sunshine," Frank said, pulling on his handlebar mustache and smiling as Faith jumped out of the truck.

"Sorry if you were waiting on Costello."

"That's all right; we've only been waiting ten minutes." Frank put his hand on the truck and Faith noticed how many calluses he had. "We'll load up and head out to the Johnson job."

Davis was already loading a pallet of bricks onto Costello. He wouldn't make eye contact with Faith; he hadn't since the reception.

"Well, I hope it goes well for you," she said to Frank.

"It will. Davis is a dream to work with. Are you going to hire him?"

She wished he wouldn't ask in front of Davis.

Davis looked over at her, his handsome face expressionless.

She bit her lip, smoothed her pale-green blouse, which was already perfectly smooth, and faced him. "If you would like an interview for a job as a bricklayer, I'll meet you in the office Monday at eight a.m."

"You're going to make him come in on Monday? We're closed on Mondays," Frank said.

"It's fine." Davis nodded once in her direction. "I'll be there." He turned and walked back into the warehouse, Faith supposed to get the mortar he needed.

She had to hand it to him, he was always working.

"Why are you making him interview?" Frank asked. "You know you're going to hire him."

"He doesn't know that, and I want him to know I really am the boss."

Frank tugged on his mustache, frowning, but made no comment.

"Why are you here so early today?" Faith asked, trying to divert his thoughts.

"Davis needs to get off early on Saturdays because he's taking dance lessons," he said.

Faith laughed. "Did he look happy about it?"

"Not especially. He mentioned that his sister Janet is taking them with him."

"So dance lessons are on Saturdays?"

"Yes," Davis answered, surprising them as he stepped up behind them. He carried a bucket of mortar. "And I'm on a monument committee that meets every week. I'll have to be done by five thirty on Tuesdays as well. Not my choice for how to use my time, but since I've been manipulated into it . . ."

"Sounds like you're involved with things that are going to help you adjust to being back home," Faith said, a challenge in her voice.

Davis, hands on his hips, glared at her. Frank looked between the two of them and said, "Well, let's get on our way, then."

Faith smiled at the two men.

"You don't need to be so smug," Davis said over his shoulder as he followed Frank to the truck.

Faith stood tapping her foot and watched them load the truck, Davis doing all the heavy lifting. She liked that he made sure Frank didn't overdo it.

He must think she was mean, but he'd brought this on himself. Now he knew that if he interfered with her dates, there would be consequences. Besides, it really was for his own good. So why did she feel guilty? She could be with Freddy as much as she wanted. Somehow, that didn't seem as satisfactory as she had thought it would.

The men pulled out, the truck backfiring its displeasure.

Faith didn't see Frank and Davis again until six when she closed the front of the shop and went back to the warehouse to find them cleaning their tools.

Davis didn't look up when she walked over to them, but Frank did, smiled, and said, "We were just talking about you. I was telling Davis you would be the perfect dance partner for him to practice with."

Davis kept cleaning his tools.

Was that how it was going to be? He was going to ignore her?

She stared at him. When he still didn't respond, she said, "Well, I'll leave you gentlemen. I have a date with Freddy, and he's picking me up here in ten minutes. I'd better go freshen up."

"You look fine to me. Don't you think so, Davis?"

"As always," Davis said without looking up.

Faith stomped back to the front of the store. She didn't like him interfering in her life, but she hated him ignoring her even more. She didn't want to examine her feelings too closely. Wanting his attention made her feel sixteen again. Faith secured her hat and pulled out the compact mirror from her purse. She applied a sheen of strawberry-colored lipstick when Freddy's horn honked from outside. Faith snapped the compact shut. She didn't need Davis's attention.

Freddy took her to a nice restaurant for dinner and then to the Bamboo Club, a little club that had just opened in Payson. They laughed and joked through dinner and then enjoyed dancing together. He was always fun. At the end of the night, he parked around the corner from Faith's house.

"Why're you stopping here?"

Freddy leaned in. "I'd rather not kiss you under Davis's eyes."

"Oh, all right." She met his lips. "You aren't scared of him, are you?" she asked after ending their kiss.

Freddy didn't say anything, but he looked sheepish. He put his Alfa Romeo back into drive and cruised it down Forest Drive, and sure enough, Davis was out on his front porch, pacing instead of smoking.

He stopped and nodded to them as they pulled up. Faith stepped out of the car and headed to her front door.

Davis waved to Freddy and called out, "Beautiful evening." Why was he being friendly? Faith headed up the porch steps.

"You on patrol?" Freddy called out from the car.

Faith paused. She preferred when Freddy and Davis ignored each other.

"Something like that," Davis said somewhat politely. "How are you?"

"Not bad," Freddy said, then waved and was off.

"What are you doing out here?" Faith asked. "Waiting for someone?"

Davis frowned. "Just trying to get some nervous energy out. Can't sleep."

Faith hesitated, her hand on the doorknob, then turned, walked down her steps, across the drive, and over to the Wilsons' front porch. She stood on the lowest step, looking up at Davis, who seemed shocked that she had approached. "Why can't you sleep? Is it just because of not smoking?"

Davis rubbed the back of his neck and met her eyes. "It started in the army. I would think about the deaths I'd seen and about Patrick. My mind won't stop. Sometimes it takes hours to get to sleep."

"Oh," Faith said. "I'm sorry."

"It's not your fault." Davis came down a step toward her.

They stared at each other. The sounds of crickets filled their silence. "I think of him all the time too," Faith whispered.

"I want to be your friend again," Davis said, taking another step toward her.

Faith's chin went up. "You're going to have to stop interfering with Freddy and me if you want to be friends."

Davis grunted.

What did that mean? Was that a yes? Faith stared up at him. The moon-light was bright enough to show the intense look on his face. What was he thinking? He took another step toward her. Her heart suddenly jumped and her pulse pounded. He looked determined.

"Good night," she said, taking a quick step back. Good heavens, why was her voice shaking? Their eyes met and held. Faith took a long breath in, and her knees shook. Why was he looking at her so intently, as if he were trying to see into her innermost thoughts?

She turned her back to him, hurried to the safety of her own front porch, and slipped inside the house. Her heart continued to race.

The thought hit her with a surge of annoyance that Davis had managed to affect her more with one look than Freddy's good-night kiss had. She frowned and set her purse down. She didn't like it that Davis could rattle her like this.

"Faith? Come up to my room," Mom called down the stairs.

Faith took a moment to pull in several deep breaths and gather herself together before heading upstairs. She entered Mom's room and found her sitting at her writing desk.

"What's wrong?" Faith asked, noticing Mom's expression.

"Oh, sweetheart. Another letter from Rose came today."

Faith took the letter, unfolded it as she sat in a chair near Mom, and read,

"*Dear Aunt Marcia and Faith,*

Thank you for your care package. Your homemade caramels may or may not have been eaten in one sitting—that is known only by me. As you can see, I also really appreciate the stationery.

Aunt Marcia, the lace you sent will fancy up a blue dress of mine that is starting to feel old and boring. Thank you! I feel so loved! And I had to smile at the licorice flavoring. I know Faith put it in to make me laugh about the time we tried to make homemade licorice. Even Patrick and Davy wouldn't eat the glommy mess. Mama Russo won't let me use the kitchen, so I won't be making licorice here, but anytime I need a good laugh, I'll uncork the bottle, sniff, and remember Aunt Marcia's face when she saw the mess we made of her spotless kitchen.

I appreciate the pattern for a maternity smock that you sent, Aunt Marcia. How did you know? It looks like it will be needed soon. My baby is due right around Valentine's Day. I haven't told

my parents yet, but since you had a sixth sense about it, you get to be the first to hear the news. I went to the doctor, and he said the exhaustion I've been experiencing is normal. I haven't told Joey yet. He won't be pleased.

I realize I was very foolish to marry a man I really didn't know. I am now living out the adage "Marry in haste; repent at leisure." Faith, I can be your cautionary tale. Be practical and realistic in your romances. I am halfway looking forward to holding my sweet little baby and halfway terrified to bring a child into this home of chaos and yelling, with a father who regrets marrying me.

Your letters and the letters from my parents are certainly the bright point of my weeks. Please pray for me that I can find a job I can do while caring for a baby or that Joey will decide to work.

Love,
Rose"

Silence filled the room as Faith set the letter sadly down on the desk. "Joey Russo sounds like a horrible man."

"Rose certainly deserved better," Mom said.

"Maybe you should call Uncle Dell and Aunt Clarice and see what they can do."

"I've thought about this situation all day. Stan's health is so poor right now, and I think caring for him is all Ella can manage. I think God wants me to step up and help Rose."

Faith's heart skipped a beat. "What are you thinking of?"

"I'm going to take some of our savings, drive to New York City, and help Rose and Joey get into their own apartment."

"What?" Faith exclaimed. She wouldn't have been more surprised if Mom had said she was going to fly to the moon. "You haven't driven since Dad died and we sold our car."

"I know, I know," Mom said. "But I feel God telling me I need to do this."

Faith rubbed her forehead. Worry for Rose was now competing with concern about Mom, who had never driven farther than the grocery store, attempting a cross-country trip.

"What about the train?"

"With all the train strikes going on, I don't think that would be very reliable, and from here it would be so pricey."

"There are so many problems with this idea. We need both trucks for the business. You know we've never been so busy." Faith frowned. "Neither truck would be reliable enough for a cross-country trip anyway. We could purchase a used car, I suppose, but I can't imagine Dad would've been all right with the idea of you traveling to Brooklyn on your own. If he were here, he would say no."

Mom's eyes welled with tears. "If he were here, he would go with me."

"I know," Faith said. A tear ran down her cheek. Dad had done everything he could to protect his wife. She picked up Mom's hand. "I'm sick with worry about Rose. I would go with you if I possibly could, but I just can't leave the business right now. Things are booming and I don't have anyone trained to do what I'm doing."

Mom pulled her handkerchief out, wiped her eyes, and blew her nose. "I'm not going to go alone."

Faith sat up straighter with surprise that her mother's plan was already in place. "Did you ask someone to go with you?"

Mom wouldn't look at her. Faith shifted back and forth. The room was silent until she prompted quietly, "Mom?"

Mom finally looked at her. Oh no. What was that sheepish look for? "I've asked Cecilia Wilson to accompany me. She agreed. We're going to take her car. I'll pay for the gas, and Cecilia will get to do a little shopping while I spend some time with Rose."

"Are you serious?" Faith jumped up with a mixture of amazement and horror.

"Perfectly serious. I knew you wouldn't like it, but I feel a real urgency to get out to Brooklyn. Cecilia is always up for an adventure. She'll do most of the driving. I'll spell her here and there, but I'll mainly be the navigator."

"Does Mr. Wilson have anything to say about this?"

"She met him for lunch and told him our plan."

"He's going to let her go?"

"I don't think James has ever been able to keep Cecilia from doing anything she sets her mind to."

Faith ran her fingers agitatedly through her hair. "Do you really think Mrs. Wilson has good enough judgment for a cross-country trip? I heard Mrs. Widbee talking about their road trip to the Grand Canyon. She said there were long stretches with no reliable service stations and that they ran out of gas more than once."

Mom said, "That's just poor planning. I'll map out all the service stations. We'll leave Tuesday and take four days to get there. I think it'll take another week to find Rose and Joey a place and get them moved in. I know it'll eat into our savings to get them set up in an apartment, but I hate the idea of them bringing a baby into a home that isn't their own."

"I'm not worried about the money." Faith shook her head. "You know I'd do anything for Rose. I'm just worried about your safety on the road."

Mom nodded. A thought came to Faith that would solve two problems at once. She wouldn't have to deal with Davis, and Mom would have someone reliable to go with. "Why don't you take Davis with you."

Mom shook her head. "I don't think you understand how much the bricklayer job means to him. He's so excited to be working at Penwilliger's. I think he almost feels that God has directed him to this job. I'm not going to pull him from it just as he's getting started."

Faith stood up from Mom's bed and walked over to the vanity. She picked up the letter from Rose and turned it over in her hand. Something was wrong with Rose and Joey, and maybe Mom could fix it.

"I wouldn't distress you or go to the expense if I didn't feel like this was what God wants," Mom said.

"I imagine living with Joey's parents is a good part of their problem," Faith said.

Mom stood and wrapped Faith up in a huge hug. "You don't mind me taking some of our savings?"

"Of course not." Faith rubbed her hand over the letter. "Rose would never ask for help, but I'm sure she needs it. As far as I'm concerned, use as much of our savings as you need to to make sure Rose and her baby are well cared for."

Mom nodded. "God willing, I'll help Rose, and I'll be as careful on the road as I possibly can."

Faith didn't say anything. She had the same feeling as when Patrick had enlisted. She hated being left behind and a loved one going off to do something uncertain, but Rose did need help, and good judgment or not, Mrs. Wilson was willing to go with Mom. Faith hugged her mom tighter, breathing in her scent and trying to push her worries away.

CHAPTER 21

DAVIS SAT ACROSS FROM FAITH at her desk, his proposal on his lap. She wore a serious-looking gray suit that matched the expression on her face. She looked every inch the successful businesswoman she was as she shifted some paper around. This was not the girl who had tagged after him when they were young—the girl he'd had to help get bubble gum off her face after she had stuffed four pieces into her mouth to try to beat her friend Katie's bubble record. All had gone well until the huge bubble popped, leaving sticky gum in her eyebrows. Twelve-year-old Davy had seen her distress, run into his house, and come back with a wet rag. He had spent a good twenty minutes scrubbing and scraping the gum off.

A smile flitted across his face as he thought of little Faith's face covered in gum, but he quickly hid it. He needed to show her he was totally and completely in earnest. He tapped his foot. Who would have thought he would be interviewing for a job with Patrick's little sister?

Faith picked up a pen and a typed sheet of questions resting on the desk in front of her. Davis braced himself and thought of soldiers diving for shelter when an enemy plane approached.

"Is your mom ready for the trip?" Faith asked.

He blinked, not expecting a personal question. "As ready as she can be. She isn't one to spend a lot of time packing. How about your mother?"

"She's spent hours packing and then unpacking and repacking." Faith sighed, looked at the paper with the typed questions, and asked, "You are applying for a job as a bricklayer?"

"Yes, ma'am."

Faith's eyebrows went up, and she stared at him, sitting up straighter. He stared back at her, not breaking eye contact. He wasn't mocking her by calling her ma'am; he was trying to show his respect. She looked down at her list of questions again. "What skills do you bring to this job?"

Davis leaned forward, eager to sell himself. "I am a hard worker. The job of a bricklayer is all about projects, and I'm a man who loves projects. I enjoy having a specific thing to do, and I like seeing the completion of a job well done. While I'm working, I'm very focused. I would rather stay two or three hours late and finish a job than go home before it's done." Faith scribbled notes as Davis went on. "I also learned how to follow and how to lead in the army."

"What do you mean by that?"

"I was in a position where I had men under my command and, of course, men over me. I learned to follow orders but also how to lead. I could only be an effective leader if my men knew I was willing to work harder than I expected them to." If his proposal was going to work, it was important that Faith view him as a leader.

She set her pen down. "What was harder: leading or following?"

Davis rubbed his chin and leaned back in his chair. "Leading was much harder. It was a tricky balance to gain respect but not get too familiar with my men. I couldn't let them think of me as a buddy they could second-guess. For all of our sakes, they needed to obey when I gave a command."

Faith leaned forward and Davis smothered another smile. She was interested in spite of herself. "Were you able to do that?" she asked.

"Yes. I set some guidelines for myself that helped."

"What kinds of guidelines?"

"I never asked my men to do anything I wasn't willing to do myself. I checked up on them—on their health, their well-being, and their gear—so they knew I cared, but I never let myself sit around and play cards with them. I wanted that distance."

Faith put her elbows on the desk. "It sounds lonely."

He sighed. "It was."

"I know about that kind of loneliness," Faith said softly. "I've felt pretty alone here at times."

"You don't have to do this alone," Davis said, leaning forward. "I know I can help."

She pushed the list of questions away. "I just don't get why you would want to work here. I know your dad would set you up in a business of your own. Is this about Patrick?"

Davis paused for a long moment, his heart beating hard in his chest as he looked her in the eyes. "It's exciting, the feeling of growth and hope in the future in our country right now. I like building things. I want to be a part of this business."

"Why our brick store?"

Davis rubbed his chin again. "It's hard to explain, but I just can't quit thinking of Penwilliger's and the possibilities here."

"Do you think you could work for a woman? Do you think you could work for me?"

"Yes and yes. If you want, I can be the best bricklayer you've ever had, but I'm hoping you'll let me do more."

"Explain what 'more' means." Faith leaned back, looking wary.

"You asked if this has anything to do with Patrick," Davis said as he sat up straighter and placed his palms down on the proposal resting on his knees. "The answer is I don't know, but somehow I feel pulled to work here. Maybe that's because of Patrick, maybe not. I just feel this is where I'll be happiest and where I'm the most needed." Davis mustered his courage and took a deep breath. Dad had helped him write his proposal up in legal terms. It represented every penny he had saved from his army salary, his college savings, and a potential loan from the bank. "If you'll let me, I want to be your partner."

Faith stared, her mouth open.

Davis put his palm out toward her. "I have some savings and would like to take a loan from the bank to buy half the business from you. I have a lot of ideas for how we can take advantage of the booming construction market."

"Partners!" Faith exclaimed.

"I envision that you would deal with customers and accounting, and I would deal with expansion and supervising the bricklayers."

"Partners?" Faith said again. Her brow furrowed in confusion.

Davis nodded. "I believe we could make a lot of money with Penwilliger Brick. Just for a start, if we take my partnership money as a down payment, we could buy our own brick factory and make our own bricks. We could contract with some construction companies that are just starting to invest in new developments. If we get on this soon, we could line up enough work to hire somewhere between seven to ten new bricklayers."

"I've never thought of trying to grow the business," Faith said slowly.

"If you're going to do it, now is the time."

"This is a surprise." Faith pushed her notes aside. "I'll need time to think this through."

Davis shifted a little in his chair. Should he say something else? He might as well lay it all on the line. He took another big breath of air and said, "My offer is contingent on you not selling your half of the business. I want to work with you, not a stranger."

Faith's eyes, round, full, and surprised, flashed to his. "How did you know I'm thinking of selling?"

"Let's just say a little bird told me."

"I'm guessing the bird was named Frank."

"The bird wants the best for Penwilliger Brick."

"So do I," Faith said, "but I'm not sure the best thing for either of us is being partners. Would you consider buying the whole business yourself?"

Davis shook his head. "I can come up with the money to buy half but not the whole business, and frankly, I need your expertise. My offer is to be partners."

Partners. The word hung in the air between them. Davis sat up straighter. "Faith, think about why Mr. Holland has offered to buy your business. He knows the construction market is booming. Penwilliger Brick has all kinds of possibilities. He sees the potential and so do I."

Faith just stared at him. Maybe she really did need time to think things over.

"Have you been happy with my bricklaying?"

"Oh yes." She gave him a small smile.

Davis leaned forward. "Partner or not, will you hire me as a bricklayer?"

"Yes," Faith said.

Davis grinned. That was a step in the right direction. Her paper with typed questions still lay on the desk. Thank heavens Faith had abandoned them. This interview had taken a decided turn from the ordinary.

"When you're deciding about being partners, this might help." Davis pushed his manila folder across the desk to Faith. "This is my business proposal and is my best estimate of what Penwilliger's is worth. It also delineates what I believe each of our responsibilities should be. I've had my dad's help. I think you'll also want to have a lawyer look at it and come up with your own numbers."

Faith took the envelope from Davis and stood up to end the interview. Her mouth was slightly open, and she looked at his proposal with something like a mix of wariness and shock on her lovely face.

"I'll continue on with Frank while you decide, and then we can see if we need to hire more men or if you want to keep the company as is."

Faith nodded and Davis came around the desk. They didn't usually stand this close. He could smell her floral perfume, and he had a sudden urge to take her in his arms. What would it be like to dance with her? He sighed a little. What would it be like to kiss her? Why was he thinking that? This was a business proposal. Their relationship should be professional. Also, Faith had a grudge about Patrick and Freddy was still a big part of her life. Kissing her seemed highly unlikely.

They stood frozen, looking at each other. He would love to know what was going through her beautiful head. He needed to stop thinking about the way she looked. Their relationship would have to be strictly business. No more sitting on the porch waiting for her to come home and interrupting her dates.

He stuck his hand out. Faith put her hand in his and shook. She dropped it quickly, but not before he had appreciated its softness. Did his calluses bother her? Freddy certainly didn't have calluses. Davis nodded to her, pulled his hat from the hat rack, and strode out of the store, leaving Faith behind.

CHAPTER 22

THE NIGHT OF THE DISCONCERTING interview with Davis, Faith sat on Mom's bed, watching her pack. *Partners?* Could she do it? Should she do it? What would it be like to be partners with someone who got under her skin?

"Faith?" Mom was waiting for a response.

"Sorry, I was woolgathering, as Granny would say. What did you ask me?"

"Rose doesn't know we're coming. Is it a mistake to just show up?" a harried Mom asked.

Faith sighed. "It is awkward, but you feel so strongly about going."

"I think she would tell me not to come if I telegrammed ahead."

"True. She was never one to want a fuss made. Remember Aunt Ella telling us about the time Rose broke her arm?" Rose had suffered in pain all through the school day because she hadn't wanted anyone to make a fuss over her. "I hate having you leave, but I think you're right. This is the only way to really help her."

"I agree," Mom said, then changed the subject. "How did Davis's interview go?"

"I think he wants to run the world."

Mom looked up from the suitcase she was carefully placing rolled clothing in—she had read in *Good Housekeeping* that rolling clothing prevented wrinkles. "Is that good or bad?"

"Let's just say capitalism is alive and well in Davis Wilson. He'd be good for our bottom line but bad for my peace of mind. He wants to buy in and be my partner."

"Really?" Mom stopped what she was doing and gave Faith her full attention, her voice filled with excitement.

"I don't think we could get along well enough to be partners."

Mom's shoulders dropped. "Couldn't you try?"

"There's no way to buy into a business on a trial basis. There are so many mitigating factors here."

"Not sure what you mean by mitigating," Mom said as she yanked a skirt off a hanger. "From my view it looks like pride on your part. Swallow it. There's no room for pride in smart decisions."

"Thank you for your advice." Faith stiffened her posture. "I'm sure you know how hard I've worked for Penwilliger Brick. I know you'll respect my decision." But would Mom respect the decision if it were selling and going to college?

"I won't force anything, but it seems clear to me that Davis would be a blessing."

"Not so much from where I'm sitting. Aargh! Let's not talk about it. Here, let me help roll."

Darn Davis! He made everything so confusing.

***

Two days later, on a pleasant, early-August morning, the Wilsons and Penwilligers gathered around the Wilsons' dark-green Buick. A light breeze lifted Faith's curls away from her face.

The car was loaded for the "big road trip," as Mr. Wilson was calling it. Janet, Carrie, Mr. Wilson, Davis, and Faith took turns asking, "Did you remember to pack . . ."

"Do you have all the maps?" Faith asked anxiously.

"Yes," Mom said, patting the bag that would sit by her feet.

"Cash?"

"Yes."

"The list of phone numbers and addresses?"

"Yes," Mom assured her.

Mr. Wilson and Davis had made sure the two women knew how to check the radiator and change the engine oil or a tire if needed. Mom had spent the last week carefully planning their route, making lists, and baking and baking and baking. The car was full of baskets of home-baked breads, cookies, meat pastries, fried chicken, biscuits, and homemade jam. She also had five gallons of water. Faith wasn't sure if the water was for the radiator or to drink, but either way she appreciated the preparation. Mom had even taken a tape measure out to the Wilsons' Buick and had measured the trunk and inside of the car so that she could choose just the right sizes of baskets, boxes, and suitcases. The boxy car was a masterpiece of packing.

Mrs. Wilson's and Mom's outfits seemed to reflect how they each viewed the trip. Mrs. Wilson wore a bright-blue dress with a perky yellow hat—she looked like she was about to set off on a fun adventure. Mom, on the other hand, was in gray traveling clothes that were serviceable and would hide dirt—her clothing was serious, as was she. Faith knew this was no pleasure trip for her mother, but a mission with a purpose: to help Rose and her unborn baby.

"Well, ladies." Mr. Wilson tucked his hands into his pockets. "Our prayers go with you."

"Amen," Davis, standing straight and tall, said.

Faith felt near tears as she hugged her mother. "Just help Rose."

Carrie and Janet hugged their mother goodbye. Davis and Mr. Wilson each gave Mrs. Wilson a kiss on the cheek, and she slid cheerfully behind the wheel. She seemed totally unfazed. Mom, on the other hand, clutched her purse tightly and looked terrified as she took her place in the passenger seat.

Faith stepped over to the open window. "You look like you might be sick."

"It's just nerves," Mom said. "Don't worry about me. I have paper sacks and antiseptic spray in case either of us gets sick."

"Of course you do." Faith couldn't decide whether to laugh or cry but settled on a weak smile. "Don't forget," she said, "I'll be waiting for you to call every night at nine p.m. to report on your day."

Mom had agreed to what she considered the exorbitant expense of long-distance phone calls in order to appease Faith. "I will if I possibly can. Don't forget that you have to wipe down the front of the stove with the vinegar mixture that's under the sink. You should harvest in the garden at least twice a week. When you do the ironing, make sure you use the spray mixture in the blue bottle for cottons and the red for linens."

"Let's get our show on the road," Mrs. Wilson interjected.

"I know I've forgotten something I need to remind you of," Mom said, twisting her hands.

"It's all right, Mom. We'll talk tonight." Faith spoke softly, having noticed that Davis was watching them, his blue eyes soft and compassionate. She didn't like the idea of him feeling sorry for them.

Mom nodded and adjusted her hat. She hugged Faith awkwardly through the window and offered an Irish blessing, "'As light to the eye, as joy to the heart, as bread to the hungry may my presence be with thee.'"

Faith blinked rapidly. She wouldn't cry in front of Davis. Her throat was tight, but she managed to say, "'May the road rise up to meet you.'"

The group watched as Mrs. Wilson pulled away. Mom had her head out the window and waved all the way up Forest Drive. The Wilsons and Faith stepped into the road and kept waving until the car rounded the corner, leaving the little group looking down the road at nothing. Faith was left with an immense feeling of emptiness.

"It's only a couple of weeks," she said out loud.

"We're next door if you need anything," Davis said behind her.

Faith nodded politely and said, "I'll see you at work."

Janet and Carrie giggled and teased each other on the front lawn. Faith supposed they couldn't understand how these small goodbyes brought back the pain of the larger ones, having never experienced a large one of their own. Oh, how she hated the feeling of being left behind. She hurried into the house to pull herself together before work. Stepping inside, she could hear the clock in the front room ticking. The house had never felt so large or empty.

She gathered her things, nearly bursting into tears when she saw the lunch Mom, even in her own busyness, had taken the time to make for Faith. She hurried out to Costello, started her old truck up, and took off. It was good to have work to distract herself with today. She cranked the radio up to some lively music, happy to take her mind off her mother's road trip.

Once at the store, she parked Costello in the back, hurried through her cleaning routine, started the coffee, and then went back to the warehouse to do a little inventory.

The warehouse bay doors were open. All the men—Juan, Lester, Frank, and Davis—were loading bricks into the two Penwilliger trucks. They talked news while loading for their delivery and prepping their mortar. Faith, clutching her clipboard, stepped a little closer, interested in the conversation but not wanting them to see her.

"Did you see the article about the Dodgers and Giants baseball game?" Frank asked.

"No," Davis responded. "I never made it to the sports section. I was pretty caught up reading about the atomic bomb explosion at the Bikini Atoll."

"You like reading about bombs. Frank and me, we have good taste. We read about baseball," Juan teased Davis.

Frank maneuvered the forklift to where the other men waited to help load the trucks. Faith, observing from behind a pallet of bricks, was happy to see that he spared his back and let the other three do the heavy lifting.

"The Dodgers' manager made a cynical comment." Frank paused to give directions to Juan. "Don't stack them quite that high. Anyway, the newspaper said that Durocher, the Dodgers' manager, pointed to the Giants' dugout and said something about the Giants' team being too nice and that because of that, they wouldn't win."

"Not a very inspiring message." Davis pushed a pallet of bricks deeper into the truck.

"Yeah," Frank said. "You think it's true, what he said?"

Lester grunted, "You gotta look out for yourself. If you're too nice, you're gonna get taken advantage of."

"I don't agree with that," Davis said. "I think life has a way of working itself out. What do you think?" He looked over at Frank and Juan.

"You don't want to be *chafa*," Juan said.

Frank rubbed the back of his neck. "The war really shook my confidence in justice. I used to believe good people would always come out on top, but I'm not so confident of that anymore."

"You gotta look out for yourself," Lester repeated.

Faith rolled her eyes at his unsurprising response. She turned her attention to counting pallets of bricks.

It was quiet for a moment, the only sound being the sound of the bricks being loaded into the trucks. Then Davis's voice came again. "I suppose it depends on what Durocher meant. If he meant good guys always stay the safest or get the prettiest girl or end up making the most money, then they probably don't win. If he meant they're the happiest long term, then I still think things work out for them."

Faith wrote, *Twenty-three pallets of red-smooth, Nineteen pallets of red-distressed.*

Lester wasn't having it and again repeated what he said before. "If you're too nice, people take advantage of you. You've got to look out for yourself."

Faith peeked around the corner to see Frank turn toward Davis. "I actually like your point. You're calling it more of a moral victory."

Lester snorted and thumped the side of the truck.

"Exactly." Davis gave Frank a small smile. "In the army I was in the same company as a guy who was a total jerk. He would steal other men's rations, suck up to commanders, and try to get out of any nasty job. It seemed to work. He was a sad sack but was able to position himself to get a desk job and get off the front lines. I thought of him the other day and what it must feel like to have to go home with himself at the end of the war."

The men finished loading and moved toward their trucks. Davis was going with Juan, a request Faith had made so he could get to know Juan better.

"What does chafa mean?" Davis asked Juan as they moved to the truck.

"Chafa," Juan said, "is like when you do bad work. It's like, how you say, bad quality."

Davis laughed. "You're right. I don't want to be chafa."

He and Juan hopped into Abbott.

Frank didn't look too excited to be working with Lester but climbed up into the passenger seat of Costello next to him. Faith watched the trucks pull out and then went back to finishing inventory.

After the inventory was done, Faith went to her desk and pulled out Davis's proposal. In addition to her regular accounting duties, she was trying to figure out whether Davis's numbers were accurate. So far, they seemed more than fair to her. It was impressive that he had been able to accurately assess the business without having access to their accounts. His numbers were right on par with what Mr. Holland had presented.

The day flew by with customers to help, bids to arrange, phone calls to deal with, and accounts to settle. Davis came into the front office around five thirty.

Faith looked up from the accounts ledger. "Is everyone done for the day?"

"Yes. Everyone's gone home."

She cleared her throat, wishing conversation between her and Davis flowed like the men's easy conversation she'd overheard this morning. "How did Lester and Frank do?"

Davis grinned. "They didn't kill each other, but Frank said working with Lester is like sucking a sour pickle—you get used to it, but it doesn't mean you don't wish it weren't sweeter."

Faith laughed, and some of the awkwardness that was always there when they were alone eased. "And how did Juan do?"

"He's great," Davis said. "He works hard, is cheerful, and has a great sense of humor."

Faith nodded. "Thanks. That's what I thought, but I'm happy to hear you agree. It was a blessing when he came through the work program during the war." She waited for Davis to leave, but he remained by her desk. Her eyebrows went up. Why was he looking at her so thoughtfully?

"Growing up, when Rose would come to visit, I always thought of her as steady and calm," he said.

"She was," Faith said, wondering at the change of subject.

"It's hard to picture her rushing into a marriage. How did that happen?"

Faith shrugged. "The war. You don't know what things were like here. Everyone had a sense of life changing, and women wondered if their boyfriends would ever come back." She paused. "I suppose it was a bit of a seize-the-day feeling."

"That makes sense."

"It's important not to rush relationships," Faith said. She couldn't keep the smugness out of her voice. "That's why Freddy and I aren't exclusive."

Davis's eyebrows shot up, but he didn't say anything.

Faith flushed and turned back to the accounts ledger.

"We could drive home together tonight and back in together tomorrow."

"No thanks. I have some more numbers to crunch, and without my mom at home, there's no incentive to hurry for dinner."

"Are you sure? You've already put in a full day."

Faith nodded. She was sure she didn't want to drive back and forth with Davis.

"Janet's making dinner for us tonight. She's not a bad cook. Would you like to join us?"

"Thanks but no thanks. I'm fine." Why was he inviting her over? Didn't he get that she wanted to keep things businesslike between them?

He stood to the side of her desk like he wanted to say something more but then apparently decided against it. He moved toward the warehouse, calling out, "See you tomorrow."

Faith didn't get home until seven. She pulled out the cold fried chicken her mother had left for her, hating the empty kitchen. She put her chicken, some lemonade, and biscuits on a tray and went out to the backyard to eat, then settled on the grass, enjoying the freshly cut smell. The lovely day had turned muggy. It was most likely going to rain overnight, and the humidity didn't feel great, but it was better than the empty house.

"Oh hi, Faith," Mr. Wilson called out from next door. "Don't you make a pretty summer picture eating there."

"Hi, Mr. Wilson. How are you faring without your wife?"

"Missing her something dreadful."

Faith tilted her head. Honestly, she had thought he might enjoy a break from his wife's chatter, but he looked totally sincere. "I just keep telling myself it's only two weeks," she said.

Mr. Wilson chatted for a few minutes and then left to "get the girls going on their chores."

Faith went inside to battle the clock. Eight fifteen. She groaned. Forty-five minutes until Mom was supposed to call. She paced the kitchen—8:20—tried to read a little of the newspaper—8:30—listened to the radio—8:40—and finally moved to the front room to play the piano. The clock absolutely crawled.

The windows were open, and she could hear kids running around outside, playing kick the can. She played some Mozart, finished, and turned to stare at the phone. It was nine. Maybe she'd play one more song. She pulled out some Schumann; it usually worked to calm her down. Five minutes after nine and her heart was racing. Why hadn't Mom called? Ten minutes past nine and she felt absolutely panicked. Were they broken down somewhere? She stopped playing and moved to the hall to stand by the phone.

Even expecting the call, she jumped when it finally rang.

"This is the operator. Will you accept a reverse-charge call from Marta Wenwilow?"

The operator slaughtered the name, but a very relieved Faith said, "Yes, yes."

"Hi, sweetheart," Mom's voice said.

Faith slumped against the wall, relieved. "Hi, Mom! How's the trip been so far?"

"Excellent. We made good time. We made it 232 miles today."

She smiled at her mother's exactness. "Did Mrs. Wilson drive the whole way?"

"I drove for 43 miles." Mom sounded like she was giving a news report.

"Did you have any car troubles?"

"Not at all. Our motel tonight is by a service station. I plan to have them look the car over before we hit the road tomorrow."

"Wonderful idea."

There was silence over the line. Then Faith spoke up. "I appreciate the food you left for me."

"It came in pretty handy for us too."

"How's that?"

"Cecilia got pulled over twice for speeding."

Faith gasped.

"I told her she was going too fast, but you know she never takes advice."

Faith laughed, picturing Mom trying to get Cecilia to slow down. "What happened?"

"Both times we were pulled over, she was able to bribe the officers with my home cooking. She got off with warnings."

Faith leaned against the wall and laughed harder.

"You take care of yourself, sweetheart."

"You too, Mom! I love you."

"Love you too. I'll talk to you tomorrow."

She hung up and stood in the hall, leaned her head against the wall, and smiled at the picture of Mrs. Wilson bribing officers.

CHAPTER 23

"I'm headed to the Penwilligers," Dad told Davis.

"Oh?" Davis was sprawled on the couch reading the newspaper, wishing he could go outside and smoke. He checked his watch. Nine fifteen. "Isn't it a little late?"

"Marcia is supposed to call Faith every night. I'm curious to get a report on how they're getting on. You want to come?"

Davis sat up. "I don't know, Dad. I think Faith gets enough of me at work."

"Nonsense," Dad said, sounding a lot like Mom. "This is just a short neighborly call."

Davis refolded the paper and stood up. Dad was right. Faith might not love his company, but it was natural to pop over to hear about Mom and Marcia's trip, wasn't it?

He followed Dad over to the Penwilligers'. He stood a couple of feet behind Dad, who tapped softly on the door. Almost immediately Faith answered. She took a look at them standing in the twilight, smiled, and said, "Come on in."

Davis exhaled. He hadn't realized he'd been holding his breath. He followed Dad into the Penwilligers' front room. She waved them to the couch and told them the number of miles traveled and that Mom had been pulled over twice for speeding. Davis shook his head.

Dad simply smiled about Mom's antics. "Thank you for the update," he said. "I'd better get back home and help Carrie with the dinner dishes."

What? Where was Dad going? He didn't care about getting the dinner dishes done. But he stood and looked at Faith with a twinkle in his eye. "You could do me a favor and play a few pieces for Davis. Since giving up smoking, he hasn't been able to get to sleep easily. The thing that helps him relax the most is when he sits on our front porch to hear you playing the piano."

Davis's face heated, and he ran his hand through his hair. He wished Dad wouldn't have said anything. He couldn't possibly know the minefield he had just shoved Davis into. Davis looked at Faith. "You don't have to play for me."

He stood to leave too, but Dad gently pushed him back down on the couch just as Faith said, "I'm happy to play for you if it helps you sleep."

Davis's eyebrows rose, but he didn't argue. He just sat back on the couch as Dad quietly exited.

Faith made her way to the piano. She didn't look friendly, exactly, but she didn't look angry either. She settled her fingers on the ivory keys and began playing. The notes floated out beneath her fingers and filled the summer air. He did feel tired. What was Faith thinking about? Davis yawned. Probably nothing. She seemed so absorbed in what she was playing.

The song ended. Would she ask him to leave? But she began playing a piece by Mozart. He relaxed into the beauty of the music, letting it flow through him.

It had been a long time since he had felt this sense of calmness. He yawned again. He'd close his eyes for just a moment.

CHAPTER 24

Faith walked over to the couch and stared at Davis's chiseled face. He had always been good-looking, but now he was something more. What was it? A strange desire to touch his sleeping face came over her. Freddy's face was handsome but soft. Davis's was all strength. What would his cheek feel like? If she stretched her arm out, she could run her finger over his cheek and down his jawline. She shook her head. Good heavens, what was she thinking? She wasn't going to touch him—not tonight, not ever.

"Davis," she said softly. "I'm done playing."

His eyes flew open, and two twin pools of blue blinked up at her.

"I'm so sorry. I didn't mean to fall asleep." He stretched and straightened. "Thank you," he said quietly.

"No problem."

He nodded, and without another word, he left. She walked to the window and shut the curtains—one of the hundreds of little things Mom usually took care of—and went up the stairs with a strange mix of feelings. Every time she played the piano it became easier to do it without the pain of wanting it to be her brother sitting at the bench pulling magic from the box of strings. She supposed she was getting more used to the piano being hers, not Patrick's.

But Davis was another matter entirely. He unsettled her. That strange desire to touch him needed to be quieted.

***

On Sunday Faith's students watched as she showed them a bag of sand and a bag of rocks. "These rocks are God's commandments," she said. "The sand is all the extra stuff we love to do."

"Like baseball?" one of her favorite boys asked.

"Exactly. For me it is dancing and music."

Faith used a newspaper to funnel the sand into a jar. She tried to put all seven of her rocks on top of the sand, but only three would fit. She asked, "Have you ever felt like that? Like you can't fit everything into your life that you want to?"

A few students agreed and a few just watched her intently. Faith pulled the rocks and sand out of the jar. This time she put the rocks into the jar first and then dumped the sand in last.

"It fits," Carrie exclaimed.

Faith grinned. All of her students looked at her. She counted it a huge success when she could get everyone's attention. "What can we take from this?" she asked.

"Put the things of God first," Janet answered. "And everything will fit."

Yay! Faith felt that connection between herself and her students. They got what she was teaching. She had needed a happy moment. Today, September 8, was a hard day, and she had to face it without Mom.

Pastor Clemmons stepped into the room with Davis, who looked sharp in his Sunday suit. How could she be partners with a man that handsome? It would be distracting to have him around. At least as a bricklayer he was out working most of the time.

The men eyed her newspaper and sand-strewn table, and the students sat up a bit straighter in their chairs. They each respected their gruff pastor.

Faith smiled at Pastor Clemmons. "It's an object lesson."

"Looks like a good one," he said. "Mr. Wilson and I are here to talk to you about a project we're starting."

Carrie and Janet looked at each other and giggled. Carrie mouthed, *"Mr. Wilson?"*

Davis shot his little sisters a look.

Pastor Clemmons continued. "We lost more than our fair share of good men during the war. I believe our total loss in Payson was thirteen."

Davis nodded.

"After discussing at length with our committee the idea of building a monument for them, we have divided up into two teams. One will find a plot of land and a beautiful design for the monument itself; the other will raise funds."

"I want to help." Allison, who was a bit of a goody-goody, raised her hand.

"Mr. Wilson will tell you how you can," the pastor said.

Davis smiled and stepped forward. "I'm here to invite you all to be on our fundraising committee. We hope this class will go door to door to ask for contributions."

There was a chorus of nods and excitement.

"We would have you work in twos and train you to do a good door approach. Please ask your parents if you can help. For those who can, we will meet again to train and assign partners."

"Can I be your partner?" Elizabeth gazed at Davis with adoration.

"Ew, no," Janet said. "You can be my partner."

"Davis and Faith should go together," Carrie said with a smirk.

Faith flushed. Why was everyone always trying to pair her with Davis?

"This is a great thing we are trying to do. A lot of good men died in the war, including my best friend. I think of him a lot. Today especially," Davis said.

Good. Faith was glad he remembered what day it was. A little voice inside her head, which sounded a lot like her mother, said, *Freddy didn't remember.* Faith bit her lip. Freddy didn't do sad. He would take her out dancing sometime next week, but sitting around her house, looking through old scrapbooks, and mourning with her wasn't his thing. It was good that he always wanted to look at the fun side of life, right?

"If we can honor them in any way, we should," Davis said.

"Amen," Pastor Clemmons agreed. The students chimed in with their own sober amens.

Davis nodded. "We'll see you Tuesday." He left with the pastor.

Faith was in no hurry to get back to her empty home after church, so she decided to walk by the Sullivans and invite Robert to help with the monument.

"Faith!" Mrs. Sullivan said as she answered the door. "How are you, dear?"

"Good. I'm wondering if I could speak with Robert."

"I'm afraid he hasn't changed his mind about coming to church." Mrs. Sullivan wrinkled her forehead. "He's awfully determined. I'm not sure we'll ever get him back there."

"Maybe on God's timetable."

Mrs. Sullivan sighed. She didn't look too excited about God's timetable.

"I'm here for a different reason," Faith said. "My Sunday School class is working on a project Robert might be interested in."

"Come on in." She left to get her son.

When Robert came back with his mother, he didn't smile or greet Faith. His mother gave him a little shove forward, and then she turned and left them alone.

"Hello, Robert," Faith said, giving him a smile and extending her hand.

He put his hand in hers and shook it slowly.

"I'm here about a project you may be interested in." Faith sat down on the couch.

Robert looked a bit suspicious but took a seat across from her.

"You might not appreciate the role of religion in your life, but maybe you can appreciate the good that can be done through a church."

Robert's eyebrows lifted.

"Our Sunday School class is going to go door to door to raise funds for a monument that will honor those from Payson who died during the war."

Robert straightened in his seat. "That's kinda cool."

Faith smiled warmly at him. "I thought you might think so. If you can make it to the church on Tuesday night, Davis Wilson is going to train us on how to ask for money."

"When would we do the actual door knocking?"

"I think that would be up to you and whoever your partner is."

"Where will the monument be?"

"I don't know. There's a committee that's finding the land and the monument design."

"I'll help," he declared. "I don't want George to ever be forgotten."

"I understand," Faith said. "It's my brother, Patrick's, birthday today. He would have been twenty-five." She blinked back tears. "I don't want him to ever be forgotten either."

"Will their names go on the monument?" Robert leaned toward her.

"Most monuments do have the fallen soldiers' names."

"I want George's name in stone." Robert looked pleased with the idea.

Faith nodded. "All right, then. I'll see you Tuesday." She got up to leave.

"This is a good idea," Robert said as he followed her to the door.

"Yes, it is," Faith said smugly, not bothering to tell him it had originated with her but was being carried out by Davis, thanks to a little blue envelope with a note inside.

She spent the rest of her Sunday afternoon reading under the apple tree in the backyard. She had spread an old quilt out and propped herself up with an oversize pillow. It felt less lonely to be outside of the house. She wandered back in for her dinner, made scrambled eggs, ate quickly, and then spent the time before her mother called looking at pictures of Patrick. The photo albums and scrapbooks captured his life with surprising accuracy.

Tears rolled down her cheeks as she thumbed through Patrick's baby pictures, schoolboy snapshots, and the accolades from his many piano competitions. She loved looking at the pictures of Patrick during his high school days and first two years of college, but she slammed the book shut when she came to the photos of him looking serious in his uniform with a grinning, happy-go-lucky Davy, also in uniform, standing by him. That familiar bubble of anger simmered inside her.

Faith lay down on the front-room couch, trying to calm her emotions before her mother called. She went over in her mind some ideas for new dance steps to try out with Freddy and was just starting to feel relaxed when the phone rang. She accepted the reverse charges, not caring what the calls were costing them. "Mom!"

"Sweetheart, how was your day?"

"I had a good Sunday School class. The afternoon has been slow. How has your day been?"

"Hard," Mom said in an open, honest voice. "I can't stop thinking of Patrick, of the day he was born and how proud your father was. It's funny, but the memory that keeps coming back to me today is of him as a five-year-old sitting enthralled in front of the radio, listening to the Vienna Philharmonic. I think I knew then that music was going to be an important part of his life. I've also been thinking about how excited he was when we brought you home from the hospital all wrapped up in a pink blanket. There was no jealousy—there never was. He adored you."

"He was always so great about letting me tag along on his adventures."

"Yes," Mom said. "He *and* Davis included you in a lot. Pretty impressive for boys four years older than you."

Faith ignored the Davis reference. "I didn't think his birthday would hit me this hard, but it's been just as hard today as it was last year."

"I know."

She could hear her mother sigh across the miles. "How are things going with Rose?" Faith asked.

"We did some sightseeing with Rose yesterday and today," Mom said. "I can't even wrap my mind around how big New York City is. I've taken a lot of pictures, and I'll tell you all about it when I get home, but the main thing is that we got Rose to open up. Her life with Joey is beyond horrible."

Faith gripped the phone tightly.

"You know I'm generally against divorce, but I don't know how she can safely raise her baby in that environment. I didn't want to be the one to step in and tell her to leave Joey, but Cecilia had no qualms about it."

"Oh?"

"She told Rose that marrying Joey was stupid but that staying with him would be far stupider."

"Good for her!" Faith said with a rush of affection for Mrs. Wilson.

"She seems to have given Rose the strength to leave."

"She's going to leave him?"

"Yes." Mom's voice got softer. "But she's embarrassed to go home. She feels like she's a failure and doesn't want to return expecting a baby and soon to be divorced."

Faith's eyes opened wide. "You've invited her to live with us?"

"Yes," Mom said. The line was silent for a moment.

"We'll make it work," Faith said with her usual optimistic outlook. "Are you ready to have a baby in our home?"

"I'm excited about it, but there are a couple of things that will be hard on you."

"Oh?"

"Rose said she will have to finish things up at work. We won't be home for another two weeks."

"Oh," Faith said. Her heart sank. It was only two more weeks, but she was beyond ready to have Mom back home.

"I'm sorry. I hate being away from you and home."

"Can Mrs. Wilson be gone that long?"

"She's in shopping heaven and doesn't seem to mind at all."

Faith swallowed her disappointment. She could manage another two weeks.

"The other thing is that Rose is going to need a room to stay in."

Faith let the silence hang heavy. Her mom couldn't possibly mean Patrick's room, could she?

Mom sighed and said, "You and I will have to share a room or give her Patrick's."

"I'll think about it," Faith said gruffly. "I'd better let you go."

"Goodbye, sweetheart. I know it's hard."

"Good night, Mom," Faith said.

She hung up the phone and rested her head against the wall. Loneliness washed over her in waves—loneliness not just for her mother but for Patrick and their father. She climbed up the stairs, opened Patrick's door, and sat on his bed.

She loved Rose and was glad she was coming, but she couldn't clean the room out; she just couldn't. Patrick should be here. They should be celebrating his birthday today, and he should be composing some brilliant birthday song. The tears came.

She hugged Patrick's pillow to her chest and ignored the soft tapping at her front door. She knew it was Davis coming for an update. He knocked again, and she waited, listening, until he finally gave up and she heard the sounds of his footsteps going down the porch.

CHAPTER 25

Davis lay in bed thinking about Faith and why she had ignored his knock earlier. Why was he so bothered by her not opening the door? She had every right to mourn Patrick's birthday in private. What had he thought would happen? That she would rush into his arms and cry on his shoulder? She had made it clear that she didn't want him in her personal life. She didn't even seem to want him as a business partner.

He flipped his pillow over, fluffing it up. Sleep wasn't going to come easily tonight; he could already tell. This would have been the time of night when he would have gone outside for a smoke. He punched his pillow. Darn Faith. Why had she made him give up smoking? *It's for your own good.* Maybe, but it was still irritating. The dancing lessons were coming along, the monument committee had met twice already, and he was pretty sure the monument was really going to happen. Smoking was the only part of Faith's interference that was still hard.

He flipped onto his back, tucked his hands behind his head, and stared at the ceiling. What was it with Faith anyway? Why couldn't he stop thinking about her? *You know why,* the same patronizing voice in his head said. Was that a crack in the ceiling? He'd have to check that the sheetrock wasn't sagging there. *You know why.* Tomorrow he'd be working with Juan again. *Admit it.* The Ford's brakes were a little loose; he'd better take a look at those tomorrow after work. *You know what this is—admit it.*

Davis sat up in bed, his fists balled. "I'm in love with her," he whispered. "Completely in love with her and she can't stand me." Fine, he could admit he loved Faith Penwilliger, and it terrified him. It terrified him that he loved the graceful way she danced and how she genuinely cared about her Sunday School class. It terrified him that he loved the way she ran her business and that he so desperately wanted to be made a partner in Penwilliger Brick. It terrified him that he wanted so much more than to be business partners and that Faith might never feel the same. If Faith let him become a partner in the business, and that was a big if, it would be torture to be near her and unable to act on his feelings. Freddy Casper was still very much in her life, and there was still a coldness between her and Davis that stemmed from the night he and Patrick had enlisted. He flopped back down, covered his face with his pillow, and groaned aloud.

***

Faith was quiet all week at work. Davis felt like something was on her mind, but he was never around her long enough to figure out what. By Friday, he was growing desperate for her to give him some inkling as to whether or not she was going to make him a partner, but she hadn't broached the subject and he didn't want to appear to be begging. He'd just have to be patient.

He spent all day Friday working with Juan. They laughed and joked as they bricked a small home in a new development. As always, the hard physical labor helped Davis forget his worries. They got done a little early, drove back to the store, and unloaded their extra brick into the warehouse, where Frank and Faith were taking inventory.

"It's a challenge to keep enough brick in stock," Faith said.

"Best decision you ever made," Frank replied.

"What's that?" she asked.

"Hiring Davis," Frank answered like it was obvious. "He's the reason we're flying through brick."

Davis stopped unloading and turned so he could see Faith's reaction.

"He's a hard worker," she said without committing herself to anything. Her face didn't change expression. She wrote something down in a ledger.

Davis grimaced. "Hard worker" was nice, but he was more than ready for her to commit to a partnership. What was she thinking? He couldn't tell one way or the other.

"Oh, he's far more than that," Frank said as he sat on a pallet of bricks. "He's far better at inventory than I ever was, he commands respect from Lester and Juan, and even though I hate to admit it, he's a better bricklayer than I am. He would make an excellent partner."

Davis smiled. Frank wasn't subtle.

"But he doesn't have your distinguished mustache." Faith gave Frank a sassy grin.

Frank patted his white handlebar. He didn't seem to take note that she was teasing. "It is a thing of beauty, is it not? There aren't many of us old-timers around who know how to properly wax a mustache."

"True, true." Faith nodded in agreement, and her eyes twinkled.

Davis chuckled.

Faith turned to Davis, all seriousness now, and said, "I scheduled four new jobs today. We need to hire another bricklayer."

"Any leads?"

"Not really. I was hoping you might find someone for us."

Davis nodded. This was progress. Surely it was a good sign that she trusted him enough to let him do the hiring.

She turned to Frank and asked, "Could you lock up for me?"

"Sure. You headed out dancing with Freddy?"

And there it was. Davis felt like he'd been sucker punched.

"I wish. I'm going to eat and then start cleaning Patrick's room out for Rose. I think if I can get everything boxed up, I'll be able to paint and maybe even do a bit of decorating before they get home."

Davis swallowed hard as his thoughts turned from wanting to punch Freddy, to Patrick's room. He couldn't imagine how hard cleaning it was going to be.

"Sounds like a lot of work," Frank said.

"I'm at the point where my granny Penwilliger would have said, 'Nodding the head doesn't row the boat.'"

"I know that exact feeling. I always have a moment before I start a project where I dread it." Frank gave her a hug.

Davis rubbed the back of his neck as he watched Faith leave. What was that saying? "Nodding the head doesn't row the boat"? He needed to get into Faith's boat and help her row.

CHAPTER 26

FAITH MADE IT AS FAR as opening Patrick's closet, but she broke down sobbing when she saw his baseball cleats.

This was ridiculous. She was crying because she could still smell his foot odor. She closed the closet and left the room, shutting the door firmly behind her. There was no way she could do it. Rose was just going to have to stay in Faith's room, and Faith would move in with Mom.

She went into Mom's room and looked around. It was immaculate and calm, as usual. It smelled faintly of lavender and seemed to be waiting patiently for Mom's return. Faith sat on the bed and tried to picture her belongings in here. Maybe a dresser there? No, that wouldn't work. Next to the window? Aargh! And would they share the bed? She loved Mom, but good grief. Music! She needed music!

Hurrying to the kitchen, she put a Frank Sinatra record on, letting her problems fade to the back of her mind. Man, she missed Mom and her dinners. It didn't seem worth it to put much time or thought into meals for one person, so Faith had been making a lot of scrambled eggs and sandwiches since Mom had been gone. Nothing was more depressing than eating boring food alone every night. Nine more lonely dinners until Mom was home. She sat at the table, eating her eggs and listening to Sinatra sing "If You Are but a Dream."

She had just finished up drying her dishes when there was a tapping on the back door. Glancing out the window, she saw Davis there in a pair of Levi jeans and a gray T-shirt. They made eye contact, and she knew decency demanded she let him in. She dried her hands and slowly crossed to the door. "Not out dancing tonight?" she teased.

"I still have a ways to go and I'll never have your grace." He offered her a friendly smile.

"Thanks. I'd go dancing myself, but it looks like I'm stuck here until I get Patrick's room cleaned out."

"I'm here to help."

Faith stared.

"I want to, Faith. Let me help."

"All right," she said. She backed up to let Davis in, keeping a good distance between them, then turned to head up to Patrick's room.

Davis looked surprised, but not as surprised as she felt that she had agreed. She remembered she needed the boxes she'd brought home and spun around to head back outside but bumped into Davis's chest. She jumped back immediately. "Boxes. I forgot them in the truck."

Davis looked at her quizzically and followed her outside. He put his hand on her shoulder and gently moved her aside. "I'll get the boxes; you could open the doors for me."

They made their way up the stairs, and Davis set the boxes down in the hallway before they stepped into the room together. Why was she holding her breath? She exhaled just as Davis did the same. They smiled at each other. Oh my. He should smile more often. She turned away before she became even more distracted.

She paused and looked around the room. Davis's kindness in being here was disconcerting. She needed a moment to settle her feelings. He had been phenomenal at Penwilliger Brick, and if she were being honest, she found him to be the most attractive man she knew. If she wasn't careful, her crush would be back. Crush? Faith shook her head. No, her feelings for Davis could be much more than a crush if she let them. She steeled her heart.

"What do you want me to do?" he asked.

"Let's start in the closet. We'll make a give-away pile and a pile to save."

Davis nodded and moved to the closet. He began by pulling everything down from the shelf and spreading it all out in front of Faith, who was seated on the bed. "You tell me to give or save and I'll make the piles." He jumped right in, opening a box of old music books that marked Patrick's musical progression through his grade-school years.

"Those are his memories," Faith said softly. She ran her hand over his David Carr Glover Book. "Let's put them in a pile of things to donate."

Davis hesitated. "Maybe your future kids will want to learn out of the same books their uncle did."

Faith couldn't meet his eyes and talk about her possible future children. "Maybe. Okay, let's keep those."

"What about this box of his trophies and medals?" Davis pulled several out of the box to show Faith. "Remember when he won the mile race?"

"I remember how happy he was."

"I was second, and boy, did that eat me up."

Faith laughed shakily. "You two were always competing."

There were ribbons from the school's annual field days. Patrick was a wonderful runner. Faith counted thirty ribbons, mostly blue, first place.

"I never tried to compete with him on the piano," Davis said as he held up one of the many trophies from state music competitions. "What do you want to do with these awards?"

"I think we have to throw those out," Faith said, her voice trembling. "I spoke with my mom last night, and we agreed that I would only save a box or two of Patrick's things. We have photographs of all those occasions, and I just don't see any use in storing them."

Davis set the box of awards and trophies aside.

It was decided that the baseball-card collection might be worth something and should be held on to, but the various baseball hats and uniforms from Patrick's years of playing would be donated to Goodwill. By the time the top of the closet was cleared out, Faith felt more confident in her ability to make the hard decisions. They placed all of Patrick's clothes into the give-away pile. Her hands shook when she put his wool merino suit in the pile.

"What's that?" Davis asked, noticing her pause.

"Patrick's suit. My parents bought it for him to wear to competitions." Oh, how handsome he had looked in it; the black had toned down his fiery red hair, the cut and fine tailoring making him look like a man.

"Didn't he wear it to a couple of school dances too?"

"Yes." Faith smiled. "I remember my mother paying to get it cleaned before one of the dances. She said it smelled like sweat."

"Well, he did take those competitions seriously."

"He told my mom it was work clothes and should smell like sweat."

Davis gave a sad little smile. "I suppose his piano competitions were a lot of work. I probably didn't appreciate how much effort he put into them. I just thought of him as a great baseball player who had a hobby of music."

They added Patrick's shoes to the pile.

"Maybe the room will smell better now," Davis said.

Faith gave him a half smile. The closet finished, she turned to pull a heavy box from underneath the bed. Opening it, she found that it was full of college textbooks. She pulled one out that was titled *Keys to Composing Music* and hugged it to her chest. Who would have thought it would be a box of textbooks that did her in? Tears flowed down her face. "He thought he was coming back. He didn't sell his textbooks. He thought he was going back to college."

Davis handed her his handkerchief, but when she looked up to take it, he was wiping his own tears with the back of his hand. Faith had never seen him cry. She had seen him break his arm in the fifth grade, step on a nail in the eighth grade, and get hit hard enough by a baseball that his face had been swollen and purple for weeks, but she had never seen him cry. It made her cry harder to hear the little gulping noises he made.

They sat in the room, surrounded by Patrick's accomplishments, hopes, and dreams, mourning him together.

Davis pulled himself together first. He moved back into cleaning, reached under the bed to pull out another box that lightened the mood. "Patrick's rock collection—remember this?"

"Oh yes!" Faith wiped her eyes. "It meant the world to him."

"He was pretty convinced that if we just looked long and hard enough around Payson, we would find all kinds of valuable rocks." Davis tipped the box so she could look into it. Their emotions took a different outlet as they laughed.

"I love how he's labeled them," Faith said. Each rock was neatly labeled: *Found 3-6-31, east bank of Sampson's Pond, in the corner* or *Found 2-18-31 behind Wilson Elementary School, near the fence that leads to Elm Street.*

"He was always so exact."

"I suppose that's what made him so accomplished." She ran her finger over a gray rock. "The thing that's funniest is that they're all so ordinary."

"To Patrick, each was an amazing find."

It was nearly midnight when the last picture was finally pulled off the wall, the to-keep pile loaded into boxes destined for the attic, and the give-away pile loaded into Davis's Ford. Faith put a small number of items in a box for Mom to look through, including a small leather diary. She turned the diary over before adding it to the top of the box. Would reading it make her feel close to Patrick again? Maybe, but it didn't seem right to read her brother's secrets.

"I can't thank you enough for your help," she said.

She and Davis stood side by side looking over the piles. "It's nothing," he said softly and stepped a little closer. Before she could move away, he grabbed her hand and gave it a squeeze. "There's nowhere I would rather have been tonight than here with you."

Faith looked at him and blinked the tears back. "It's hard," she said.

"For me too."

Faith gave his hand a squeeze back and then said, "Is there anything you would want? I know Patrick would have liked you to have something." That felt like the right thing to offer. Was this the beginning of forgiveness? Was this what Pastor Clemmons had meant when he said it was a process?

"Do you mind if I take the rock collection?" Davis asked.

"Not at all," Faith said. Her eyebrows lifted in surprise.

"I know it's silly. They aren't worth anything, but the memories . . . I think I was with him when we found every one of those rocks."

Memories. She nodded, and their eyes met with mutual understanding. He looked as exhausted as she felt. "Davis, thank you. I couldn't have done it without you," she said in a shaky but sincere voice.

"I'll be back Monday afternoon to help you paint. Can you get the paint purchased before then?"

"Yes." Faith followed her mom's advice, swallowed her pride, and accepted his help. "I'll go first thing Monday morning."

He said goodbye and turned to leave, clutching the box of rocks tightly to his chest. Faith sighed. Yes, Davis had talked Patrick into enlisting, but he and Mom were the only two people alive who understood the goodness and potential that was lost when Patrick died.

She stood at the window, watching Davis walk slowly down the front porch and then back toward his own home.

CHAPTER 27

Monday morning Davis, in a T-shirt and blue jeans, sat on the Penwilligers' front porch, tapping his foot. Would he and Faith have another bonding moment today? Make progress toward being partners?

She pulled up in her rickety truck, and Davis's eyes were immediately drawn to her brightness. He smiled and hurried down the steps to help carry the cans of paint. "Are you going to paint in that dress?"

"Of course not, but I had to dress up to go buy the paint. My mother would be mortified if I went to town in jeans. D'you want to set up while I change?" She handed him three paint cans.

Davis had a tarp taped down in Patrick's room before Faith came back wearing a green T-shirt and faded overalls. Her hair was wrapped in a matching green kerchief. She looked pretty in her work clothes—really pretty. She tugged at her kerchief like she was self-conscious. Had he been staring too long? He cleared his throat. "Which color on which wall?"

"The blue will go on all four walls, but this little nook is going to be soft yellow, for Rose's baby."

"Sounds good. I'll get started over here." Davis carefully dipped his roller and, without further comment, started. They painted in silence for a while before Faith spoke again. "How have you been sleeping lately?"

"Better," Davis said. "I'm not craving smoking anymore." The only thing keeping him awake at night was thoughts of Faith and Penwilliger Brick.

"I'm glad."

Davis smiled at her.

Faith's brow scrunched, and she stopped rolling paint. "Was it . . . was it the horrible things you saw in the war that kept you up?"

Did she really want to know? Did she really care? "Yes," Davis said. "It's been hard to reconcile the things I saw with what I want to believe about the world."

"Do you mean that good guys finish last?"

Davis stretched to roll the blue to the top of the ceiling. "You must have been talking to Frank. He heard that quote on the news and it's stuck with him."

"Do you believe that?" Faith asked. "That evil is winning?"

"Have you followed the Nuremberg Trials?" Davis asked. He would answer her question with what he saw currently unfolding in the news.

"I've read a little bit in the paper."

"I was reading an interesting story about a man named Raphael Lemkin who's at the trials, lobbying for a new word."

"A new word?" Faith shook her head.

"*Genocide.* It means trying to exterminate a race of people like the Nazis did," Davis said. "If the word were to have a legal meaning, then countries would be obligated to do something about genocide."

"But surely what Hitler did to the Jews will never happen again," Faith said.

"That's my hope. Evil won't win if we don't let it. The trials and people like Lemkin are fighting to make sure justice is served and that evil men don't finish first. You wouldn't believe how the Jews were treated in the concentration camps unless you saw it yourself. One of my buddies in the war, Louis Green, was a Jewish soldier from Chicago. He talked to me about the persecution of the Jews. I think we need to make legal consequences precisely so that history *doesn't* repeat itself."

Faith shivered. "Aren't these such calming colors? I think it'll be a wonderful room for Rose and her baby."

She obviously wanted a change of subject. Davis rolled for a few moments and then said, "You never did like talking about unpleasant things, did you?"

"If my talking about things could change what happened, then I would talk, but it doesn't."

Davis frowned. "That's well and fine, but sometimes you do have to step up and take a stand against evil."

"Don't lecture me."

Silence filled the room.

Davis rolled hard and fast, frustrated. Somehow they had gone from a nice moment to something that felt a lot like their argument from the night he and Patrick had enlisted. Current events hadn't been a good idea.

"Slow down, soldier; the blue is supposed to evoke peace." Faith gave him a little smile. She spoke again, and her voice was soft. "I'm sorry. I asked the question and then I didn't like the answer. You're right. I don't like thinking about evil."

Davis let out a huge breath. She was right. This was meant to be a peace offering. He and Faith didn't have to agree about everything, and really, her ability to look for the good, not the ugly, was one of the things he loved about her. He slowed his pace. They rolled for another half hour without much talking.

"Yellow here?" he said.

"Yes, please. Use this little brush for the edges."

"Got it," Davis said.

"You can start the second coat now."

"The day is hot enough; the paint's drying fast," he said. They worked well together. Could Faith see that?

They finished the room a little before one. Faith looked up at him, her pretty brown eyes wide and sincere as she repeated what she'd said to him when they'd cleaned out Patrick's room. "I couldn't have done this without you."

"It was no problem at all." He sighed. There was nowhere in the world he'd rather be than helping Faith. He'd do anything for her if she'd let him. Did she know that? How obvious were his feelings? How pathetic he was, totally smitten with Patrick's little sister, a girl who had shown no interest in him. A girl who had a dance partner she spent most of her free time with. He hammered the lids back onto the cans. "You can keep these for touch-ups."

Faith nodded. "The Penwilligers really owe the Wilsons."

Davis stepped closer to her. "I don't want you to feel obligated to me."

She dropped the brush she was holding, and it fell to the tarp. Davis took another determined step toward her. The moment seemed right. He would be direct with her. "Can we be partners, Faith? Will you commit to not selling? To staying with the store?" He was asking a lot. He was asking her to commit to not leaving for college, to staying in Payson.

She looked up at him, her beautiful eyes big and round. There was a long pause. What was going through her head? "I've been thinking a lot about college lately."

Davis's heart sank. She was being pulled to college. He couldn't blame her.

But she smiled at him. "I've been thinking how much I've learned the last two years—far more than I ever could have in college. I've learned accounting, salesmanship, people skills, and how to take care of a business. I'm a business-woman, and I see the potential of my store."

Davis blinked. Was she saying what he thought she was saying? He took another step toward her. "You're going to stay? We'll be partners?"

"I know we can build something spectacular. Yes, I would like to take you on as a business partner." She extended her hand, which he ignored. He just grinned at her. He had expected her to say no.

"That's great news! This is going to be phenomenal. I'm going to work my tail off for the store, Faith. You'll not be sorry!" He hadn't felt this kind of euphoria in years.

She smiled up at him. She looked happy. "I know you'll make our business better."

"Our business," he said with energy. "Our business—I love the 'our.'" His excitement carried him a step closer to her, and before he even realized what he was doing, he wrapped his arms around Faith, picking her up for an enthusiastic hug.

She gasped as her feet left the floor, surprise in her eyes.

He set her down but kept his hands around her waist and lowered his head toward Faith's. She seemed to move toward him, and for a fraction of a second, he thought they'd meet in the middle for a kiss, but then she moved back against the wall and twisted her head to the right. He let go of her quickly, realizing what he'd almost done, his eyes wide. He hadn't intended to try to kiss her. He had simply gotten carried away. Would she take back her offer? She looked down, and he couldn't fully see her expression. Oh no, the new paint. He yanked her forward off the wall, and she gasped again.

"Wet paint," he rushed. His cheeks felt hot, and he immediately let go again, stepping away from her.

"Do I have paint all over my back?" She turned.

"It's in your hair and, um, not exactly your back."

She groaned and gathered the paint cans as Davis stood frozen in place, and then she stepped out of the room, calling over her shoulder, "Thanks again for all the help. We'll talk more about the partnership on Monday. Freddy's picking me up soon, so I, uh, I-I'd better get cleaned up."

Davis let out an exhale of relief. She wasn't going to scold him for the attempted kiss—the first time he'd ever been turned down for a kiss. His cheeks still felt a little flushed, but embarrassed or not, at least the partnership was going to happen.

He finished cleaning up and put the supplies away. The room really did look good. He and Faith worked well together. Partners. They'd be partners. He grinned, and a memory from the war came back to him. One of the older soldiers had shown him how to track the enemy. The soldier had said to pay attention to the little details, like the grass, claiming he could tell which way the enemy was going just by the way the grass was leaning. Leaning, he'd said, was telling. Faith had leaned in to him. It had been a fraction of a second, but she had definitely leaned. He knew he shouldn't be so irrationally happy about it, but he whistled as he left the Penwilligers'.

CHAPTER 28

FAITH WAITED FOR HER MOTHER to call, sitting in the hall under the phone. She was ruminating about the almost-kiss, alternating between relief that it hadn't happened and wondering what it would have been like. She and Freddy sometimes kissed after they'd been out dancing, but there was no commitment behind those kisses. Everything with Freddy was just for fun. They had never even agreed to exclusive dating.

But Davis? Kissing him would mean something. It would be . . . what? Intense. That was the word. Faith stared at the phone. Yes, it was good the kiss hadn't happened. She was glad, wasn't she? After all, she couldn't kiss her business partner, who she had unresolved issues with.

The phone rang, rescuing her from her thoughts. "Mom!"

"Sweetheart!"

"How was your drive today?"

"Long, but I don't care. Every mile is bringing me closer to home and to you."

"I can't wait. I did a little fundraising for the monument project today."

"Oh?"

"My Sunday School class is working hard."

"That's wonderful, dear."

"Oh, and the room is almost ready for Rose. I just need to buy some bedding." She didn't add out loud *and touch up some paint from when Davis almost kissed me.*

"Thank you, sweetheart. I know it must have been hard."

There was silence, and then Faith admitted, "Davis was a big help."

"Oh?" Mom said with a hint of hope in her voice.

"I have some news that will make you happy. I've accepted his offer of partnership."

"Thank heavens!" She sounded relieved. "I've been praying."

"It's just a business partnership," Faith said, irritated at how extremely pleased Mom was. "Don't get your hopes up that it will ever be more than that."

"How's the house?" Mom asked, ever the expert at changing awkward conversations.

"It misses you almost as much as I do. How's Rose doing?"

"She's awfully quiet. Of course, listening to Cecilia talk nonstop, we're both pretty quiet."

Faith laughed. "Three more days! Give Rose a hug for me. I can't wait to hug both of you in person."

CHAPTER 29

DAVIS TUCKED HIS HANDS INTO his pockets as he waited for Pastor Clemmons to start the meeting. "Thank you all for being here," he said to Faith's Sunday School class. "Mr. Wilson is going to demonstrate a good door approach, and then we'll choose partners."

Alan Armstrong elbowed his way over to stand by Janet. The kid obviously knew a good partner when he saw her.

Davis looked away from his sister and stepped to the front of the classroom. "A good salesperson is going to make a cheerful first impression. You want to dress in your Sunday best and carry yourself with confidence. Offer your hand and then introduce yourself." He walked over to Faith, and she jumped a bit. "Hi," he said, extending his hand. She accepted his hand. He'd take any contact he could get. "I'm Davis Wilson, and I'm here to tell you about the Payson Monument project."

"I'm too busy." Faith tugged her hand away, gave him a smirk, and slammed a pretend door in his face.

Ouch. Too close to the truth.

The class laughed.

"That will certainly happen. Rejection happens all the time."

Faith flushed. Good. She knew he was referring to his attempt to kiss her.

"Anyway," he went on, "that's all right. You've got to shake it off and keep trying. We'll move to the next house and try again." He pretend-knocked on a door, which Faith pretend-opened.

"Miss Penwilliger, my, you look lovely tonight. That hat certainly brings out the beautiful red highlights in your hair." Might as well show her that he did, indeed, plan to keep trying to gain her good opinion. Frank would have been proud of Davis's attempt at sweet-talking.

Faith looked a little uncertain as she touched her green hat and said, "Why, thank you, Mr. Wilson."

The students giggled.

"A little sincere flattery never hurt a door approach," Davis said with a smile.

Faith's cheeks were pink. Good. At least he was affecting her.

He continued with his demonstration. "I'm here representing a wonderful cause. The church has a special committee that is raising funds for a monument to honor our hometown heroes who lost their lives in the war." Davis turned to the students. "A great talking point here would be to ask if they knew any of the soldiers from Payson who lost their lives in the war."

"Everyone knows someone," a boy called out.

"Exactly. Let's get them thinking of those they loved and lost before we pitch them for money."

"Crafty," Robert Sullivan said.

"For a good cause." Pastor Clemmons rubbed his hands together.

"Now," Davis continued, "you are going to approach them as if it is a given that they will want to contribute."

"How do you do that?" Carrie asked.

"You simply say that funds will be collected by November first and that every bit helps. Ask them if you can put them down for a donation."

"Isn't that kind of pushy?" a quiet girl asked.

Pushy? He'd been far too pushy when he'd tried to break up Faith and Freddy's dance partnership. "In the army I just told my men what to do. I've learned that being that pushy or bossy doesn't work in civilian life." There was a better way. "You have to help people see what they want." He looked at Faith. He hoped like crazy she would eventually want the same things he did. "We need to help our townspeople realize that the monument is something they'll be proud of, something they'll want to be part of. We can do this."

There was a chorus of amens.

"Okay, then," Pastor Clemmons said. "Let's pair up and practice the door approach with our partners. Don't forget, you and your partner will be assigned a section of town that you'll canvass on your own time. Make sure you choose someone you can match schedules with."

There was a general positioning and hustling around as everyone paired up.

Davis watched Faith approach an awkward girl who stood alone. Typical Faith, looking for someone to help.

"Oh, Miss Penwilliger, I would love to be your partner." The girl gave a relieved smile.

Lucky girl. He would have loved to work with Faith. She made everything fun.

Robert Sullivan made his way over to Davis and asked him confidently, "Would you like to be partners? I want to get a ton of donations, and I think we would be amazing together."

Davis shook hands with him. The duos made their way into corners of the meetinghouse and practiced their door approaches. Every pair was silly and giggling, except Robert and Davis. Robert practiced his door approach earnestly, asking Davis for feedback on what he could do better. The boy certainly cared about the monument. Davis suspected Robert's efforts were a credit to Faith's influence.

CHAPTER 30

FAITH PACED ON HER PORCH and waved to the Wilsons, who waited on their porch. The Wilson home was once again bedecked with yellow ribbons, but this time half of them had been shared with the Penwilliger home. Faith had painted a sign that said, *Welcome home, Rose, Cecilia, and Marcia.*

Shouldn't they be here already? She gazed anxiously up the road.

Finally! Just as dusk descended, the Buick came cruising down the road and made a sharp stop right in front of the Wilson home. Three doors flew open nearly simultaneously as the travelers emerged from the dusty car. Janet, Carrie, Mr. Wilson, Davis, and Faith all descended on them.

"What is Mom wearing on her head?" Carrie gasped.

Everyone paused in their rush to welcome the arrivals and stared at Mrs. Wilson. She had a very interesting hat on.

"Isn't it marvelous?" Mrs. Wilson asked as she patted what looked like an upside-down ice-cream cone that was dripping long trails of pink and silver ribbons down the back of her head. "It's the latest rage in the city—hats that evoke feelings."

Faith smothered a smile. It certainly did evoke feelings.

Mr. Wilson stared, his mouth agape, then gulped. "How many did you buy?"

"Seven!"

"Seven?"

Mrs. Wilson seemed to think it was a good time to change the subject. She opened her arms to her husband, which seemed to break the spell that her head topper had caused.

Faith ran to her mother.

Huge hugs were given all around and everyone talked excitedly. Mr. Wilson attempted to give his wife a welcome-home kiss without being stabbed by her hat. Faith looked over at them and laughed.

"Missed you so much," Mr. Wilson said.

"Drove the last four hours without stopping," Mrs. Wilson replied.

"Janet got a boyfriend while you've been gone," Carrie said.

"I did not," Janet said hotly. "Carrie burned dinner every time it was her turn to cook. Davis had to make us something every time she was supposed to."

Faith squeezed Mom even tighter. The back of her mind, though, was noting how sweet it was that Davis would step up and do the cooking for Carrie. Davis was like that—he pitched in and did things but didn't need the credit.

"His name is Alan." Carrie grinned.

"Oh, stop!" Janet said.

Over Mom's shoulder Faith saw Davis hug his mother and kiss her cheek while carefully using one hand to hold the cone out of the way.

"I never want to eat scrambled eggs again!" Faith said to Mom with her arms still wrapped tightly around her. She planted kisses all over Mom's cheeks. Mom smiled ear to ear and hugged and kissed Faith back.

"Did you hear Davis is the new partner at Penwilliger Brick?" Mr. Wilson asked his wife as he smiled over at Faith.

Faith returned the smile, hiding her feelings. She had no regrets about college—that decision felt right—and she was glad the Wilsons and Davis were so pleased with the partnership, but what would it be like to be business partners?

"Marcia may have mentioned that to me four or five times," Mrs. Wilson said. "I sense wonderful things from that *partnership*," she emphasized.

Ready to change the subject, Faith turned to her cousin, who had been the only quiet member of their party. Rose looked as beautiful as ever with her dark-red hair and gray eyes. She had always tended toward the thin side, but now her cheeks looked too hollow, and there were dark circles under her eyes. She was still in regular clothing, and Faith would never have guessed she was expecting. "How are you feeling?"

"Pretty tired. I might just grab my suitcase and head in if you want to show me where I'm staying."

Mrs. Wilson popped the trunk, and the group came over to admire Mom's outstanding packing.

"I can see it was no easy feat to get seven hatboxes and all your luggage into the car," Mr. Wilson said drily.

Janet and Carrie took the hatboxes into the Wilson home while Davis unloaded Rose's two suitcases. Rose paused on the front porch, touching the welcome-home sign. She looked like she was going to burst into tears. Davis moved past her, and Faith followed behind Rose with Mom's suitcase.

"There you are," Davis said cheerfully to Rose. "It's so good to see you again. It's been a while."

"I was happy to hear you made it home safely," Rose said.

"Thank you," Davis said. "And I'm happy to see you've made it to your new home safely."

Rose's eyes welled up with tears. Davis smiled at her and left, calling out, "See you all tomorrow."

Faith put Mom's suitcase in her room and then came to Patrick's—now Rose's—room to see what her cousin thought.

Rose stood by the bed, looking around the room quietly. Faith had pulled an old crib down from the attic, cleaned it up, and purchased yellow-and-white bedding for it. She had stenciled little ducklings in the nook and even painted a pretty blue pond for the ducks. Rose's bed was covered with a creamy ivory quilt. On Patrick's old desk Faith had filled a vase with yellow and white daisies and blue forget-me-nots.

"If you want to decorate differently for the baby, we can repaint any color you want, and we can do something besides ducks."

"Oh, Faith!" Rose said, putting a shaking hand to her mouth. "I don't deserve this. I can't believe you did this for me." She sank down onto the bed, looking exhausted.

"It was my pleasure," Faith said, feeling for the first time the full importance of preparing the room for Rose. "It's so exciting to have you here and to think of the baby."

Rose, choked up with emotion, whispered, "Thanks."

Faith stepped back. It was strange to see her confident cousin looking so unsure of herself, as if she were surprised to find that Mom and Faith would welcome her and her future baby. "I'll let you settle in. I imagine a nice long bath would be just the thing."

Rose gave her a tremulous smile.

Faith went downstairs, thinking how wonderful it was going to be to have her cousin living with them. She and Mom would make sure Rose knew how much they wanted her here, and soon there'd be a baby in the house.

An hour later Faith came into Mom's room and shut the door. "Tell me all the juicy tidbits you couldn't talk about over the phone, like what does Mrs. Wilson wear to bed?"

Mom smiled, put down the book she'd been reading, and patted the bed next to her. Faith happily settled in, resting her head in Mom's lap. Mom ran her fingers through Faith's hair and said with amusement, "I imagine Cecilia has a very nice white nightgown at home; unfortunately, she forgot to pack it."

"No!"

"Oh yes."

"What did she wear?"

"Her underwear."

Faith sat up in amazement to look her mother in the face. *She's not joking.* "Ew," she said and plopped back down.

"I did suggest she buy a nightgown, but every time she went out shopping, she just came back with more hats."

Faith shook with laughter, and Mom joined in.

"She's not embarrassed by much, and I think that's been helpful to Rose."

"What do you mean?"

"Rose's devastated and humiliated to be getting a divorce. Cecilia was so matter-of-fact about it and treated the situation like it was obvious that Rose had to leave."

"So it was really that bad?"

"Joey was taking her paychecks and drinking them. He spends his time in bars and with other women. I don't know what he was like before the war, but he's a bitter, angry man now, and he has no plans to ever work again." Mom shuddered. "Let's not talk about him."

"Divorce," Faith whispered.

"I never thought I would say this because I believe firmly in the sanctity of marriage, but I'm glad she's divorcing him."

Mom continued to stroke Faith's hair while Faith caught her up on the logistics of the partnership with Davis.

"How has it been working with him?"

"All right."

"You're making a face," Mom said.

"It's a little irritating to see how the customers and bricklayers all naturally turn to him as the voice of authority."

"I can see how, after all your hard work the past two years, you would feel underappreciated," Mom said.

"It's annoying. It's like some people just can't handle having a woman in charge."

"It was hard for me to see Cecilia be the one who saved the day with Rose. I planned and organized the trip, and yet somehow Cecilia was the one who was able to see clearly what Rose needed."

"Because she encouraged her to leave?"

"Exactly. I couldn't get past the idea that our family has never had a divorce. Cecilia had a different perspective than me, a healthier one. She was able to give Rose the help she needed. I guess what I'm saying is that a fresh set of eyes is never a bad thing and that it doesn't matter who gets the glory in the end."

"I know you're right," Faith mumbled into the bedspread. "It's just going to be hard to work closely with Davis when I have mixed feelings about him."

"I think . . ." Mom paused and rubbed Faith's back. "I think the root of those feelings needs to be addressed."

Faith ignored her. "Freddy isn't that excited about the partnership either."

Mom made no comment.

"Did you see the box of Patrick's things I left you to sort out?"

"Yes, I did. Thanks again for getting the room done. I know it was hard."

"Sounds like we both did some hard things the last couple of weeks."

Mom kept rubbing with soft, comforting circles.

"With Davis as a partner, I could leave him in charge and go with you the next time."

"I don't ever want to leave home again," Mom said. She thumped Faith's back as if to emphasize her words.

"Good, because I don't ever want to eat three weeks of my own dinners again."

CHAPTER 31

DAVIS SIGHED AS HE LOOKED at Faith sitting beside him in the old red truck. She had signed the partnership papers but had looked like she was sucking on a sour pickle the entire time. He had a lot of work in front of him to convince her they wanted the same things. He pulled behind the store and parked by the warehouse doors, and she popped out of the truck before he could be a gentleman and open her door.

They entered the store to find Frank, Lester, and Juan waiting for them with a bottle of champagne.

"Congratulations!" Frank said, smiling wide. "Here's to the next chapter for Penwilliger Brick."

"You aren't going to put your name on the store?" Lester looked at Davis, his tone implying Davis was being cheated.

"No, it'll stay Penwilliger Brick, a name that conveys quality and family service."

"Thank you." Faith gave him a nod.

"We don't want to change the Penwilliger brand—we just want to expand."

"Congratulations," Juan said. "You married now?"

Davis smothered a smile. He knew Juan understood what was happening but was using this opportunity to show that he thought Faith and Davis should be a couple.

Faith scowled. "No!" she said firmly. "Business partners. We just work together."

"Partners?" Juan questioned. "Freddy is your partner, yes?"

"Yes. Freddy is my dance partner."

Juan looked from Faith to Davis and then back to Faith. "Partner means like brother, yes?"

Frank laughed. "Brother. That's the right idea for Freddy."

Davis smiled. Juan knew perfectly well what the word *partner* meant. Davis was going to treat him to lunch the next chance he got.

"Right idea?" Juan put a fake confused look on his face.

"Freddy isn't my brother!" Faith flushed and narrowed her eyes at Juan, who just grinned.

Davis slapped him on the back, earning a glare from Faith.

She reached to pour them each a few sips of champagne and swiftly changed the subject. "Thank you for thinking of the champagne, Frank."

"Our expansion will be happening almost immediately." Davis tapped his foot. Bubbles of pride floated inside him. They had two new bricklayers hired. Their business was going to thrive.

Faith looked at him and shrugged. He knew she was having a hard time ceding some of the control to him. He'd made the decision about who to hire. Faith had agreed that the new men, Andrew and Ivan—both of them GIs—seemed to be good hires, but she had commented, "Make sure they know they work for me too."

Even so, Davis took a moment to simply feel happy. It was real. The papers were signed. He silently admired how sharp his new business partner looked in her navy-blue suit, pink polka-dot blouse, and cute pink hat.

He tugged at his collar and wished he had put a suit on too, but it was such a hot day, and it had just been Dad doing the legal paperwork for them. But next to Faith, he had felt shabby and too casual as he'd signed the papers in his father's law office. His clothing choice today didn't reflect how serious he was about this partnership, and he needed Faith to know it would work.

Lester and Juan left for their job, and Frank followed them out to give some last-minute instruction.

"Faith," Davis said.

"Hmm?" She set her cup down on the counter and turned to him.

"Do you remember when we went to see *The Wizard of Oz*?"

"I remember." She tilted her head, and her eyes softened. "Why?"

"I was just thinking about Patrick."

Her lips twisted in a wry smile. "He fell in love with the music."

"Patrick and I were thirteen."

"Right, and I would have been nine." She rubbed her finger around her champagne flute that rested on the counter. "You were kind to let me tag along."

Davis shrugged. He didn't remember ever being annoyed with her tagging along. "Do you remember what happened during the movie?"

Faith tensed. "The bullies?"

"Yeah, those three older boys sitting behind us. Remember how they saw Patrick crying and started making fun of him?"

Faith flushed in anger. "I remember. The music had touched him deeply, and those awful boys ruined the experience."

"They seemed so old to me at the time. College-age boys."

She frowned. "Patrick was a musician, not a fighter."

Davis sighed. Maybe he had chosen the wrong story to make his point. Still, he'd try to remind her of how well they had worked together. "Do you remember what we did?"

Her lips turned up in a teeny, quick smile. "Oh, I remember."

Davis had whispered to little Faith to go out and buy some sodas. He had instructed her to fake tripping on the way back and get the college boys as wet as possible. She had come back in carrying two sodas and had done the job thoroughly, and the boys had cursed at her. Davis had jumped up, called the usher over, and told him that the "ruffians" were swearing in front of a little lady. The college boys, mad and still cursing, had been asked to leave.

"My point is that we work well together. Penwilliger Brick has a wonderful future ahead."

She smiled and raised her glass. "To a very bright future."

"To tomorrow." Frank returned, smiling at Davis and Faith.

Davis's memory made him pause at the words. He turned to Frank and said quietly, "That's what we always said during the war when we were miserable—that we were fighting for our tomorrows."

"I like that." Frank's leathery, lined face broke into smile lines as he repeated, "Here's to tomorrow."

"May it be bright," Davis added.

"Hear, hear." Faith tilted her head to the side and said, "Penwilliger Brick—we build tomorrows." She lifted her glass.

"That's beautiful." Davis, too, lifted his glass. "We should make a sign and put it in the front window."

Glasses clinked and everyone sipped their champagne. The bubbles in Davis's drink tasted like optimism and hope—until Freddy Casper walked through the front door. He went straight to Faith, picked her up, and swung her around.

"Hiya," Freddy said. "What are you all dolled up for?"

He set her down, and she smoothed her suit jacket. "We signed the partnership papers today."

"You and Davis?"

Faith nodded, and Freddy turned to eye Davis, his eyes narrowed.

Davis resented the suspicion, but it was well-deserved. He had, after all, tried to break up their dance partnership. He nodded at Freddy.

Freddy smiled and shrugged, and the look of suspicion was gone. He turned his broad smile on Faith. "I came to ask you to cut out early and go dancing at the Bamboo Club. There's a new band taking the stage, and I want to see if they can jitter our bug."

Davis met Frank's eyes and knew he was in total agreement—grown men should not talk like that.

"I'd love to," Faith said, "but we took the morning off to get the business contract signed, and I'm afraid we have a backlog of work."

Davis nodded. They really did have a backlog. They needed to design a plan for how Ivan and Andrew would be trained and make some phone calls regarding bids. Bless the business and its busyness.

Freddy shrugged and said with good nature, "No problem. This ducky shincracker is ready any time you are."

Ducky shincracker? The man sounded sillier than Carrie.

Faith gave Freddy a hug and a kiss on the cheek. "Thanks for being so understanding. Friday will give me something to look forward to."

Davis gritted his teeth. Yes, being Faith's business partner would bring lots of sweet moments, but he would also have a front-row seat to her relationship with Freddy, and for the sake of getting along, he couldn't interfere.

"Hang in there," Frank whispered. "Remember what Churchill said: 'We shall not flag or fail. We shall go on to the end.'"

Davis raised his champagne flute.

***

A week later Davis and Faith met at the brick store before it opened. They sat together in the front office, papers spread out over the walnut desk. Davis rubbed his chin. Could they afford their own brick factory? In the long run it would save a ton of money, but it was a large chunk of money up front. He startled out of his thinking at the sound of a knock.

Faith jumped up and opened the door to let her cousin in. "My, you look nice, Rose," she said.

"Thanks."

Davis glanced over at Rose as she smoothed her loose-fitting light-brown blouse, absently thinking that she did look pretty. He turned back to the numbers.

"What's up?" Faith asked her cousin.

There was a long pause—long enough that it caught Davis's attention—and he looked back up. Rose twisted her hands awkwardly, but even though she seemed nervous, she looked so much better than when she'd arrived. Just a few weeks with the Penwilligers and her cheeks were rosy and no longer hollow.

He stood and pulled another chair over to the desk.

"Thank you." Rose sat down and looked from Faith to Davis and bit her lip. "I'm wondering if you might need a part-time secretary and accountant. As you know, I have lots of experience, both at the Pentagon during the war and for a law firm in New York after that."

Faith looked at Davis. He shrugged, trying to communicate that this was her choice. She said warmly, "That would be wonderful, Rose. I should have thought of it myself. We can give you work you could do from home when the baby comes, and you can spend the next few months until then learning how we run things."

Rose's face absolutely lit up. "Thank you," she said.

"Don't thank me. I know you'll be fantastic, and I'm ready to work fewer hours."

The cousins smiled at each other.

"Do you want to start tomorrow?"

"I'll be here anytime you want me."

Rose chatted with them a bit about the business and then stood, shook their hands, and left with her head held high.

"The dignity of work," Faith said.

"She'll be a good employee." Rose had a hard path in front of her, and Davis was glad they could help. He looked at the door she had just exited and lowered his voice. "I'm glad the divorce is going through so she can focus on her future."

"I'm sure you are," Faith said in a brusque voice.

He turned back to the paperwork, wondering what he'd done to irritate Faith.

CHAPTER 32

SHOULD FAITH JUST ASK ROSE if she had feelings for Davis? They'd be a good fit in many ways. They were both hard workers, both serious. But somehow it felt wrong. Davis wasn't meant for Rose. Faith shook her head. Rose deserved the best, and so did her baby. If Davis were to fall in love with her, it could be a happy ending for all of them.

Faith unpinned her hat and hung her suit coat up on their coatrack. Mom was at her junior cultus club, but Rose had come straight home.

"Oh hi, Faith," Rose mumbled behind a full laundry basket.

Faith rushed forward. "Let me take that. It looks heavy."

"I'm all right."

Faith took the basket anyway. She started as she got a look at Rose's pink and blotchy face. "What's wrong?"

Rose shook her head and sat down on the stairs. Faith put the basket on the floor and sat by her cousin, placing an arm around her.

She buried her head in Faith's shoulder and cried a little while Faith just held her.

"Did something happen today after you left the brick store?"

"Your mom and I went to the divorce lawyer. I can't believe I'm getting a divorce. I'm caught in ripples."

"What do you mean?"

Rose tugged Faith's hand and pulled her off the stairs and into the front room. They sat on the flowery couch.

"The ripple effects of the war. The first hit was Patrick dying. That caused a ripple. Your dad got caught in the ripple that widened and spread, carrying grief with it."

Faith nodded. "I know what you mean. The first ripple for me was Patrick enlisting. I never thought he would go. I thought he had a higher calling. He was supposed to be a musician who wrote music that changed the world." She brushed a tear off her cheek and said angrily, "Life hasn't been the same since the night I found out he was enlisting. I feel like I'll never get over the ripple effects of the war."

"I'm caught in a ripple too. The war made me impulsive. It felt like the world was ending. Patrick died, your dad died, and three of the boys I went to high school with were killed. I got caught up in the sadness of it all."

Faith touched her cousin's cheek softly and Rose continued. "I married a man I didn't know. I didn't know his beliefs, his drinking tendencies, his work ethic, or his family." She paused, emotion catching her. "I was caught up in Joey's looks, the fact that he was a soldier, and the feeling that we had to act quickly before he shipped out."

"It happened to a lot of—"

Rose cut her off. "No excuse. There's no excuse for my stupidity. I married a man who is both lazy and cruel."

"I think you can plead war and youth."

Tears rolled down Rose's cheeks. "I just—I just can't stand being the first divorcée in our family."

Faith tugged her cousin closer. "Oh, sweetie," she said. "You know Uncle Elwood and Aunt Bessie should have divorced long ago."

Rose snorted and made a little half-choking sound.

"Are you laughing or crying?"

"I'm right in between."

Faith laughed shakily, wiped her eyes, and hugged her cousin. "I know two good ripples."

"Hmm?"

"The baby and having you here. You don't know how much my mom needed something to focus on."

"You mean besides hoping you and Freddy will break up your dance partnership?" Rose asked with a mischievous glint.

Faith just shook her head.

"There's another good ripple I can see," Rose said. "You have become such a strong, competent businesswoman. I'm in awe of all you've accomplished the last two years. You learned so much."

Faith squeezed Rose's hand. She *had* learned and grown a lot.

"Tell me about Freddy," Rose said. "How did you end up spending so much time with him?"

Was Rose being critical of Freddy like Mom and Davis? She looked sincerely interested. Faith would try to explain it. "Well, things were really overwhelming after Patrick and my dad died." Faith leaned back against the couch as Rose nodded with a look of sympathy. "My mom couldn't manage the store, and I had to take over. I was working long hours and then coming home to sadness."

Rose put her arm around Faith's shoulders now.

Faith gave her a wavery smile. "I felt so lost. It was like I didn't even recognize myself. I'd always been the happy girl. The girl who smiled. The girl who laughed and joked and danced. One day after work Freddy came into the store. He was home from college, working for his dad's company and was bored. He . . . well, he, uh . . ."

"He came in and flirted with you?"

Faith nodded and her face flushed. Did that make her sound shallow? She had loved Freddy's flirting. It had made her forget her problems and feel like a normal eighteen-year-old.

"Anyway, I realized I was going to have to give up on going to college because I was needed to run the business. Suddenly I went from a high school senior with her head in the clouds to a businesswoman with serious responsibilities."

"Oh, honey," Rose said. "I knew things were hard. I guess I just didn't know how hard."

"Well . . ." Faith gulped. "Freddy helped me feel like me again. He brought dancing back into my life. I know people think he's shallow, but he made me happy." She flinched, suddenly hearing Davis's voice in her mind. *"Made you happy? . . . Does he* still *do you good, or is he just a habit?"* Why hadn't she said *makes* instead of *made?* Freddy still made her happy, didn't he? "Enough about me," she said. "Is there someone you might be interested in?" She leaned toward her cousin.

"What?" Rose exclaimed. "Are you crazy? I'm not even divorced yet!"

"Oh, well . . ." Faith rubbed her hand through her hair. "I mean, someday you'll remarry, right?"

Rose sighed and rubbed her belly. "That's hard to imagine."

The two cousins chatted awhile more, but it wasn't until Faith was lying in bed that night that she realized Rose hadn't answered her question.

CHAPTER 33

DAVIS WAS TAKING INVENTORY OF the bags of mortar powder in the warehouse when he heard Freddy's unmistakable voice in the front office. He no longer waited on the porch when he knew Faith was coming home after dancing. Frank had been right; he'd been too heavy-handed trying to interfere with her dates. He could admit that he'd been wrong to try to boss Faith and Freddy. He'd been wrong to sit out on the porch, making sure there were no good-night kisses. He wouldn't attempt interference again, but he couldn't help but be irritated every time Freddy visited her at work. It seemed the man worked only a couple of hours a week and often popped in to kill time.

"Hi, doll," he said. "You set for the Bamboo Club tonight?"

Davis moved quickly away from the door and deeper into the warehouse. Faith and Freddy went out dancing every Friday night. And every single time, Davis's instincts screamed at him to interfere, to do everything possible to stop them from being together. But he had to bide his time—ignore his instincts, so to speak. It was like being on the front line and being shot at. His first impulse told him to get out of the foxhole and run, but that was the most dangerous thing he could do.

Still, he nearly groaned aloud at the thought of Faith in Freddy's arms again tonight.

Davis paused and stared absently at a pallet of bricks when a realization hit him. He wasn't defenseless anymore. He might not be a master at dancing, but he had finished his lessons, and he could certainly do more than bob in place. The Bamboo Club, huh? Faith didn't dance every single dance with Freddy, did she? Maybe he could dance one with her.

***

Davis parked Betsy, feeling more than a little foolish. The Bamboo Club was Payson's only dance club. It was small and only open on weekends.

He tugged at his necktie, standing at the building's entrance. The music from inside blasted, and laughter floated out to him—the kind of loud, carefree laughter that he didn't relate to anymore. He turned around. This wasn't going to work. What had he been thinking? His family hadn't seen him leave. He could hurry back, and no one would be the wiser that he had ventured out.

A couple he didn't recognize jostled him as they pushed their way in. Good heavens, they looked young.

He rested his hand indecisively on the door. Faith was inside, dancing in Freddy's arms. Davis needed to show her that he, too, was fun. That he, too, could dance and joke and be lighthearted. He took a big breath, pulled the door open, and walked inside.

He blinked under the bright lights. The laughter was even louder inside. About thirty couples danced in the middle of the small dance floor. A refreshment table was set up along one wall, and chairs for those not dancing were run along another. A young man stood by a record player, tapping his foot to the music.

Of course, Freddy and Faith were already on the floor. She had some kind of flowy silver dress on. It swirled with her when she twirled. Freddy's bow tie matched her dress, which annoyed Davis immensely. He grimaced, then realized the look on his face was probably the opposite of what he was trying to achieve. He plastered a grin on and walked over to a girl who sat on a chair. "Would you like to dance?"

"Sure." The girl was cute with a button nose and lots of brown curls. She looked like a little doll. Then she stood up. Oh my, she was small. He loomed over her.

He grabbed the girl's teeny hand and led her onto the dance floor, his smile still plastered on his face. Then Faith noticed him. She stumbled in her dance, and Freddy had to catch her elbow. Davis looked down at his dance partner and grinned bigger. Fun. He needed to look like he was having fun.

"I'm Davis Wilson. What's your name?" he asked his partner. She was about a foot and a half shorter than him.

She said something in a high, squeaky voice that sounded like, "Lots of Crying." That couldn't be right.

He craned his neck down to hear her better. "Pardon?" he said. "I didn't quite catch your name."

The next record started. It was a waltz. Davis began to sweat. Nothing in his dance lessons had covered how to waltz with someone who didn't even come up to his armpits.

The girl looked overwhelmed by his looming height. "Lottie Ryan," she called up to him in her high-pitched voice. Well, that made more sense than Lots of Crying.

Davis continued to smile. He was pretty sure Faith was watching him, and even if his cheeks were starting to hurt, he was determined to show that he was fun. He was a good time.

The waltz began, and there was a very awkward moment when Lottie looked up and Davis looked down. Obviously, she couldn't do anything about their height difference. It was up to him. He hunched over, and they began a very awkward waltz.

What was Ms. Rogers's advice on the waltz? Having to hunch over was throwing him off. He did manage to keep the smile plastered on, but by the time he waltzed Lottie around the room twice, he was sweating, had knocked into three other dancers, had heard lots of snickers, and his neck was getting a crick from looking down in such an awkward way. A flash of silver drew closer, and Faith and Freddy glided by. He couldn't glance over; it was requiring all his concentration not to trample Lottie, but he'd show Faith he was having a wonderful time.

He let out a rather loud, bellowing laugh.

Lottie gave a little shriek and stopped dancing. She put her hand over her heart. "Mercy," she said.

"Sorry," Davis said loudly. "I'm just having so much fun."

"You are?" Lottie's high voice went even higher in its skepticism.

"Oh yes," Davis said, hunching back down and holding out his arm. They began their painful waltz again. His smile was genuine when the dance came to an end.

Faith and Freddy approached.

"Well, well," Freddy said, "looks like the old man is dancing." He laughed. "That was the most interesting waltz I've ever seen."

Davis wanted to hit the smug look off Freddy's face, but then, wanting to hit Freddy certainly wasn't a new sensation for him. *Smile.* He flashed them a big grin. "I'm putting my dance lessons to good use. My, it's fun," he said.

Faith's eyes narrowed. She stared hard at him, and he just grinned back. Hopefully, he looked like he was having the time of his life, not like an empty-headed fool.

One by one Davis asked the women without partners to dance. He jitter-bugged, lindy-hopped, waltzed, and foxtrotted. No, he wasn't great. But he was out there making awkward conversation with women, laughing, smiling, and pretending it was all super enjoyable. He stepped on toes, stumbled a couple of times, and bumped into several more dancers. It wasn't graceful, but he kept going, doing his best to look the picture of happiness.

He took a break after an hour of solid dancing to drink some lemonade. Elinore, the redheaded girl at the refreshment table, handed him a cup.

Suddenly there was Faith right at his elbow. "Are you having fun?" she asked.

"So much fun." He took a long sip of his lemonade, hoping his lie didn't make him choke.

"Really?"

Davis nodded but then coughed on his lemonade.

Faith just stood there staring at him. What was she thinking?

Desperate for a conversation starter, he blurted out, "How's Rose's divorce coming?"

"Fine." Faith frowned. "It'll be finalized next week."

He opened his mouth to ask her to dance, but then Freddy swooped in and Davis was left with Elinore. "Do you want to dance?" he asked her.

"I guess I could leave the table for a bit."

A swing dance played. Davis wasn't great at swing. It was too modern for Ms. Rogers to teach, but Janet had shown him the basics.

Then an idea struck. If he could just end the dance right next to Faith, he could ask her to dance the next one with him. Surely the next dance would be a waltz after the fast-paced swing. He could hold her in his arms. The thought propelled him forward. He tugged Elinore along with him as they danced their way across the floor.

He was pretty sure what they were doing couldn't be classified as swing. Freddy and Faith moved right, so Davis pulled Elinore right. Good heavens, Freddy covered a lot of ground. Davis did a little hop, step to cover more ground. Darn. Elinore hadn't come with him. He turned to find she had fallen to the dance floor. She glared up at him.

"Upsy-daisy," he said and pulled her back to her feet.

Elinore gasped but came along as he did his version of the swing and continued to follow Faith and Freddy.

"Did you ever hear what Ginger Rogers said about dancing and men?" Elinore asked him.

"No," Davis answered, his eyes following Faith and Freddy's movements.

Elinore pulled on his hand, and he turned to find her still glaring at him. "She said that part of the joy of dancing is conversation but that the trouble is some men can't talk and dance at the same time."

Davis nodded. He'd process the insult later.

The accident wouldn't have happened if that darn Freddy Casper hadn't been trying to move across the dance floor away from him. Davis, intent on catching up, failed to see how close he and Elinore were to the refreshment table.

He grabbed her hand and swung her hard. The pull gave her momentum—too much momentum—and she flew past him, right into the refreshment table. The legs of the old table held for a moment, then groaned and collapsed. Cupcakes flew off, arcing high into the air. They peaked and then submitted to gravity, hitting dancers and spattering across the floor.

The punch bowl, though, was the really spectacular part. It soared up and over the dance floor, spraying the dancers with sticky liquid.

Girls squealed, men hollered, and the fake smile finally left Davis's face. He could stop pretending he was having fun. This—this was a full-scale disaster.

CHAPTER 34

Saturday, the morning after the Bamboo Club fiasco, found Faith, Mom, and Rose eating breakfast together.

"Good heavens," Mom said and set the orange-juice pitcher down. "Did anyone get hurt?"

Faith laughed a bit. "No one was hurt, but we all got doused in lemonade. They had to shut the club down for the night to clean up. Plus, everyone was sticky and wanted to go home and change."

"Poor Davis," Rose said.

"Poor Davis, my eye," Faith responded. "He was acting so strange. You should have seen him pulling his partner all over the dance floor. It was the oddest swing dancing I've ever seen."

"He seems like such a steady man," Rose said. "I wonder what possessed him." She sipped some orange juice, her brows scrunched together.

Faith buttered her toast. "Freddy thinks Davis was out to get him."

"Get him?" Mom's eyebrows rose sky-high.

Faith nodded. "He's been wary of Davis ever since the night of the dance competition when he rode home with him from the Swingin' Stars Club."

"Oh?" Rose leaned back in her chair.

Faith flushed and explained. "Davis was inappropriately trying to prevent me from going out with Freddy."

"He was trying to scare Freddy off?" Rose said.

"Pretty much. So I showed him what being interfered with feels like, and he's backed off since then."

Rose's eyes and mouth were round *O*'s.

"Anyway," Faith went on, buttering her toast so hard the knife went clean through, "Freddy was convinced Davis was following him across the dance floor for some unknown, threatening purpose."

Mom snorted.

"Well, whatever was going through his head, he stayed to help the club owners scrub lemonade off the floor."

"Which reminds me, your silver dress will be fine," Mom said. "I put it to soak. The lemonade should come right out of it."

Faith nodded. "Long night for Davis last night, and he'll have another long night tonight. We're meeting to look over some inventory numbers Rose prepared."

"On a Saturday?" Mom asked.

"Poor Davis," Rose said.

Faith frowned. Why was Rose worried about Davis?

***

Inventory was the worst, but at least Faith didn't have to do it alone. She and Davis had already spent three hours seated at the big desk, going over the numbers. All they had spoken of was bricks, numbers of pallets ordered, and numbers of pallets used. The quiet man surrounded by stacks of papers didn't seem like the same one who had danced so energetically last night.

Faith, from her side of the desk, pushed a stack of papers aside. She needed a break from numbers. "Did it take a long time to get the lemonade cleaned up last night?"

Davis's face went a bit pink, and he looked up at her. "Uh no, it was fine. I was home by midnight."

"Rose was worried about you having two long nights in a row." Faith fidgeted, tugging on her blue blouse.

"That was kind of her." He turned back to the numbers he'd been looking at.

Did he have feelings for Rose? Maybe she should just ask. "Davis?"

"Hmm?"

"Nothing."

He looked up again. "It's something. What is it?"

"Do you like Rose?" Faith asked in a rush.

Davis's mouth dropped open. The pen in his hand dropped to the desk. "Like, as in 'like to date'?"

"Never mind." She felt her face heat. That question, based on the shocked look on his face, had been a mistake.

"I can honestly say that never occurred to me."

"Ah, well, let's look at those numbers," Faith said, grabbing a random handful of papers. She wouldn't meet his eyes. Why did she feel relieved?

The room went still. Davis had quit moving papers around. She peeked across the desk to find him staring intently at her. "You must know what everyone in town seems to know," he said.

She furrowed her eyebrows. What did he mean?

"You're the only woman I have any interest in."

Her heart skipped a beat, and she looked back down at the papers.

"I love working with you, but, Faith, there could be so much more for us." He reached over and gently lifted her chin to look him in the eyes. She pulled out of his grasp.

"Do I have any chance at all with you?"

Faith met his eyes but didn't answer.

His shoulders dropped. "Because of Freddy?"

Faith nodded, then added, "And Patrick."

Davis frowned. "Faith, Patrick did the right—"

"No he didn't!" she interrupted. Patrick was an easier topic to fight about than Freddy. She glared at Davis. All her pent-up feelings rose to the surface. "He was a musi—"

"He did what his heart told him he had to!" Davis looked mad.

"He was *not* a soldier; he never should have—"

"You're wrong," Davis said. "You don't know what it was like to know in your heart that you had to—"

"No, you're wrong! He only went because, just like when you were kids, you convinced him—"

"That's not true!"

"You led and he followed! He wasn't a soldier! He—"

"Who do you think fought the war? *Professional* soldiers?" Davis crumpled a piece of paper and dropped it onto the desk. He leaned away.

"He shouldn't have gone. He didn't have to go. He was my parents' only s—"

"He wanted to go." Davis's fists balled.

Faith threw the crumpled paper to the floor. "Patrick wouldn't have wanted to leave his music! He wanted to be like you. You talked him into—"

"I did not!" Davis stood abruptly.

"He was their only son," Faith said. She stood too, and they faced each other across the desk, each of them with clenched fists and flushed faces.

"He was no Freddy Casper, finding a doctor to say he had flat—"

"Freddy does have flat feet."

"Funny. That never stopped him from dancing." Davis slapped the desktop with his open palm.

"Why does this conversation have to include Freddy?"

"The same reason our fight the night I told you Patrick and I were enlisting included Daisy."

"What does that mean?"

"I already told you." He moved closer to her. He was flush up against the desk—towering over it, really.

The room was silent.

Davis looked like he was struggling to calm his breathing and regain composure. "For whatever it's worth, what you said about Daisy that day was exactly right. She—"

Faith put her hand out to silence him. She glared at him across the desk, folded her arms, and said, "I was only sixteen. I didn't have any right to comment about your relationship with Daisy, but you didn't need to attack me that night and tell me I was a spoiled princess." Her voice shook a little. It still hurt, that moment when her hero had denounced her.

"I was immature and thought everyone would be impressed with my enlisting. Your response took me off guard. I shouldn't have said what I did." He paused and rubbed his face. "But I thought about every word you said about Daisy."

Faith leaned away from him. "We don't have to talk about her." She was still embarrassed by the memory of what she had blurted out.

"You were right when you said you were meant for me." His hand reached across the desk and brushed her elbow.

Faith flinched. "I had had a crush on you for years. I was naive."

"You were right," he repeated. "The best thing that happened to me was her writing to break it off."

Faith didn't say anything. She couldn't. She was too confused—part anger and part sadness.

He reached out again and gently grabbed her arm. "But you were wrong about Patrick. He wanted to fight. He felt called to fight." He stopped talking and looked at Faith as if waiting for her to interrupt. She gripped the edge of the desk, and her lips pressed tightly together as she glared at him.

He took a big breath and looked at her with a sad expression in his eyes. "Faith, you have to understand the type of evil we were fighting against. When we liberated Buchenwald, Eisenhower said nothing had ever shocked him more. Right in the middle of that beautiful valley was pure evil. The emaciated"—he stopped, a memory catching him—"the poor skeletons who greeted us, too weak to get up, cheering from their beds, five to a bunk, packed—absolutely packed—in . . . their hollow eyes will haunt me till the day I die."

Her gaze was directed at the wall behind him, but she could feel him lean closer to her.

"We brought the local townspeople to tour the camp. They claimed they knew nothing. That valley is the birthplace of Goethe, a bedrock of German culture. But all the culture in the world can't cover up that kind of stink."

Faith's head whipped back toward Davis, her lips trembling. "Do you think I'm like the German townspeople, living in my own selfish world, ignoring evil?"

"No, no," he said adamantly. His hands gripped the sides of the desk. "I love that you look for beauty in everything. No, I'm just saying that is what Patrick fought for. Good prevailed because of men like Patrick who fought. They weren't professional soldiers; they were decent men who answered a call."

"He wrote to us the month before he died that he had a beautiful composition that was developing in his head. He never got to put it down on paper. We'll never hear his music—what he could have created. The possibilities were unlimited." Faith's voice and hands shook wildly.

"I know. He knew how much the music and his training meant to your family. That's why he sent me that night to tell you we were enlisting. It broke his heart to know he was going to break yours, but, Faith, after Pearl Harbor, *he* came to *me* and told me he was going to enlist. He made the decision first; *I* followed."

The room went silent again, and they stared at each other for a long moment.

"I need to go home." Faith stood abruptly and left the papers on the desk. She grabbed her purse and hat.

Davis said nothing but just watched her leave. The door gave an ironic jingle as she closed it quickly behind her.

Her heart pounded all the way home. Patrick had been the one to choose to enlist? He had decided before Davis? It was too much to take in. She replayed Davis's words all through her short drive home. By the time she went through the front door she was crying. Stupid, stupid, hateful war.

CHAPTER 35

IT HAD BEEN A MONTH since the big argument, and politeness marked every conversation and interaction between Faith and Davis. He was determined to prove himself a good partner. Even if Faith could never care for him in the way he cared for her, even though she went out dancing several times a week with Freddy, he hoped she would at least respect him as an asset to the success of Penwilliger Brick.

November first arrived, the day of Frank's retirement, and Davis and Faith were awkwardly working together to make sure he had a good party. "Where would you like the table?" he asked her.

"Where do you think?" she asked ever so politely back.

"I'll defer to you."

Did she roll her eyes?

"Let's put it right in the middle of the warehouse, and then I'll load it with the refreshments."

"Excellent," Davis said as if talking to a respected general.

Faith spread the red tablecloth out. "It was good of your mother to lend us the decorations from your reception."

Davis nodded. The reception felt like forever ago. Back then he had felt so lost and sleepless. A lot had changed. He slept well now. The thoughts of death didn't plague him like they once had. He was a partner in a flourishing business, and he was in love. He smiled wryly. The old man on the train had been right when he'd said to just get on with life. If only Faith loved him back.

He looked around the warehouse. Even with the awkwardness between them, today was going to be a great day. Mom's patriotic bunting hung from the walls, making the big room look festive. Davis and Faith, with a little help from Rose, had transformed the warehouse. They would surprise Frank when he returned from his morning job.

Frank's wife, Edith, entered from the front just as Juan and Lester came in from the back.

"I'm hungry," Lester complained. "When do you think Frank will be back?"

"He and Ivan should be back shortly. We'll yell 'Surprise' right as they walk through the door." Davis shook his head. Lester had worked with Frank for at least twenty years, and all he could think of was his own hunger?

Rose came in carrying a basket of fried chicken. "Aunt Marcia is coming with more food," she said.

Davis hurried over to relieve Marcia of a huge box. He'd lent her Betsy so she could drive the food over.

"Ooh, yummy," Faith said as Rose pulled out a layer cake with *Happy retirement, Frank!* written on it. They placed fresh rolls, corn, and Marcia's famous honey butter on the table. Andrew, Juan, and Lester helped Marcia unload the rest of the food from Davis's car. The table was set for a feast.

"Let's turn the lights off," Rose suggested.

The group waited in silent dimness.

Funny, Davis thought. *Even in the darkness I know where Faith is.* She was on his left, about five feet away, standing next to Marcia.

They heard Costello pulling up behind the warehouse, the engine loud.

"No way we wouldn't hear him coming," Faith whispered to her mother.

The back door opened, and a shaft of bright light flooded in.

"Why are the lights off?" Frank's voice sounded confused.

Everyone yelled "Surprise," except Juan, who, getting into the spirit of the occasion, jumped at Frank and let out a blood-curdling scream. Faith and Marcia gasped as Frank fell to the warehouse floor and curled into a fetal position.

Davis hurried to flip the lights back on, and Faith, Edith, and Marcia all ran over to help Frank up.

"My living stars!" Edith exclaimed. "Has he had a heart attack?"

"What are you trying to do?" Frank gasped, sitting up, his face pale.

"Surprise you," Faith said.

"Well, it worked." He looked around at the decorations and smiled. "You didn't have to do this!"

"We wanted to!" Davis said.

"We love you, Frank!" Faith said.

"I hope my retirement party is a little calmer," Lester said.

Juan grinned from ear to ear. "I got you."

"Oh yeah, you got me," Frank said. "I thought you were a robber."

Davis couldn't help smiling a little at the picture Frank and Juan made.

"Here to steal your bags of cement powder?" Edith asked.

"Idiot," Lester said to Juan. "It's a surprise party, not a let's-kill-the-old-man party."

"Hey!" Frank boomed. "I might be retiring, but I'm not an old man. I'm in the prime of my life."

"Right, dear." Edith rolled her eyes. "You're the guest of honor—come dish up."

Everyone followed Frank eagerly, grabbed food, and found seats—the women on the few chairs, the men on bags of cement powder. Frank looked like he had gotten over his scare as he laughed, chatted with everyone, and ate.

Marcia sat by Davis and said, "'Men are like bagpipes. No sound comes from them until they're full.'"

Davis smiled. He loved her Irish sayings. "There's real truth in that one!"

After the meal, Faith announced that she wanted to say a few words. The group gathered around her, and Davis leaned against the warehouse wall. He knew how much Frank meant to her.

"Frank, this might be the hardest speech I've ever given." She looked down at a note card. "All my earliest memories of the brick store have you in them. You've always been a constant in my life, but I didn't appreciate what a constant meant until"—she paused and swallowed—"until my dad died."

The room was silent. Davis longed to stand by her and put his arm around her shoulder. He straightened against the wall. Comforting her wasn't possible. There was a rift between them. He smiled at her, trying to show her his support. She met his eyes for a moment, and he thought he saw confusion.

Faith turned back to Frank. "There aren't many sixty-eight-year-old men who could accept an eighteen-year-old boss. Not only did you accept me graciously, but you also made sure I succeeded." She had the room's complete attention. "You've been my sounding board, my strength, and my sanity, and I've been dreading this day for a long time." She cleared her throat. "Thank you for staying two years longer than you wanted to. I've watched your mustache go from brown to white over the years, but it has always been beautiful and constant, just like you."

"Hear, hear!" Davis called out.

"Amen!" Juan said.

"We love you, Frank," Marcia said.

Frank smoothed his mustache, his eyes bright. Edith cried beside him.

"So even though this gift isn't compensation for your generosity to Penwilliger Brick, we hope it's something that'll remind you of how much we adore you," Faith added. She handed a box to Frank. Edith stepped closer to watch as paper and ribbon fell to the floor and Frank reverently pulled out his gift.

"A Hallicrafter shortwave radio," he said with reverence.

Edith laughed. "That answers what he'll be doing during retirement."

"We know how much you love following world news," Marcia said.

Davis stepped forward holding an envelope. Faith had said he should be the one to make their big announcement. "Frank, you taught me all the tricks of the trade. You're an excellent teacher whom I respect immensely. I've loved working with you, and I'm going to miss our talks about everything from the news to the best way to barbecue meat. You are irreplaceable."

Frank gave Davis a salute.

"Here's a well-deserved thank-you from the Penwilligers and me." He passed Frank the envelope and gave him a hug.

Frank opened the envelope, pulled out a paper, and stared for a long moment without saying anything. "Ten-percent ownership of Penwilliger Brick." Tears welled in his eyes.

Edith gasped and put her hand to her mouth.

"I didn't know we were doing gifts," Lester said.

Davis and Faith looked at each other, and Faith rolled her eyes. Davis shook his head as if to say, "Yep, that's Lester—you get what you get."

Marcia and Juan came over to add their congratulations.

"I have a little something to say," Marcia said, surprising everyone. She hated the spotlight. "What you did for the war effort was significant. You are every bit as much of a hero as the soldiers who fought. When the men were gone, you stepped up and helped keep Penwilliger Brick from closing. You are the reason we are still in business today."

Frank pulled his handkerchief out and blew his nose.

Marcia took a moment and collected herself. "Charles would thank you, if he were here, for helping Faith keep the business going."

"It was nothing." Frank's chin trembled.

"What you've done has meant everything to Faith and me."

A few tears trickled down Frank's weathered cheeks and landed in the curls of his mustache.

"And," Marcia said, "I leave you with an Irish blessing: 'May the raindrops fall lightly on your brow. May the soft winds freshen your spirit. May the sunshine brighten your heart. May the burdens of the day rest lightly upon you. And may God enfold you in the mantle of His love.'" She gave Frank a hug and stepped aside for Juan.

"Is your heart normal again?" Juan asked.

"Yes," Frank responded drily. "My heart is back to normal."

Juan thumped him on the back and said, "You looked very funny." He did an imitation of Frank falling to the ground and curling up.

Frank sniffed. "It wasn't funny. I got dirt on my mustache."

Juan snickered, and the others surrounded Frank, chatting and smiling. Warmth flowed freely, and even Lester seemed happy as he ate a big piece of Marcia's chocolate cake.

CHAPTER 36

"WHAT ON EARTH WAS YOUR mom wearing on her head?" one of Faith's Sunday School boys asked Janet and Carrie. They were gathered in the classroom waiting for Faith to begin her lesson.

"None of your business," Janet said.

"It's the latest style from New York," Carrie responded in defense of her mom.

"It looks like she has a nest on her head."

Faith silently agreed.

"Does she worry when she's outside that birds are going to come roost?"

Janet flushed, and—oh dear—Carrie looked like she was going to deck someone. Faith cleared her throat. What could she say to sidetrack the teasing? Pastor Clemmons, Davis, and Robert Sullivan entered her classroom while she was thinking of what to say. Good timing. She exhaled and smiled at the men.

"We have some fundraising totals to report," Pastor Clemmons said. He beamed. This must be positive news.

Faith nodded at Robert, who smiled back.

"We want to announce the total to your class first, as a thank-you for all the hard work you've done." The good pastor nodded at the teens, and the students sat a little taller in their seats. "The grand total is impressive," he said. "We will be able to build a marvelous monument." His eyes squinted as if he were looking far into the future and liked what he saw.

Faith's Sunday School class had collected donations for over two months. The entire town had been canvassed by the energetic teens. She looked over her class. Faith's students had put real effort into the project, and she couldn't be prouder of them.

Robert stood tall but twisted his hands. It must have taken some talking to get him to come back to the church. Faith supposed Pastor Clemmons had gone to his home and brought him so he could report what he had fundraised.

"Robert," Pastor Clemmons said, "no one worked harder than you and Davis. I'd like you to announce the grand total." He handed Robert a piece of paper.

Davis rested his arm across Robert's back.

"Seven thousand eight hundred and twenty-five dollars."

There was a moment of shocked silence and then cheers all around.

"And over two thousand of that came from Davis and Robert's efforts," Pastor Clemmons said.

"That was all Robert," Davis said. "I've never met a better salesman."

Robert tugged at his sweater and stood up straighter. Janet looked at him with admiration in her eyes.

"Speech, speech, speech," one of the boys called.

Robert flushed but looked pleased. "The men who died deserve this monument. This is more important than my baseball or any junk we'll do at school this year."

"Hear, hear!"

Over the hubbub of self-congratulations, Davis met Faith's eyes and gave her a smile and a salute. She smiled in return and let herself gaze back at him. He kept his eyes on her for a long moment.

As they filed out of the church, energy still high among the teens, he stepped behind her and said quietly, "I admit it was a good idea."

In a soft voice, without turning to look at him, she said, "I admit you carried it out well."

***

Sunday dinner was a happy affair that evening. Faith told Mom excitedly about the fundraising and how pleased Robert Sullivan had been.

"Do they have the location yet?"

"It looks like it'll be on the west side of Collier's Park."

"And all the boys' names will be engraved in stone?" Mom asked.

Faith nodded and reached over to squeeze her hand. "Never forgotten."

"Well done," Rose said.

Faith smiled at her pretty cousin, who finally looked like she was expecting. With three in the household, the meals had transformed back to the dining room. They passed around the steaming spareribs, vegetables, rolls, and fruit.

"This looks absolutely marvelous, Mom!" Faith said. It had been nearly two months since she had had to cook for herself, but she still felt immensely grateful each time she sat down to home-cooked food and warm conversation.

Rose nodded and shot Mom a smile, and the trio held hands while Mom said grace.

"Amen."

Conversation and laughter flowed throughout the meal. At one point Mom said, "Davis told me yesterday that there are some promising things on the horizon for Penwilliger Brick."

Faith nodded. "He's found a brick factory that may be willing to sell to us. It's up past Lima."

"That seems kind of far."

"It's doable."

"Three-hour drive?"

"Yes, and if we can buy this factory, it'll be huge for our business. We could even hire bricklayers in the area around the factory so we could contract for jobs up there." Faith sat up straight, feeling nerves course through her. "Davis and I are going to go Friday to check out the brick factory and make an offer if it looks good."

Rose nodded. "According to the books, the business is doing remarkably well—the numbers are there for expansion."

"Rose has helped us with number crunching, and we're all feeling great about our future. I'd say it looks brick solid."

"Ha, ha," Rose responded.

"How are the new bricklayers working out for you?" Mom asked.

"Oh, they're marvelous," Faith gushed. "Andrew and Ivan are making fast progress."

"Hard workers?"

"Both GIs," Faith said.

"That doesn't always mean much," Rose said, looking down at her plate. "Not all GIs are like Davis Wilson."

Faith bit her lip. Davis had said he didn't have feelings for Rose, but did Rose have feelings for him? If so, Faith certainly couldn't blame her.

Mom put her hand on Rose's arm to give a little comfort.

There was a loud honking out front; the horn beeped in a rhythmic pattern.

"Sounds like Freddy," Mom said with a frown. "Where are you off to?" Faith didn't usually go out with Freddy on Sundays.

"He wants to go on a Sunday drive. I'll be back by eleven."

Rose rubbed her belly. "Long past my bedtime," she said.

Faith smiled, but she didn't have her usual energy as she headed out the door. To tell the truth, she'd rather stay in tonight. Freddy honked again.

As Faith headed out, Mom inexplicably said, "'Pains and patience will bring a snail to America.'"

CHAPTER 37

ON A CRISP NOVEMBER DAY, Davis stood in the Penwilligers' kitchen waiting for Faith.

"Do you think the red hat is all right?" Faith asked Davis. He shifted from foot to foot, looked at her quickly, and then looked away. The bright-red hat perched jauntily on the top of her head. She looked gorgeous. Didn't she know how pretty she was? But she smoothed her matching red cardigan and looked at him anxiously.

She had let him into the kitchen while she put the lunch Marcia had made them into a basket. They had a three-hour drive ahead of them, an important decision to make about buying the brick factory, and then the same long drive home. He'd be alone with her for hours today, and during those hours he would have to concentrate on *not* noticing how pretty she looked. He cleared his throat and simply said, "You look very businesslike. Do I look all right?" He wore the charcoal suit that Janet had said made him look like Cary Grant and a tie she'd claimed "brought out his eyes," whatever that meant.

"Yes," Faith said. "You look very . . . *businesslike* too."

"Well, should we be off?"

She grabbed her gloves, and Davis led the way to his Ford. The air was brisk and smelled like fall. He hurriedly set the food by the trunk and then rushed to open Faith's door for her. The door creaked. The ride wouldn't be as smooth as Freddy's Alfa Romeo, but Betsy would get them there.

"Thank you," Faith said.

Davis nodded, loaded the basket of food into the trunk, and hurried around to settle himself behind the wheel. This was going to be a great day. Brick factory purchased or not, he had Faith all to himself.

"Your car smells nice."

"Thanks." He had cleaned it for her last night, literally scrubbing small spots of dirt with a toothbrush. It was as clean as Marcia's kitchen now. His chin went up. His Ford was no Alfa Romeo, but he could vouch it ran well and there wasn't a speck of dirt inside.

"Did you clean it for me?" Faith played with her gloves, pulling them off her hands slightly and then back on again. She looked nervous.

He evaded the question with one of his own. "Ready?"

He'd confessed his feelings for her, and she'd said it would never work out. Since then they'd been polite to each other, and they were running the business efficiently. How would he describe his relationship with Faith now? *Awkward business partners* probably summed it up best. His feelings were still there, strong as ever, but he did everything he could to keep them buried. He glanced over at her. She didn't need to hear him say how much he wanted to impress her. She could interpret the ultraclean car however she wanted.

Faith exhaled. "Ready."

Davis started the car, shifted into drive, released the clutch, and they were off. They were quiet as they made their way out of town. This would be a long three hours if they couldn't think of anything to say to each other. He glanced over at her again. She sat on the edge of the seat, looking anything but relaxed.

"I like the lemon smell."

"Thanks," Davis said.

"What is it?"

He cleared his throat. "It's, uh, it's a leather polish I used on the seats. It buffs them up nicely and smells good."

"It's a nice car."

"But like you once said, it's no Alfa Romeo."

Faith groaned. She looked sheepish. "Sorry for insulting your car. I was really mad about your interfering with my date."

Davis grinned. It was a good sign that she didn't say Freddy's name. Calling him a date sounded pretty generic. "Betsy accepts your apology."

Faith laughed. "You never did have much creativity with names."

His shoulders relaxed. This teasing was good. It was progress. He liked the teasing Faith so much better than the serious, polite businesswoman of the last two months. "What would you have named her?"

She tapped her chin, and Davis turned his attention back to the highway. She was too distracting. He needed to concentrate on the road.

"She's such a lovely color of green. Maybe Greenelda."

Davis groaned this time. "You should never be allowed to name anything. Good heavens. Your poor future children."

She blushed and changed the subject. "I can drive part of the way if you get tired."

"That would be nice. I'll have you drive when we get to Dayton so I can take one more chance to look over the numbers Rose prepared." He flipped the radio dial. "You mind if I put some music on?"

"No, I love having the radio on."

Bing Crosby's beautiful voice rang out as he sang "I Can't Begin to Tell You." Davis glanced over at Faith. The words would be his words if he could express his feelings. She squirmed in her seat. Did this song make her uncomfortable?

"Chickery Chick" came on next. She seemed to like the silly song, bobbing her head to its rhythm.

They listened to the radio together all through the time Davis drove, and he occasionally commented on the song. Faith was quiet but very fidgety during the love songs and spent most of her time looking out the window, admiring the beautiful fall leaves that remained on the trees. That probably wasn't a good sign.

When Davis pulled into a gas station in Dayton, the attendant cleaned their windows and refilled the tank while Faith took a minute to go to the ladies' room.

Then Davis turned the driver's seat over to Faith, stretched his long legs, tipped his seat back, and pulled out the sheet with the numbers to look at again.

"You don't mind a woman driving Greenelda?"

"I don't mind you driving," Davis said.

"I pass?"

"You're a great driver."

She smiled, the little dimple on her cheek popping out. Man, he would love to kiss that spot. He shook his head and turned his attention back to the numbers.

They continued in silence again until another love song came on. Faith turned off the radio and said, "We'll keep it quiet while you go over the numbers."

Davis talked numbers with her as they made their way down the highway. "Don't forget we want to bargain for their delivery trucks as part of the package."

"Right. You lead off in the negotiations," Faith said. "They'll take you more seriously, and then I'll add details in."

"Good plan. Want the radio back on?" Davis asked as he finished up with the papers and slipped them into his briefcase.

"Let's listen to a news station."

Davis's eyebrows went up. She wanted news? He turned the dial until he found a local station that rebroadcast national news. The announcer was reporting on the recent midterm election. "The Republican party captured control of both houses. The Democrats lost eleven seats to a now-Republican majority of fifty-one. The house nearly reversed itself as the Democrats lost a 242 to 191 majority to become Republican-held with a 246 to 188 advantage."

"I guess that's pretty bad news for Truman," Davis commented.

"Not sure the country is buying into his post-war policies," Faith said.

"I did hear that his daughter, Margaret, made her debut singing at the Metropolitan Opera."

Faith smiled at Davis and said, "Pride in your children's musical accomplishments goes a long way, huh? Probably helped Truman feel better about the election results." She looked thoughtful. "Nothing made my parents happier than watching Patrick play in a piano competition."

Davis nodded. Good. It was the first time she'd mentioned Patrick since their fight. "I could never figure out what the big deal was. I thought piano was fluff, that the real stuff of life was sports."

Faith laughed softly. "I remember you coming over after a competition that Patrick had won. You said something like, 'That's great! Now, let's go hit some balls.'"

Davis smiled sheepishly. "That sounds about right."

"You were good for him."

"Thanks." Tears stung Davis's eyes. She might think he was responsible for Patrick enlisting, but at least she acknowledged that there had been a lot of happy, good times growing up. Time for a lighter topic. "Let's hope President Truman feels consoled by Margaret's talent," he said.

The radio announcer went on to report sporting news.

"I listened to that game last night," Davis said.

"What game?"

"The Army–Notre Dame football game. Did you hear what the newscaster said?"

"Sorry, my mind was wandering."

"Oh, what on? Are you thinking about buying Harris's factory?"

"Something like that." Faith rubbed the steering wheel.

"I wish I could have been at the game." Davis slapped his open palm on his knee.

"Who won?"

"You really weren't listening to the radio? They just said it ended tied zero to zero."

"Doesn't sound too exciting."

"It was kind of painful to listen to."

"You wanted army?"

"Of course!"

Faith jumped as he burst into "The Army Goes Rolling Along."

She laughed. "Stop, please, you're hurting my ears."

Davis only sang louder, and she laughed harder. He glanced her way. She made quite the cheerful picture in her bright-red hat and cardigan. It was a good sign that they could laugh together, right?

She pulled into the warehouse and parked. They stepped onto the gravel drive and eyed the building.

"It looks in good repair," Davis said.

"Positive sign that it doesn't need to be painted," Faith added.

"Let's go find Mr. Harris."

Clive Harris turned out to be a short, plump man around seventy. He eyed them without smiling as they shook hands all around. "Let's go see the factory," he said without any preamble. He motioned them through the double doors that led into his warehouse.

Mr. Harris's tour took two hours. Davis and Faith asked hundreds of questions that he answered in his gruff, brief way. They met all five of his employees during the tour and saw every corner of the factory, and then Mr. Harris finally ushered them back into his office. He motioned for them to sit at a little table and held a chair out for Faith, indicated one for Davis, and seated himself. "What do you think of my factory?" he asked bluntly.

"It's well run," Davis responded.

"It also looks like it has been well maintained," Faith said. "Are you interested in selling?"

Davis took a long look at the serious Mr. Harris. Did he really want to sell? He hadn't smiled once or even tried to promote his factory.

"If you're the right buyers," he answered curtly.

"Why are you selling now?" Davis asked.

For the first time, they saw emotion on his plump face. "I had three sons; they were all killed in the war. Tommy and Bryant fought and died at Iwo Jima. Clive Jr. was captured in the Philippines. We didn't know till the end of the war that he died on the Bataan Death March."

"I'm so sorry," Faith said.

"My wife didn't want them to fight. That's the worst of it. I pushed them all to enlist, and now they're gone." He cleared his throat. "All my wife wants now is to retire down by her sister in Florida. Selling my factory and taking her to Florida is the least I can do." The room was completely silent. Davis couldn't look at Faith. Mr. Harris's situation hit far too close to home.

"She'll come to understand it wasn't your fault," Faith said. "Give her time."

Davis's eyes flew to Faith. She smiled sweetly at Mr. Harris. Did she mean it? Was it possible she no longer blamed him for Patrick enlisting?

Mr. Harris cleared his throat and said matter-of-factly, "I don't have any children left to take over for me. My daughters have both married well—one to a doctor, one to a professor. Nobody in my family wants my factory."

Davis moved to the edge of his seat. Excitement made his foot tap. He looked Mr. Harris in the eyes. "We want it."

"I have some concerns about the two of you," Mr. Harris said.

"Concerns?" Faith asked.

"Well, yes. For one thing, you're awfully young, and for another, it's mighty unusual that one of the partners is a woman. I don't want to sell my business to any fly-by-nighters."

Faith opened her mouth, probably to defend herself, but Davis beat her to it. "I can assure you, Mr. Harris," he said, "Miss Penwilliger is most serious. She has run her business competently." He paused. "More than competently. She has run her business expertly the last two years. I must say that she is hardworking, creative, honest, and thoroughly responsible. She was able to hold her business together during the war years because of those qualities." He stopped talking.

Faith blinked rapidly, surprise written on her lovely face. Surely she must have known that was how he felt.

He added one more comment for good measure. "She's no fly-by-night. Miss Penwilliger gave up her dreams of college to stand by Penwilliger Brick Store. She has shown in every way possible how dedicated and loyal she is."

"Thank you," Faith whispered. She turned to Mr. Harris. "And I can assure you that while Mr. Wilson is young, he embodies the best of America. He is hardworking, skilled, smart, and completely dependable. You couldn't find a better man in all of Ohio."

His heart beat erratically. Did she mean that? She sounded so sincere.

Mr. Harris just grunted, but two hours later Faith and Davis walked out of his brick factory with huge smiles on their faces.

"Congratulations, Miss Penwilliger," Davis said. "It looks like you are the proud owner of a brick factory."

"Co-owner," Faith corrected. "How does it feel to see your plans working out?"

He stopped in front of his car. "I'm exhausted. I feel like I've been through my mom's clothes wringer."

Faith laughed.

"We should have eaten before we went in."

"What time is it?"

Davis glanced at his watch. "After three."

"Let's take our lunch to a park."

They ate Marcia's delicious lunch in Davis's car overlooking a cute little park, the November air too cold for eating outside. They chatted happily about the future of their brick business and how to best manage the new factory as they ate their way through Marcia's roast-beef sandwiches, potato salad, and chocolate cupcakes.

The autumn light spilled across Faith's face, and Davis had the insane urge to run his finger over her cheek where the sunshine played. He turned and looked out at the golden-orange trees. He didn't know much about women, but it seemed like today he and Faith had made some progress—yes, in buying their own brick factory, but also in getting more comfortable with each other. Today felt like . . . He searched for the right word. Today felt like friendship, and he wasn't going to do anything silly like touch her cheek to ruin this new olive branch between them.

"See that monument across the park?" he asked instead.

"Yes."

"The monument my committee is working on is going to look something like that."

"I like it," Faith said.

"I've been thinking a lot about monuments lately." Would she appreciate his thoughts, or would they just annoy her? Yes, Freddy Casper was still a big part of her life, but things were changing between Faith and Davis. He could feel it. He could open up to her. "Have I ever told you about the village in France that my grandmother came from?" he asked.

"No, I don't think so."

"It was decimated during the first Great War. Every major building was a pile of rubble, and something like 80 percent of the homes were destroyed."

"Unimaginable," she said. "Did they rebuild after the war?"

"Yes, except for the church. The town decided to leave the church in ruins as a symbol of how horrific war is. I went there with my family when I was twelve. The rubble was a profound reminder of the losses the town sustained."

Faith's eyes crinkled like she was concentrating and trying to figure out what he was saying. Davis chose his next words carefully. "We were all affected by the war, but some of us know things will never be the same." He lowered his voice. "I won't ever be the same. I'm not the carefree college boy Davy. I've seen too much."

Faith nodded. "And I'm not the sixteen-year-old girl you left behind. The war forced me to learn a lot in a very short amount of time. I lost half my family. Rose isn't the same either, my mom isn't the same, Robert Sullivan isn't the same."

"Exactly," Davis said. "It's pretty painful to watch others going back to regular life as though the war didn't change anything. Figuratively speaking, there are many who are rebuilding the bombed church with the idea that they can make things the same as they were before the war.

"I sometimes think, though, that we need a pile of rubble to remind us of the sacrifices that were made by men like your father and Patrick." He reached out to touch her hand. "Some things in our lives are like the church that burned down. They're gone, like Robert Sullivan's first faith, like our carefree college days, and I think"—he paused again—"I think that's all right. Robert can build a new, deeper faith. You and I missed college, but we have other experiences, outside of college, that we've been educated by. We will always miss Patrick. The real monument is the fact that we can't replace him." He watched in silence as a tear slid down her cheek and then said quietly, "We were both changed by the war."

"Yes," Faith said. "How do we get past our feelings of loss?"

"Looking to the future. Having hope and a plan. Brick by brick."

"I like that," Faith said. "Brick by brick."

Neither of them spoke. The silence built, but it felt companionable. They sat together just looking out over the park for some time until she finally said, "We should go."

He returned the basket to the trunk, and they left to go back home. Back to a promising future.

They turned onto the highway, and Davis flipped the radio on. Faith had gone quiet again. "You like this song?" he asked.

She fidgeted, and from the corner of his eye he could see she was twisting her hands together.

"You like this song?" he asked again.

"Hmm? What song?"

"This song . . . the one playing on the radio right now."

"Bing Crosby is always great."

"What? Faith, this is Sinatra."

What was going on with her? Why did she suddenly seem nervous? They had had a connection today, and he'd been feeling so good about it. They'd made progress in their friendship, hadn't they? So why was Faith so tense now?

CHAPTER 38

FAITH HAD BEEN NERVOUS THROUGHOUT the entire ride home. She had admitted to herself what she needed to do, and she dreaded it. She sighed and rolled over in bed. Sleep evaded her for a long time.

Saturday morning she helped Mom and Rose with chores around the house.

"You're unusually quiet," Mom said as they folded laundry together.

Faith sighed. "It's a long road that has no turning."

Mom gave Faith a long look and replied, "'The longest road out is the shortest road home.'"

"I know, but I can't help thinking 'when a well is dry, we know the worth of water.'" Faith picked up a towel and began folding it.

Rose turned from the ironing board, where she was pressing a blouse. Her brow was creased, and she set the iron down.

"Perhaps that's true," Mom said, "but 'when the apple is ripe, it will fall.'"

"It's just going to be hard," Faith said. "You must crack the nut before you eat the kernel."

Mom countered with "'God's help is nearer than the door.' You can do this, Faith."

Rose gaped at them.

Faith smiled, feeling a bit better about the daunting task in front of her. She sat up a little taller. "'A mother's eye is a good mirror.'"

"Rose and I can finish up here. You go on. 'You'll never plow a field by turning it over in your mind.'"

Faith nodded and ever so slowly went to grab her coat and hat. She hated knowing she would make someone sad.

As she left, she heard Rose say, "What on earth was that conversation about? Where is she going?"

"To Freddy Casper's," Mom answered.

Even though it was nearly noon, Freddy was just finishing his breakfast when Faith arrived at his home. The maid left them alone in the lovely breakfast nook.

"Hiya, kiddo," Freddy said. "What's cookin'?"

"Let's go for a walk." Faith extended her hand.

Nearly an hour and several miles of walking later, he said, "I still don't understand why. We're perfect partners."

She squeezed his hand. "I've been thinking about that word a lot—*partners*."

"Because of your business partner?" Freddy's words came out bitter.

She sighed. "Maybe." She rubbed his hand. "I think there are different types of partners. There's a pard'ner, what Frank calls his buddies that he chats with. Then there're business partners you need to be able to work with. There're dance partners you need to move well with and have fun with. That's what you and I are. But there's a higher type of partner, a marriage partner, a lifelong commitment."

Freddy grunted and dropped her hand. "Are you saying if I want to remain dance partners we have to get married?"

"Not at all. I'm saying you came into my life exactly when I needed you, and I've loved being your dance partner, but we aren't lifelong partners, and it's time for both of us to move on."

"Why can't we keep dancing while we date other people? You can find your future husband, and we can keep dancing."

Faith shook her head and rubbed her thick tweed skirt. "That doesn't seem fair to you, to me, or to my future husband."

"We could start dating exclusively. I adore you."

Faith bit back a teeny smile. Freddy wasn't ready to date anyone exclusively. Life for him right now was all about having fun. "Freddy," she said, placing a hand on his arm. "My mom has a saying. She says that a relationship isn't about gazing into each other's eyes with adoration; it's about looking to the same goals."

Freddy kicked a rock. "I never get your mom's sayings. She doesn't like me. She always has some weird saying for me. What does that mean anyway?"

Faith was surprised he had even noticed or cared what Mom thought. "It means the person you enter into a romantic relationship with should be someone you're compatible with in your goals." She patted his arm. "I'm sorry, Freddy."

He complained all the way back to the house about Davis Wilson breaking them up. Faith just listened. Behind his fun-loving ways there *were* deeper feelings.

Freddy walked her back to her car. Faith gave him a kiss on the cheek, and he finally stopped protesting. "I'll miss you, kiddo," he said.

She nodded. "I'll miss you too." She was grateful there were no tears. "No one can jitterbug like you can."

She was thankful that Costello started smoothly for once. It had been more exhausting than she had thought it would be to tell Freddy their partnership was over. It wasn't just the end of a relationship but the end of an era, the end of their dancing and laughing.

She thought she would feel sadness, but all she felt on the drive home was relief. She spent the afternoon in her room, just thinking.

Dinner began with Mom and Rose eyeing her and being overly polite.

Faith finally set her fork down. "I'm fine, ladies."

"Was it horrible?" Mom asked.

Faith sighed. "It wasn't pleasant, but it had to be done. He took it pretty well, all in all. To be honest, he's probably going out dancing tonight without me."

"I'm sorry," Rose said.

"It's not a big deal."

Rose said, "Well, it'll be a big deal to Davis. Just ask him how he feels about Freddy Casper."

"I'd like to be the one to tell Davis that Freddy and I are over, if you two don't mind."

Rose and Mom exchanged a look, but they both nodded their agreement.

Mom asked, "How are you two getting along these days?" The hope in her eyes was irritating.

"Oh, fine. Just lovely." Faith cut her spareribs a little aggressively and stuffed a big bite into her mouth.

Rose's eyes twinkled, and she leaned toward Mom. "Have you seen the movie *The Philadelphia Story?*"

"Yes."

"Remember the tension between Cary Grant and Katherine Hepburn?"

"Oh stop!" Faith said, waving her fork at her cousin.

"Yep, the romantic tension is pretty much oozing off them."

Mom looked uncomfortable with romantic tension being discussed at her dinner table. She said, "Here, have more potatoes; the baby needs to eat too."

"Yeah," Faith said. "Have some potatoes and put lots of them in your mouth—maybe enough that you can't talk."

Rose just laughed. She didn't seem in the least bothered by the idea of Faith and Davis. Maybe Faith had misread her cousin's interest in him.

Rose said, "'Methinks the lady doth protest too much.' I'm just saying that if you're in the room, Davis's eyes are on you. Cecilia spent all of the drive home from New York discussing her hopes for you two. I thought her judgment might be in question—after all, I had seen her taste in hats. Then I got here and realized that Davis is, indeed, madly in love with you." She smirked and took a sip of water.

"'Madly in love?' Good grief, what does that even mean?" Faith got her words out, then stuffed a big bite of potatoes into her mouth.

"I think it means he helps around your house, hoping to make your life easier," Rose said.

"It means he wants to be near you, so he takes a job as a bricklayer and then waits for weeks, hoping you will take him on as a partner." Mom was getting in on this too?

"It means he takes on all the unpleasant little things at the brick store so you won't have to," Rose said.

"It means," Mom said, waving her fork in the air, "that he gave up smoking for you and took dance lessons hoping you would dance with him."

"And," Rose added, "he hasn't asked a single girl out since coming home. The poor man is too besotted with you to even look twice at any other woman."

The two women looked like they were enjoying ganging up on Faith, and her head turned from one to the other as they continued.

"It means that he spent hours helping you sort Patrick's room because he didn't want you to have to do it alone," Mom said quietly.

Faith paused in her aggressive chewing.

"It means," Rose said, "that he tries to impress you by working after hours making phone calls and figuring out how to expand the business."

Faith swallowed. "He wants the business to do well for his own investment."

"Nope, I'm pretty sure he's mainly thinking of you. I see him get off the phone and say things like, 'Faith will love that.'" Rose smiled.

"It means"—Mom really seemed to be getting into the spirit of the conversation— "that he has done hours of canvassing for your monument project, without complaining, I might add."

"That's because he likes Robert Sullivan."

"Don't change the subject. He likes Robert Sullivan and likes canvassing with him, but he loves you and is on the monument committee for you," Mom said.

"He's a good man," Rose said.

"If you love him, don't let your pride stand in the way of telling him so," Mom said firmly.

"Okay, ladies, I see what you want."

Mom and Rose leaned expectantly toward Faith, but she just smiled at them and continued eating.

She might look calm outwardly, but inwardly her heart raced. She knew what she needed to do, and she hoped Davis wouldn't say yes to her for Patrick's sake. He wouldn't do that, would he? He'd confessed he had feelings for her two months ago when they'd had their second big fight. Were those feelings still there, or had she killed them with her angry, unjust accusations? Did he think of her as just a business partner after all?

CHAPTER 39

THE WEEK AFTER THEIR TRIP to buy the brick factory, Davis and Faith stayed after hours to do employee reviews. They agreed that everyone was flourishing except Lester. Davis felt strongly that the man needed to show Faith more respect or find another job.

When they wrapped things up, Davis stretched. It had been a long day. "I'll put these away." He unlocked the filing cabinet where they kept personal information and slipped the manila employee files in.

Faith watched him from the desk. She was unusually quiet, like she had been during their trip to purchase the factory. He searched for a topic of conversation now that they were done discussing their business. "How's Rose feeling these days?"

"Rose?"

"Your cousin," Davis said. Was Faith all right? She had a funny look on her face.

"Yes, Rose likes dancing."

Davis laughed. "Where's your mind, Faith?"

"Sorry. I'm woolgathering, I guess." She stood and walked to the old radio set that sat on a shelf behind the desk. She turned it on and fiddled with the dials. Davis watched her movements. Odd. She seemed in no hurry to go home, and it was long past dark. His mom and Marcia were probably both unhappy to be waiting to eat dinner. What was Faith doing? She kept turning the knobs until the radio settled on a slow song. A love song. That was odd. His eyes went wide. Why was she putting a love song on?

"Dance with me." Faith extended her hand.

Surprise froze Davis in place.

She took a step nearer. Her pretty brown eyes were large, and her face was serious as she looked up at him like he was a brick project she was trying to figure out.

His feet didn't move, but he leaned toward her. "You want to dance with me?"

"Yes." Faith's simple one-word answer sent warmth through him.

"You know I'm not a good dancer, right? I mean, you saw me make a fool of myself at the Bamboo Club."

"Davis," she said, and he had to lean forward to hear her. "You just need the right partner and you'll be fine."

His hands shook, but he opened his arms, and she stepped right into them, as if she had always belonged there. In the most heavenly, trusting way, her arms went slowly up around his neck.

They began to sway together to the music. And suddenly, there, in the middle of their office, Davis completely understood the purpose of dancing. He hoped the music would never end as he pulled her more securely into his embrace. He didn't feel clumsy like he had in the Bamboo Club. He felt, he felt . . . how to describe it?

Just when he thought the moment couldn't get any better, Faith rested her head on his shoulder. His heart rate accelerated. What was going on? What about Freddy?

As if Faith could read his mind, she said, "Freddy has moved on to a new dance partner. I hear he and Joan Young had a marvelous time together over the weekend."

Bubbles of happiness and hope burst inside of him. Did this mean what he thought it did? He pressed his hand to her back, and she moved perfectly with him.

She sighed against him. "Davis?"

"Yes?" His breath moved over the top of her head.

"If it's drowning you're after, don't do it in shallow water."

"Drowning?" he asked, confused. He tilted away from her so he could see her face. "What are you talking about?"

"I didn't mean to say that out loud. It just means don't do things halfway."

She buried her head in his chest. They had stopped dancing, but the soft crooning song still played, and he kept his arms wrapped around her. Whatever strangeness was going on with Faith, at least he got to hold her.

She took a deep breath in. "Davis, you were right about everything." She spoke quickly and softly, but he could hear every word distinctly. "Patrick wanted to fight. I needed to forgive you—there was never anything to forgive in the first place."

He took a step back and gripped her elbows. Her face was straight ahead, as if she were speaking to his shirtfront. "I've been unfair to you, and the thing is . . . the thing is . . ."

He gripped her elbows tighter.

"The thing is—I-I've had a hard time admitting this—but the thing is, I'm in love with you."

Davis never could remember exactly what happened next or in what order. He must have pulled her back to him and picked her up. They ended up in the office chair with Faith on his lap as they kissed each other, his hands running through her beautiful hair, then holding her face, then her waist, and then moving back to her hair. She responded warmly, matching him kiss for kiss.

"I need to breathe," Faith finally said.

He laughed. "I suppose that's a reasonable request." He kept her snuggly pulled to his chest as she laughed too.

"Finally," he murmured.

"I love you."

"I love you too," he said.

"I'm happy," Faith said between more dizzying kisses.

A feeling of safety, contentment, and joy engulfed Davis. Completely out of breath, he pulled away from her lips and buried his face in her hair.

"I didn't think you cared." He pulled her tightly to him again and just held her, their hearts beating wildly together.

Faith began to laugh against his chest. "Davis, this chair isn't meant for two."

"Uh-huh." He rubbed her back and said cheerfully, "I blame this on you. I came into the office to discuss our employees. You, on the other hand, had ulterior motives." His happiness made his face feel like it would crack in two with the largeness of his smile. "You shouldn't surprise a man like that. You could have given me a heart attack. Ambushed. You completely ambushed me. You could have told me a little more gradually." He had no real complaint.

"I would have." Faith reached up and touched his face. "But it's hard to find a chance to be alone with you. People are always around at work or at home, and I wanted privacy. I didn't know how you were going to react."

He kissed her again—a nice, sweet kiss. "How could you have not known how I would react? I think every single person in Payson knows how I feel about you."

She smiled up at him and ran her hands through his hair. He loved the tenderness and familiarity of it.

"It was good judgment on your part for us to be alone when you told me you love me," he admitted. "I honestly don't think anything or anyone could have stopped me from kissing you once you said those words. I've never felt so surprised or happy in my entire life."

Faith made the sweetest, most contented little sighing sound.

"Come on," Davis said. "Let's leave Costello here and I'll drive you home."

They closed the office and made their way out to Betsy, holding hands. The night was cold, but Davis didn't feel it. She loved him. He couldn't take it all in.

He opened her door for her and then hurried around to the driver's seat. He reached over and tugged her hair. "You sure hid your feelings well."

She pulled him in for another kiss. "I've just had some things to work out."

"Freddy?"

"Yes."

Davis took half a second to feel sorry for Freddy.

"And Patrick."

"I think Patrick would have been pleased." Davis touched her cheek softly.

Faith said, "As long as he didn't have to watch us kissing, he would have been fine. He was well aware of my feelings for you. One time he told me not to gush about you in front of him. He said it was nauseating."

Davis laughed. "I'd like to hear you gush."

"Oh, there will be plenty of gushing about my husband."

Davis grinned.

Faith put her hand on his arm, and even in the moonlight that flooded the old car, Davis could tell she was blushing. "I don't mean to assume we're getting married."

Davis pulled her in, tucking her securely under his arm, and said emphatically, "Of course we're getting married—as soon as our mothers can reasonably put it together."

Faith pulled his head down to show her approval of his plan.

"One thing though," Davis said. "I get to name the children."

"Betsy? There's no chance."

"Greenelda? Over my dead body." Davis laughed. "There will have to be some compromising."

A train whistled from far away.

"Faith?" he said.

"Hmm?"

This feeling. He had never thought he would experience anything like this. He turned the key and started Betsy. How could he express to her what this meant to him? What she meant to him? This feeling was euphoric, and he was shocked that life could contain this much happiness. This . . . this was floating. This was walking on air. He turned his car up the road toward home, trying to put his thoughts into words.

"What were you saying?" she prompted.

"I really—" His voice shook with emotion. "I need you. You're what has kept me going these last few months. I hope you know there hasn't been a moment since seeing you get out of the truck my first night home that you haven't been disturbing my peace."

Faith laughed. "Disturbing your peace?"

"I just didn't think I deserved you. I didn't know how to get what I wanted."

She squeezed his arm again. "I love you. Even when I didn't want to love you, I couldn't help it. I think my subconscious has known for a long time that we should end up together. That I need you too. That you're my partner."

"Maybe that's why you made me take dance lessons—your subconscious knew I needed to get better to be your partner."

She snuggled closer against his side. "I'm going to make you practice dance steps with me every night."

He was perfectly happy with that plan. "I thought I had no chance."

"I had to forgive you for coming home without Patrick. I spent the last four years blaming you for him enlisting, and I guess it's just been another process of growing up to admit he's gone and that it was his choice to fight."

They drove for a few moments together in silence. Davis passed their homes and kept right on driving. He didn't want the night to end, ever.

His voice shook as he said, "I need your joy and sweetness in my life. I need you."

"I need you too." She tugged his hand up to her cheek. "My pride just hasn't wanted to admit it."

"Faith?"

"Hmm, love?"

Davis couldn't help another smile. She seemed to be enjoying trying out endearments.

"Let's get on with life."

CHAPTER 40

"Thank heavens you're home," Mom said as Faith stepped in. "What kept you so long? I've been frantic with worry. It's two a.m." She looked agitated standing in the doorway in her white flannel nightgown, hair in curlers.

"Davis and I drove for a long time, then ran out of gas out on West Ridge Avenue. We had to walk home." She stepped toward her mother to try to calm her down.

Mom gasped and put her hands to her face. "Are you drunk?"

Faith laughed. "No, Mom, you know I don't drink, and do you really think Davis would get me drunk?"

Mom stared and said slowly, "No, I know Davis wouldn't do that, but your cheeks are flushed, and you have an odd smile on your face. And how did your hair get in that state? It looks absolutely wild. Where's your hat?"

Faith's cheeks warmed. "That's all Davis's fault, and if you want an explanation, you'll have to get it from him. I'll just say that he got a little carried away."

Understanding dawned on Mom's face. "No explanation necessary," she said primly.

"Do you want the good news now or in the morning?"

Mom stepped closer to Faith and took a good look at her. "Are you saying what I think you're saying?"

"I'm engaged."

Mom wrapped her arms around Faith and hugged her ecstatically. "I've wanted this to happen ever since he got home. You don't know how happy this makes me."

"I'm happy too. I've never felt this kind of happiness before."

"Oh, sweetie." Mom kissed her cheek. "Cecilia bought a hat when we were in New York City. She's saving it for your wedding, and it is really something."

Faith laughed. "I can't wait to see it."

EPILOGUE

October 1949

"Can you believe how many people are here?" Faith asked Davis.

"It's impressive," he said, bouncing little Patrick gently in his arms to keep him asleep. "Frank and Edith are over there, and did you see how many of your old Sunday School students are back from college?"

Faith squeezed her husband's arm. "It's turned out so wonderfully."

"I'm really proud of what Payson has accomplished."

"Do you remember how mad you were the day of your reception, when I tricked you into starting the monument committee? Could you have guessed then how well it would turn out?"

Davis leaned down to kiss her cheek, their baby cocooned between them, and whispered into her ear. "I remember the day of the reception well—and no. In my wildest, happiest dreams I couldn't have guessed how well it would all turn out."

She smiled, knowing her husband meant far more than just the monument they were dedicating. Penwilliger Brick was thriving. They had thirty employees. Her brother's and father's fights for tomorrow had certainly paid off. Mom continued to miss her husband and son, but oh, how she fussed over and enjoyed her grandson, Patrick, and Rose's daughter, Liza.

Faith and Davis had settled into a darling new home on three acres just outside of town. It was brick, of course—Davis had done much of the work himself, with Frank coming out of retirement to help. Faith had painted a sign that hung in their kitchen: Tomorrow is worth fighting for. Their home was filled with love and happiness.

Rose, Liza, and Mom came over to say hi. Mom picked up Liza, who wiggled like crazy to get down and play.

"Go ahead and set her down, Aunt Marcia," Rose said. "I'll chase her for a while. She's too much of an armful to contain."

Faith admired the picture they made, Liza in her pretty green smocked dress, white sweater, and patent leather shoes on her chubby legs, her red ringlets flying, and her pretty mother following closely behind with a smile.

"That'll be Patrick before you know it, giving us the chase," Davis said.

"No doubt. Let's just enjoy this stage while he wants to cuddle in our arms."

Mom, missing having a little one in her arms, reached for Patrick, and Davis gently transferred him, keeping the blanket wrapped tightly around the sleeping infant.

Mom smiled at Faith and said, "I was just thinking, dear, of one of my father's favorite sayings: 'Hindsight is the best insight to foresight.'"

Faith thought about it for a moment. "I believe that's very true. You think our monument is a bit of hindsight?"

"Yes, our looking back is going to help us move forward."

Faith's eyes misted. "I have a saying too. 'Forgetting your debt doesn't mean it is paid.'"

Patrick made a little sigh in his sleep, and Mom said solemnly, "The debt we owe our boys is certainly one we can't forget."

Faith nodded.

Pastor Clemmons stepped to the podium, and the crowd politely clapped. He didn't wait for the clapping to stop but launched briskly into his speech with his usual gruffness. "We are here today to dedicate this monument to the thirteen men—boys, really—from Payson who lost their lives during the war. I knew many of them. They were typical boys. They had their strengths and they had their weaknesses. They had triumphs and they made mistakes. What made them heroes? When the time to fight evil came, they rose to the occasion—they answered the call.

"And so, we honor them, not because they were perfect but because they gave the greatest gift any man can give for another—their lives. Their names are carved in stone to be forever remembered by the citizens of Payson. We dedicate this monument to them, to their sacrifice, and to their families, who also sacrificed." The pastor cleared his throat. "I leave you with words from John 15:13. 'Greater love hath no man than this, that a man lay down his life for his friends.'" He sat down to a chorus of amens and applause.

Robert Sullivan came forward to take a giant pair of scissors from the mayor. He looked out at the crowd, and his eyes rested on Faith and Davis. He nodded at them and stepped over to the large yellow ribbon that surrounded the beautiful stone monument. Robert raised the scissors, cut the ribbon, and looked out at the cheering crowd. There were tears in his eyes.

ACKNOWLEDGMENTS

It's humbling to look back at the help I've received from others in creating this book. I've appreciated and needed the advice: proofreading and plotting help from Paula Kremser, Alice Patron, Esther Hatch, Audrey Mangum, Lisa Rowley, and Heather Tomlinson, who were my earliest readers. Their encouragement helped me keep going, and their knowledge improved this book from rough draft to completed manuscript.

Jessica Parker and my daughters, Sierra, Jenna, and Caroline gave me a younger point of view. These four women are absolutely fantastic proofreaders. Their advice was spot-on, from word choice to pacing to style to character development. They give me confidence in our public schools!

Finally, I love being part of the Covenant team. It means so much to know that in a profession that can feel solitary, I'm not alone. Special thanks to Kami Hancock, editor extraordinaire, Samantha Millburn, Amy Parker, Jessica Bybee, and Kevin Jorgensen and to the many other team members who work tirelessly to design, market, and promote Covenant's books. Thank you for seeing something in my writing and making it worthy of sharing.

QUOTED IN THE SERGEANT AND THE GIRL NEXT DOOR

Many of the quotes appearing in this book are Irish proverbs of unknown origin that have been passed down through the generations. A few of the other quotes' origins can be traced to specific works, as follows:

Edmund Tilney, *A briefe and pleasant discourse of duties in Mariage, called the Flower of Friendshippe* (imprinted at London: Henrie Denham, dwelling in Pater noster Rowe, at the Signe of the Starre, 1571), https://quod.lib.umich.edu/e/eebo/A13778.0001.001?rgn=main;view=fulltext (see also https://www.bookbrowse.com/expressions/detail/index.cfm/expression_number/180/marry-in-haste-repent-at-leisure).

William Shakespeare, *The Tragedie of Hamlet, Prince of Denmarke*, Project Gutenberg, https://www.gutenberg.org/files/1524/1524-h/1524-h.htm.

Winston Churchill, "We Shall Fight on the Beaches" (speech delivered to the House of Commons), June 4, 1940. Reproduced in *The Guardian*, https://www.theguardian.com/theguardian/2007/apr/20/greatspeeches1.

ABOUT THE AUTHOR

LAURA RUPPER SPENT HER FIRST six years of life in Metlakatla, Alaska. There was no TV reception on the island, so a great love of books was born. In addition to reading, Laura loves creative activities, from painting to new ways of teaching fourth-grade math concepts. Boring chores, like laundry, leave her daydreaming of magical worlds and interesting characters. She has three beautiful daughters, an extremely nice husband, and one giant dog. Laura is an eclectic reader but, no matter the genre, she believes in happy endings.

Follow her on her website and social media:
laurarupperauthor.weebly.com
Instagram: @authorlaurarupper
twitter@laura_rupper